THE SAVIOR

THE ACES SERIES, BOOK #1

New York Times Bestselling Author

CRISTIN HARBER

This is a work of fiction. All of the characters, organizations, and events portrayed in this novel are either the products of the author's imagination or are used fictionally.

www.cristinharber.com

DEDICATION

For Claudia Connor, who taught me that inspiration and the God's-honest-truth might be served best with chips, salsa, and margaritas.

CHAPTER ONE

THAT TUESDAY WAS just like any other except that it would become one of the most important days in Liam's and Julia's lives. Liam rolled his shoulders back, unable to find a comfortable way to sit next to his girlfriend. Though a commuter-packed Metro wasn't the most comfortable place to start.

The train descended into a tunnel, and he straightened. The underground lights whirred as they passed with a rhythmic hum. The seesawing normally eased him into a hypnotic form of relaxation, but not that night. With every stop closer to the restaurant where he'd requested a secluded table, the ring box weighed heavier against his chest.

"Are you feeling all right?" Julia brushed her hand across his cheek.

"Of course." Liam cleared his throat. Who knew proposing could give him a nervous high?

"Oooh-kay." Her eyebrows arched, but her laughter was soft and as sweet as cotton candy. "If you say so."

Hell if he hadn't spoken too fast… too loudly… too everything that might ruin the surprise. Shrouding his nerves, he gave a playful side-eye. "Oooh-kay, yourself, sweetness."

"I still think you're up to something," she joked.

He kissed her cheek. "You just have a creative imagination."

Her easy laugh rolled off her tongue. "That's why they pay me the big bucks."

Which was a joke. When he'd discovered how reporters were paid, he quickly understood why Julia had teamed up with her best friend, Chelsea, a federal agent, to sensationalize true-crime stories for a big-name publisher. Not that their contracts meant they were paid better, but Liam saw similarities with her job and his decision to pick up freelance military-contracting work.

The dark-purple sky lit their Metro car as it surfaced again. They rounded a bridge toward DC, and if he hadn't known how soon autumn was, he would have said the skyline almost seemed as if it still belonged to the summer.

A few weekends ago, the summer sun still hung high at night when he'd sat Linda and Frank down to ask for their daughter's hand in marriage. They were close enough to be his parents and had said as much when they'd happily given their blessing.

"Liam?" Julia's eyebrows arched. "Earth to Liam. Come in."

"Sorry." He focused. "What?"

"I can still catch up with Chelsea tonight..." She twisted a lock of hair. "If you need to concentrate on work."

He bristled. No way in hell.

Julia nudged him. "What's up?"

"I'm not changing a date night for Chelsea."

"I was just offering to change our plans if you had elsewhere to be."

He grumbled.

"Ease up, all right? It was just a thought."

"I *am* at ease."

She giggled. "I can see that—and you don't have to hate on Chelsea for everything."

He *didn't.* What he was trying to do was propose. Liam readjusted his suit jacket as they slid into a station. The doors opened, and people pushed in and out. Commuters headed home. Hill rats headed for happy hour. Tourists took up too many seats with their gift-shop bags. But an older man was the one who commanded Liam's attention.

"Do you know that guy?" Liam asked under his breath.

The old man gripped a metal pole and stood rather than taking an empty seat. The train picked up speed again. Outside their car, dim lights whooshed, methodically humming as they remained underground.

"Nope." Julia rolled her thumb over Liam's knuckles.

The man still stared.

A cold shiver pricked at the back of Liam's neck. "Because he's looking at us." He cracked his neck and stretched to check their surroundings. There wasn't anyone in the man's direct line of sight.

"People do weird things on the Metro."

That didn't make Liam any more comfortable. The overhead speakers crackled with the announcement of the next stop, and the cars slowed. Liam tapped his foot, hoping the old man would get off at the next stop. If he didn't, maybe they would switch trains.

The doors opened. The influx and exit of riders freed up new seats. Still, the older man didn't take one.

"Let's get off here," Liam suggested.

"I thought we were getting off at—"

The doors closed again. He tapped his teeth together. The prospect of proposing had made him paranoid. "Never mind." Then he captured the older man's gaze and gestured to the seats. "Open seat now, buddy."

Julia shifted uncomfortably, and her eyes bugged. "Let him be."

"No need," the man responded with a thick accent then smiled at Julia. "Are you a reporter for the Post?"

"I am." She smiled and scooted to the edge of her seat.

Liam's neck hairs stood on end, and he placed a protective hand on her knee, urging her back.

She gave Liam a quick glance but had her attention pulled back as the man asked, "You're Julia Nyman?"

As he tightened his grip, Liam felt his heart pound without reason. They were having a simple conversation. Julia's picture had accompanied her reports before.

Her head tilted. "I am. Have you read—"

But that was all the small talk the man offered. He gave her a wave and took a seat several rows up so that he'd still face them.

Mental warning bells chimed. Flattening his lips, he took Julia's hand. "We have to go."

"We can't go anywhere right now," she said, pointing out the obvious as the Metro continued. "What is your problem tonight?"

It had been proposing. Now? Liam glanced the length of the car. "Call it a feeling."

The speakers crackled and announced a temporary hold for single tracking. Dammit. He wanted off that train.

Adrenaline surged. He pulled out his phone—no cell service—then returned it to his pocket. The man had been staring down the car, beyond them.

Liam twisted and followed the man's line of sight. This time, another person made Liam's skin crawl. The second man held no expression but wore a long overcoat. The nighttime temperatures were dropping but not enough to warrant another layer of clothes.

His instinct shouted that there was a threat, but when he turned for the old man, Liam saw that he'd taken a book out, and the new man stared blankly ahead.

Either the man in the coat was a threat, or Liam had lost his mind. He calculated the distance to Metro Center, the most densely packed station, and wondered when the hell they'd start moving again. His thoughts raced as he suddenly questioned whether proposal nerves caused paranoia or he'd never had a more mission-critical moment in his life. *What is under that asshole's jacket?*

Fuck it. Liam nuzzled against Julia's cheek, and she jumped at the unusual public display of affection.

"Listen," he whispered.

"What are you—"

"*Listen to me.*"

Julia froze. She had to know something was wrong. He'd never spoken to her like that before.

"I need to check on someone."

"Who?"

"No one. I'm sure. I just have to double-check." Because his gut instinct was never wrong.

"What's going on?" Her voice wavered.

"Lean against the wall and make yourself small." He cupped her cheek. "If you hear me shout, drop to the ground and get under the chair."

Her frightened eyes widened. "Okay."

"Everything will be fine." His thumb ran along her cheek.

Because this situation was what he did—his life had been built on a team that destroyed terrorists and violent plans.

"Everything...will be fine," she repeated, lips trembling.

"It will." He touched her chin then stood. "Promise."

Julia sank against the window, awkwardly twisting her legs to keep the sexy blue dress down.

"Be right back." Then he let intuition lead him to the back of the Metro car. His casual stroll hid the rage curled in his fists until only an arm's length separated Liam from the other man.

Menace-fueled eyes showed Liam he wasn't wrong.

"Julia! Now!" Liam swung.

Commuters gasped and screamed in surprise. Liam ripped open the man's overcoat and found a weapon fit for carnage.

Fists flew. Hands grasped for the weapon. Liam reached for the man's neck. Fingers on flesh, he curled his grip tight, jamming against a pressure point and counting the seconds to choke the gun-wielding bastard out.

"*Oof!*" Liam doubled forward when the knee hit his groin, grip faltering.

The gun came loose, and they wrestled for it. Liam took a hard blow to his head. His eyesight darkened, stars exploding.

Pop. Pop.

Gunfire? The blasts sounded too far away. The pain in his head throbbed, his vision skewed, but Liam kicked the weapon free. He and the man fought for it again, their hands slipping, the gun barrel pointing back and forth—

Pop. Pop.

Liam rolled away as the man fell, covered in blood. *Dead.*

"Julia!" Liam pushed off the ground and lost his balance but steadied himself.

People grouped at the other end of the car, and he pushed his way through the tourists and commuters, growing sick on their terror polluting the hot air.

"Julia?"

The small crowd parted, and the shocked, stuttering cries fell quiet. He searched their faces and followed their trembling eyes.

Julia… Her lifeless figure lay by their seats. Dark pain sliced into him, dragging Liam into the depths of an inexplicable black hole.

Her deep puddle of blood spread wide like morbid angels' wings on a dirty subway floor, and he dropped to a knee next to the high heel that had slipped off her foot.

Julia was gone, and it was his fault.

His eyes shut, and his dead heart ached. He clasped a hand to his chest and felt—*the engagement ring.*

In that agonizing instant, all that he knew and loved faded away.

CHAPTER TWO

US MARSHAL CHELSEA Kilpatrick ignored her vibrating cell phone. Besides the fact that she detested talking on the phone, she was certain that any second, a brilliant answer would pop to mind and end years of work searching for Zee Zee Mars.

The phone vibrated again. “Son of a Slurpee—” Her train of thought disappeared. If work didn’t require phone calls, she’d change her voicemail to say, “You know I won’t answer. Hang up and send a message.” Whoever had made the mortal mistake to call twice in a row instead of text was about to hear her riot act.

Chelsea glanced at the cell phone and groaned. Mac Cabello. His timing never failed. She was sure that her partner had some kind of homing device able to detect when Chelsea was neck deep in her study of the ongoing Zee Zee Mars investigation.

Well, Mac would grumble that the investigation was never-ending instead of ongoing. Though both *ongoing* and *never-ending* seemed semi-interchangeable. Zee Zee Mars’s infamous case had been interwoven throughout Chelsea’s law enforcement career, whether she was assigned to the woman on the US Marshal’s Most Wanted Fugitive list or not. Which, technically, she wasn’t.

Her primary responsibilities included prisoner transportation, serving federal warrants, and an ungodly amount of paperwork. Adrenaline-fueled fugitive apprehensions were few and far between. Calhoun, her boss, allowed her to lead the Marshal’s investigation and work alongside the FBI, who also targeted Mars. But only as Chelsea’s time allowed—which meant she *made* the time.

Not only had the case become a small obsession, but she had a side job writing about Mars.

She answered the call. "Hey, Mac."

He grumbled, "You sound chipper."

What a grouch. "Chipper" shouldn't be a complaint. Chelsea rolled her eyes. "And you sound like you need a smoothie."

"Wouldn't hurt, but that's not why I'm calling."

Mac was a hundred percent helpful fifty percent of the time. That was the best way she could think to describe their hot-and-cold relationship. When they were first partnered, they got on fine. She even appreciated his overbearing habit of "handling the situation." Not because she wasn't capable, but because he had several years of experience. She was nothing if not eager to learn from the surly man with high hopes of moving up in the ranks.

"What's up?"

"Where are you?" he demanded.

Sometimes less was more with Mac. "Following up on—"

"Thought so. You're re-walking the crime scene?"

Well, so much for staying off the Zee Zee Mars topic. Here came the lecture about returning without giving him a heads-up. They had an agreement that if she and Julia, her best-friend-slash-co-writer, re-walked a scene, they'd check in. However, checking in with Mac about Zee Zee Mars was always a complaint-filled conversation about how Mars would never be caught. It was easier to forget to loop him in. "Yeah."

The uncomfortable part of their talk would be when he learned she was alone. Julia had a date night. Mac's lecture would be a doozy.

"Maybe for once that saved you," he muttered. "Come out front."

"I'm sorry?"

"You weren't at home. It wasn't that hard to figure out where else you might be."

If Mac hunting her down hadn't made her worry, she would've denied that work was her life. Chasing Zee Zee consumed a significant part of Chelsea's work and free time. The criminal had made it personal without even knowing it, with bombings on her birthdays, at her favorite places, and even had a calling card that resonated with Chelsea—black calla lilies.

They were elegant and mysterious, the opposite of the white ones that had decorated the house she'd grown up in, which had become a symbol of everything that she hated—unflawed perfection.

But Mac *was here.* "Coming."

Crossing the second floor of the library at night required her to move with small, careful steps until she reached the main staircase. Zee Zee's bomb had ripped through the law texts of the local university, and though it only affected the upstairs of one wing of the library, the whole of it would remain closed at the start of the school year until they determined there was nothing left to learn from the scene. They had almost missed the black calla lily wedged in a textbook on DNA and genetics in an entirely different part of the library. Who knew what else had they missed.

Chelsea stepped under the yellow tape strung across the hallway and took the stairs down. She exited the university library and waved to Mac, who sat on a bench near the bike racks, then locked the doors behind her.

Even though the start of the new school year was just underway, the campus seemed too quiet since the sun had gone down.

"What are you doing?"

"Let's have a seat."

"Mac?"

"Come on." He motioned toward the bench and didn't wait for her to follow.

Anxiety drummed quietly in her chest. Nothing he was doing was normal, even if over the last few months, he'd become even more of a grouch.

What could be so serious? Maybe he'd been transferred? Though their boss Calhoun would never let Mac leave. They had an advantageous relationship. Calhoun always had a Yes Man on staff, and Mac could count on his ever-increasing authority—even if he did have to deal with her and Zee Zee. Even with Calhoun's help, Mac might even blame Chelsea for slowing his ascent of upward promotions.

Or maybe Chelsea was overthinking their dynamic.

Mac slapped the spot next to him on the bench, and hesitantly, Chelsea sat down.

"Were you working? Or getting…" He gestured blankly. "Pictures or something?"

She was sure that Mac thought writing a book with Julia was a joke. He wasn't keen on true-crime reporters, which was what Julia did in addition to working on their Zee Zee Mars book, and he would make bad jokes about how Chelsea could play Zee Zee if their agent ever sold the movie rights. He somehow thought their dark hair and noses were similar.

"I always thought that Calhoun was batshit," Mac said, "letting you do whatever you want."

She tried to bite her tongue but corrected him. "I can't do *whatever I want.*"

He snorted. "I thought that your *research* would get you and Julia killed."

"Zee Zee has never killed anyone."

"Not yet," he said.

"Not yet," she admitted. At the rate the explosions were coming, increasing in size, spreading out across the country, Zee Zee would slip up. Someone would die. "You're right."

"Fuck." He dropped his head and shook it.

"What?" She'd never seen him gut-shot before. "Mac?"

"There was a shooting. As soon as I heard about it, I headed your way."

Her stomach bottomed out. "Who? What happened?"

Mac's brow knitted. "Tonight, on the Metro."

Her mind raced. Terrorist attack? Random violence? "What happened?"

"Julia was shot."

Chelsea faltered. She hadn't understood. That didn't make sense. Julia was on a date. "*Mac?*"

"I'm sorry." He pursed his lips then braced a hand on her shoulder. "Julia died."

CHAPTER THREE

One Year Later

TWO NEVER-ENDING HOURS inched by as Liam stayed in the same spot on the Nymans' couch and waited. It was the same position he'd manned after the funeral when the Nymans' house had been full of mourners.

After the funeral, he'd waited for his mind to go numb. Mostly, he'd waited for an alarm clock to ring and wake him from his nightmare.

Somehow, the time had passed. Slow days and lonely nights crept by. The weeks changed to months. The seasons rolled their usual paces with falling leaves, snowstorms, then slips of green turned into spring and summer.

Fall had returned, and after more than a year, Linda planned a celebration of life where friends and family could smile instead of cry at Julia's memory. Liam wasn't sure what to feel, but if her parents needed him there, then that's where he would be. They were the closest thing he had to family.

Everywhere he looked, family and friends huddled as they had after the funeral. But today, laughter and reminiscent grins mixed with hugs and favorite stories. But Liam didn't move, just as he didn't the year prior. Guilt pinned him down, shining a neon sign as the reason Julia had been killed to anyone who looked his way.

A gentle hand rested on his shoulder.

Pain knotted in his throat, but he cleared it. "Linda, do you need something?"

She kept her hand on his arm as he stood. Few dared to talk to him, much less touch him, and he didn't blame them for staying away. But

Linda gave a soft smile. "I'm fine."

How could anyone in this house be fine? "Are you hungry?" he offered.

Casseroles decorated the dining room table. He wasn't sure what to expect for a celebration of life, but it involved large pans of food to go with smiling pictures. He didn't know when they arrived, but he hadn't been paying much attention.

"Can I join you?" She took a seat next to where he'd been most of the afternoon then gestured toward the couch. "Sit."

"Of course." The cushion was still warm when he eased back down. His new suit dug into the folds at his elbows and arms, and the waist bunched at his back. He hadn't thought to buy a new suit after the shooting, and he had to go shopping that morning. Off-the-rack suits could never accommodate the bulk of his muscles. Either his thighs threatened to rip the inseam, or the waist was too large. His resentment for the day grew every time he repositioned uncomfortably.

"You holding up all right?" he asked.

"I was about to ask you the same thing." She glanced about the room. "You haven't spent much time talking with others."

"I'm having a hard time celebrating."

"No one's celebrating her death," Linda said as though he were one of her kindergarten students. "We're rejoicing and remembering everything we loved about her."

Liam grumbled. A year ago, he spent most days trying to forget so that the pain would stop. Weeks passed, and his grief evolved. He wanted to cling to every memory. But as the seasons changed, he didn't know what the hole in his chest meant. Sadness? Solitude? No matter what feelings were there, he would always feel the guilt.

"This isn't how it's supposed to happen," Linda said.

He nodded.

"Have you ever heard of Swedish death cleaning?"

His eyebrows arched. "Uh, no."

"It's a gift parents give their children and loved ones."

"When they die?"

Slowly, she nodded. "At a certain age, you clean. You rid yourself of what you do not need, and when it comes time for your death, you've helped to prepare your family."

"I wasn't prepared. That's for damn sure." He drew a deep breath. "I'm not sure what I am, to be honest."

"I wasn't either." She paused, and he could only offer a sympathetic nod. Linda continued, "But I'm grateful for every moment I had. I know you are too."

Guilt seared his throat. For a year, he hadn't been able to find the words to ask for her forgiveness, and now, she was trying to comfort *him*. He didn't need comfort—he needed… He didn't know. "Don't worry about me," he finally managed. "I celebrate her in my own way."

They sat quietly, and he noticed the celebration had thinned. Frank and Chelsea cleaned discarded plates and cups from a nearby hutch.

"Have you talked to Chelsea?" Linda asked.

He wondered how so many people could stomach the idea of eating. Celebration or not. They'd gathered because someone had died. No matter how much time had passed.

"*Liam?*"

He jerked out of his thoughts. "Yeah, sorry. Chelsea?" He pinched the bridge of his nose. "No. Nothing other than a wave hello."

"You should ask her to tell you one of her stories from when they were kids. Most are hysterical." She squeezed his shoulder. "Those girls were a handful."

Linda evaluated the quieting living room. "I'm worried about you."

He turned to Linda. "Don't."

She gave a motherly smile. "That's what I do."

"I'm fine."

She raised an eyebrow.

Unable to take the scrutiny, he shifted. *Does she want me to apologize? Does she hate that I didn't save Julia?* He tugged at the dress shirt collar. "Are you sure you don't need something? A glass of wine?"

He glanced at Chelsea, who stood in the corner, appraising what else she might need to clean or tidy. He could see a tinge of sadness and exhaustion shadow her face. Even if Chelsea had shared funny memories, he could recognize someone haunted by the same demons.

Linda wrapped her arm behind his stiff shoulders and offered a concerned hug, and then, stood. "Oh, I forgot to mention. You had a package delivered here earlier today." She held up a hand as someone waved goodbye to her. "I asked Chelsea to put it in Frank's study."

"Thanks." His curiosity piqued.

Linda walked away, and Chelsea caught his gaze. The corners of her eyes tightened, making her seem as if she was glaring. He wouldn't blame her if she were. He hadn't protected her best friend nor mingled today while offering his memories.

But she lasered in on a rogue plate with a crumpled napkin and crossed the living room to retrieve it. She searched the living room again for missed trash then headed to the kitchen.

Not wanting to risk another conversation about Julia, he slipped from the living room and escaped to the study.

The murmur of guests down the hall was dulling. He wanted the event to end so he could go back to the numbness.

A manila envelope was propped on the base of a desk lamp. The scrawl across the front only listed his name, no recipient or sender address.

Liam sat at Frank's desk and picked up the envelope, noticing a framed family picture. He closed his eyes and wanted to fade from the house. But wishing to disappear made him feel empty. Damn it! He wanted to celebrate Julia. But not in the same way as most of those people who arrived hours ago. He didn't know half of them, and nothing about the gathering seemed to honor her.

Or maybe he was just an asshole.

Liam unbuttoned his collar and took a deep breath. He pushed from Frank's desk and left the study, heading upstairs. He didn't know where he was going until the door to Julia's old bedroom waited in front of him.

This was what he needed. He'd said goodbye a year ago. Mourned and struggled with grief and guilt. But he somehow hadn't returned to this room.

Carefully, he turned the doorknob as though moving too fast might disturb the time that had been frozen on the other side.

Nothing had changed. It wasn't as if Julia still lived there, but her bedroom was the same from the day she left for college, and Linda hadn't touched a thing since Julia had died. The bulletin board held pictures and cards. The bedroom had a cotton-candy air about it. Soft and sweet, as though if he touched anything, it might melt away.

Liam remembered. He felt. And he knew that life was moving on, but he didn't know how to get beyond the bleakness that shadowed each day. He dropped onto the side of the bed and waited to feel less hollow.

But he didn't feel anything—not even the guilt that he always clung too. Liam squeezed his hands into fists, crumpling the envelope he'd still held, and flung it across the room. The impact barely smacked the wall, and it dropped. The unfulfilling throw agitated his frustration. "Fucking hell."

Liam reached for the pillow and launched it. Hints of Julia's scent clung to the linens. The pillow crashed into the window. The blinds clattered, then her desk lamp crashed over the edge. *Finally!* That was what he needed. Noise. Damage. Not a damn celebration!

A knock sounded on the bedroom room, and his irritation flared at the interruption. He sucked in a deep breath and held it until his lungs burned.

"Liam?" Chelsea called quietly.

"Everything's fine. Don't worry about it."

She rapped softly again, and he pinched his eyes shut.

"What?"

"If I missed the invitation to throw things, I'd like to invite myself anyway."

He rubbed his forehead.

"I'm coming in whether you like it or not." The knob twisted, and the door cracked.

"Be my guest." As if he had a choice.

Chelsea passed him and righted the lamp and drapes. She swept the pillow off the ground and tossed it back on to the bed. "Could've done better."

"*What?*"

She shrugged. "Two out of ten."

He didn't have a clue. "For what?"

Chelsea glanced about the room. "Aftermath?" She shrugged again. "Though I missed your technique."

He frowned. "Did you need something?"

She crossed her arms. "Someone woke up on the wrong side of the rainbow today."

"Go away, Chelsea."

She sighed and shook her head. "We're supposed to be full of joy and life today. Didn't you know?"

Maybe everyone could find a happy place today because they weren't the one to blame for Julia's death. "I missed the memo."

Chelsea turned and nearly left but stopped. "My partner says that when people are too deep in pain, it's impossible to realize they're not alone."

Ha. Today proved he was alone on a dreary island. "Got it."

Her dark eyes narrowed, and she pursed her lips. "Now I know how Mac feels when he shares words of wisdom. You're not alone, Liam."

A part of him always believed Chelsea blamed him whenever she wasn't with Julia. He couldn't fathom the level of her resentment now. "*No one* knows how I feel."

"I do. I promise you."

Liam glowered. "You can't."

She snorted. "Why's that?"

"Because..." His fists balled at his side. "Because I didn't mean for this to happen."

Her dark eyes widened and jaw dropped. "Liam—"

"I should've been able to stop it." He paced the small width of the bedroom with the day's smiles and laughter mocking him. The celebration echoed in his thoughts, reminding him of pain he had learned to cope with over the past year.

"You can't do that to yourself," she whispered.

"I can." He stopped. "And I deserve it."

"Can you please cut the empathetic bull-cocky?"

"I don't think I should." He rubbed his temples and shook his head. "Leave. Before I say something I shouldn't."

She crossed her arms, and her jaw set. Dark eyes narrowed as though she might pounce. "Has anyone told you to shut up yet?"

His chin snapped up. "What?"

"Because maybe that's what you need." Her lips pursed. "Someone to tell you to stop with the selfish woe-is-me pity party."

He drew back then shook off his shock. "You have no idea what I need."

She stepped closer. "I know this wasn't your fault."

The hell it wasn't. "Chelsea, go."

She inched even closer. "You did *everything* you were supposed to do."

"You have no idea what I did." He never spoke about the shooting. The nightly news reports didn't do justice in their condensed, minute-long explanation of the worst night of his life. Chelsea didn't know what he'd said, what he promised. She didn't know shit.

He stalked to the door and threw it wide. "Get out."

Chelsea's bravado cracked. He couldn't pinpoint how. Maybe he saw a minute detail like her eyelashes flutter or her frown deepen. Whatever he'd noticed, for a moment, he saw past the unaffected woman ordering him to get over the past. Her loss, loneliness, and sorrow weighed heavily against his chest, and Liam deflated. He tilted his head and urged her out of the bedroom. "I just need to be alone."

She met his gaze like she wanted to read his mind, and her voice lowered, "You'll always have her. Even when you stop blaming yourself."

He didn't know what to say.

Then again, he didn't have to. She left as quickly as she'd come in, and he was left in the wake of her words.

Exhausted, he pivoted and noticed the manila envelope on the ground. He wanted to forget Chelsea's unsolicited advice and scooped the envelope off the floor. After another inspection for a return address, Liam tore it open.

Paperwork slid out. His stomach turned as he caught a glimpse of a crime scene report. Sweat pricked the back of his neck, and again Liam checked the envelope.

Shaking, he moved to a small desk and chair by the window and dropped onto the seat, then like a sadist readying for a painful fix, he picked up the contents and knew the horror he was about to relive: photocopies of original handwritten accounts taken from the scene, an evidence list, and a bureaucracy's worth of heartache from the FBI, DHS, Capitol Hill, and the Metro police. But he didn't know why.

"Everyone has something to say." He skimmed the first page then the second. For twelve months, he'd avoided most of the public reports and media, only sitting through necessary conversations with law enforcement.

Eyewitness accounts said as much as he'd expected. No one had pinpointed the older man as an additional shooter, and every agency known to man had assured him there wasn't an old man with dark eyes and salt-and-pepper hair.

Liam flipped to another page. Uncertainty twisted in his stomach. A shadowy picture showed a person stepping from the depths of a tunnel. Scrutinizing the poor photo, Liam narrowed his eyes, but it was impossible to see details.

The next page was an enlargement, too blurred to do any good. Then Liam flipped another page. The shadowed figured stepped up a ladder. The following picture showed that he'd slipped off his coat and added a hat.

"What the hell...?"

He rechecked the back of the pictures but found no label, no detail on who had tagged them as evidence. But there was a time stamp and a platform location.

The pictures came in sequential order, seconds apart. He shuffled the pile of papers of the reports he'd skimmed. Police reports detailed each 911 call. Liam checked the time stamps. Two minutes had elapsed between the first call and the man emerging from the tunnels.

A chill spiked over Liam's skin, and he scattered the pages on the desk, haphazardly sorting them into piles: police reports, threat assessments, eyewitness statements, and photographs.

This man in the photographs was the old man, the guy Liam was told hadn't been on the train. He hadn't given a witness statement because he *must've* stepped out at a previous station. At least that was what investigators told him.

He rechecked the piles—still no ballistics report. *Why was that impossible to get a hold of?* That would have proved that the man Liam attacked hadn't shot Julia. His weapon hadn't discharged, or some other idiotic excuse he'd heard.

There was another shooter. And suddenly the missing old man and these pictures confirmed his sanity. Maybe Liam wasn't to blame after all.

But why…?

He grabbed the manila envelope and rushed into the hall. The house was quiet. He checked the dining room and the living room but didn't find anyone, not even the Nymans. The side door to the expansive backyard opened, and he spun around.

Chelsea jumped then rolled her eyes. "Jeez, Liam. You almost scared the vanilla wafers out of me."

"Where did this come from?" He held the envelope upright.

She shrugged. "I don't know."

"You don't know what?" He shook it as though she needed to look again. "Where it came from or who it's from?"

"Both." Chelsea walked to the kitchen sink and pulled open the cabinet. She pulled a new trash bag free and lined the can then slid the can back into place. "What's going on with you?"

He searched the kitchen wildly as if it could offer answers. "Where are Linda and Frank?"

"I'm not sure you should bother them like this."

"Like what?" He stared at his name on the envelope.

"Like you're losing your mind."

His jaw clenched. "Where are they?"

"Probably relaxing. Which you might want to consider."

He ignored Chelsea and paced. *Who would have this?*

He could call the FBI agent who had taken his statement. Maybe he could call in a favor at work. But dammit, his contacts were rooted soundly in war zones, not in the city of agencies and red tape. He had absolutely zero connections in the United States.

Except for… he turned.

Except for *Chelsea.*

CHAPTER FOUR

THE CELL PHONE vibrated in Chelsea's purse on the counter. The spastic buzz was loud enough to break her concentration—and apparently, Liam's also.

He stared pointedly. "Are you going to answer that?"

"No." Somehow, phone calls only served to exhaust her. Given the emotional roller coaster of the day, she considered ignoring phone calls part of self-care. "Everyone I'd talk to just left this house or would know better."

She walked to the dining room.

Liam followed and asked, "Better than what?"

"*Then to call.*"

He scowled. "People don't call you?"

"They text me." *How does he not understand that in the age of messenger apps?* Though truth be told, texts were starting to bug her too. But at least she'd check them—unlike her voicemail, which remained perpetually full. "You're a phone guy?"

"I'm a..." He shook his head and returned to sorting the piles of paper on the dining room table. "Never mind. Will you look at something?"

The dining room chandelier cast a dramatic light over the long dark-wood table. Just hours earlier, it had been covered with an assortment of pastries, antipasti, and casseroles, and now that she'd cleaned every last crumb from the Nymans' first floor, Chelsea didn't know what to do with herself. "Sure, I guess."

Reliving the best parts of her best friend had been uplifting. The last year had been a process of healing and moving forward. But the celebration of life reminded Chelsea still how much work there was to do when it came to the hole in her heart that Julia's death left.

She leaned against the wall and watched as Liam inspected the papers, his consternation deepening with every page studied. His behavior worried her as he fussed over his documents. "I can come back when you have this—" She gestured. "Organized."

He methodically rearranged the paperwork. Each page checkered the mahogany table as he reviewed them, then squared the papers.

"Gimme another second," he grumbled. "Paperwork isn't my thing."

"Good thing it's mine." *Though what kind of paperwork?* She hadn't the slightest clue, but he had piqued her interest. She inched from the wall. "Want some help?"

He didn't answer, and she edged closer. *Evidence. Documentation. Pictures.*

Oh, coconut cupcakes. Her throat tightened, and she crept the few inches back to the wall. If that had to do with Julia, Chelsea didn't want to help. Her stomach lurched at the possibilities—crime scene photos, autopsy notes, or worse. She wasn't one of those tough-talking, gun-slinging crime fighters that could leap from building to building. She didn't like bloody crime scenes and cursed more like a kindergarten teacher than a sailor.

Other than her badge, there was nothing about her that would give her away as a typical Marshal—if there were such a thing—except her upper-body strength. She didn't look the part. Some might go so far as to say that she didn't *play* the part—if "some" were her partner, Mac. He once joked that her gravestone would one day read, "Here lies a rule-following, candy-cane-cursing woman."

When she glared, he'd tacked on, "And brought Zee Zee Mars to justice."

That line on her gravestone, she would take, because one day, Chelsea would catch the criminal.

Julia wouldn't be there to see Chelsea arrest Zee Zee Mars, and a lonely sorrow melted the funny memory.

She looked at Liam. He hid his emotions well as he focused on the table, but she could still feel the cloud that had lingered around him throughout the day. She hoped he'd move away from blaming himself. A guy like that might carry that burden forever. They had superhero brains and lived action-movie lives—invincible. She couldn't imagine what the mortality he must grapple with and didn't want him to suffer. Even if she didn't know much about him, she knew he'd treated Julia like a princess. That made him okay in her book.

"All right. Can you look at this?" he asked.

Chelsea sucked in her cheeks and prayed her gag reflex didn't trigger. "What've you got?"

He tipped his head toward the dark pictures and paperwork. Julia's name was on the top of a report.

Son of a blueberry muffin, she'd do anything to avoid crime scene photos. Dread curled Chelsea's toes as she quickly begged God to be easy on her. It'd been a tough day despite her smile, and she wasn't sure how much she could take.

Chelsea held her breath, and as she came closer, her dark silk blouse felt like a straight jacket. She stopped at Liam's side and stole a peek at the pictures—and choked on relief. No lifeless, bloody pictures waited for her inspection.

Dizzy and teetering in high heels she that hated, Chelsea swallowed the last bits of panic and placed her hands on the edge of the table.

"You okay?" he asked.

Another breath in and out, and she reassured him, "Tired, I guess," and picked up the closest set of papers—photocopies of handwritten statements. Then she moved to a concise form that summarized the event with a few checked boxes. But the dark CCTV shots didn't make sense. "What's the context?"

He didn't speak but angled to watch her and the papers.

She refocused on the CCTV pictures then moved on to a highly redacted report. Most of the text had been blacked out, and as she flipped the page, she didn't learn much.

His eyes burned into her as she read what little was there then turned the page again.

"There." He tapped the paper. "*This*."

The top paragraph had been completely blacked out, but the page had more text to read than the previous ones, and as she went over the lines, trying to quilt the context together, Liam shoved his hands into his suit pockets and stepped closer to read over her shoulder. "Fourth paragraph."

Her eyes dropped, skimming.

"It says the bullets recovered don't match the FN-P90 submachine gun found."

She read what he said then did so again. "What the donut holes is going on," she muttered and turned back to the first page. Any information indicating which agency or who wrote the report had been redacted. Chelsea turned back and reread the paragraph in question. "I don't understand."

Crossing his arms, he arched his eyebrows in a way that made the skin at the back of her neck tingle. But he didn't explain.

"Liam… the news said—"

"I don't know what they said. But I know what I was told and what this says here."

She cleared her throat. "The news said there was a shooter. *One* shooter."

"I was told the weapon that misfired shot Julia. It might've been chaos, but those shots didn't come from our side." Liam jerked his head toward the table, pinpointing another document. "Read."

She put the report down and skimmed the statements from the officers.

"Now the CCTV pictures," he ordered.

Again, Chelsea cleared her throat. "I'm not sure what I'm looking for."

"You know *exactly* what you're looking for."

Another shooter? Another gun? Yes, that was what she was looking for—an answer that explained why the public information didn't mention anything of the sort.

"Dammit, tell me what you think, Chelsea."

Pain coated his demand. She didn't know how he'd spent the last year, but reliving the tragedy today of all days had to hurt. "*Liam—*"

"The first day I met Julia," he abruptly changed the subject, "she told me that if I ever hurt her feelings, she had a best friend who would hunt me down."

The unexpected story made her heart squeeze in a happy way. She'd had that wonderful feeling several times that day, and even if it took Liam all day to share a happy memory, she was glad he did. Chelsea let a grin grow. "Good thing you were a good guy."

He let the tiniest flicker of a smile fight to the surface, but then he shook his head. "What do you think?"

I think today made Liam crazy. But she didn't understand why he had this information. "I think you saved a lot of lives that day. Even if you couldn't save everyone."

He shook his head.

"You disarmed a shooter on mass transit," she gently suggested, pointing out the obvious.

Tapping the redacted report, he said, "Different weapon."

"Reports are wrong all the time." Chelsea placed a hand on his bicep, hoping to ease the blow but pulled away when his muscle tensed.

"Sometimes." He blew out a breath and scrubbed a hand through his hair. "God, I wish we knew where this envelope came from."

She sucked on her bottom lip. There were sickos out in the world. Maybe someone was screwing with him. The timing of the delivery was questionable. Maybe it was a bad joke gone wrong. Maybe that sounded too cruel to be real, and it was merely a report that included a mistake.

"And who is this?" He tapped the CCTV pictures.

She picked them up. They were grainy. The cameras' focus had been on the commuters lined up, waiting for the train. She squinted, cataloging each person for anything that would appear out of sorts.

At the mouth of the tunnel... *Who is that?* She narrowed her eyes, trying to focus on the image, then she flipped to the next picture. The small blur was larger. Chelsea checked the time stamps—seconds apart. Again, she flipped to the next picture and the next and the next until she had no doubt that the small blur of an image had materialized into an out-of-focus person who emerged from the tunnel and melted into the crowd.

Her stomach tightened, and a curious tingle skated over her forearms as she placed the pictures in a neat pile, squaring them as Liam had done. She rechecked all that she reviewed already, now noting the time stamps on the 911-call readouts and the witness statements. "If," she whispered, uncertain why she kept her voice low, "there was another weapon—"

"And shooter."

Her mind raced. Nothing made sense. "Why didn't anyone see them?"

"Because all attention was on me."

She stared blankly.

"There was a fight. All eyes were on us and the FN-P90."

That didn't change her confusion.

"It's a memorable weapon," he offered.

"True—" She waved the point away. "But Julia?"

"Julia did exactly what I told her to. Get down and stay put."

"What you're suggesting—"

"I'm not suggesting shit. That report says there was another gun but doesn't say what kind."

"That would be..." Pins and needles numbed her fingertips, and a heavy weight lodged against her chest. "That really sounds like..." *A conspiracy theory.* But she wouldn't say that. She couldn't. Calling Liam paranoid seemed cruel and unnecessary. Especially since his imaginative complot had some credence of truth. "It sounds like a stretch."

He glowered. "Right."

"I'm sorry that wasn't what you wanted to hear." She took another hard look. "You don't know where it came from?"

He shook his head then shoved the pages he'd neatly organized toward the center of the table, squaring them into one pile. "Thanks for your opinion."

"What are you going to do?"

He picked up the pile and tapped it on the table until the edges aligned, then he turned around. "Thanks again."

"Wait."

But he didn't and walked away.

Chelsea followed. "Liam?"

"That's all I needed." He crossed the living room.

She trailed him. "Would you stop for a second?"

"Got things to do." He powered toward the stairs.

She grabbed the back of his shirt, and Liam spun. They stared at each other. His green eyes flared with ice-cold determination, and she gritted her teeth. An unspoken showdown exploded—who hurt more, who lost more, who spent the last year searching for answers when senseless crimes didn't have explanations.

"You don't get to be the only one in pain," she said.

His jaw ticked. "I never said that."

"And you don't get to ask for my help then act like a turd."

His face froze. "A turd?"

"Yeah." She pursed her lips, refusing to repent for her lack of f-bombs and five-dollar-word name-calling. She used them when necessary, but he didn't need to know that.

"Don't worry about it. I've got it covered."

She nearly tipped back in her high heels for how hard her eyes rolled. "You have *it* covered? You don't even know what *it* is!"

"And neither do you. Which is what I want."

Indignant, she straightened her shoulders. "And why is that?"

He jerked away, but she snagged his arm again. Liam pulled free but didn't storm off. "What is going on with you?"

"I already let Julia die on my watch. I'm sure as shit not going to point you toward an early grave too."

Her jaw fell, and her heart broke. For the second time, she wanted desperately to reassure him Julia wasn't killed because of him—but *after* she set his butt straight. "You do not get to pull the uber-protective man card to keep me safe." She was a US Marshal for crying out loud.

"I can pull whatever I want, Chelsea."

Gah! He was infuriating. "Go blow your chauvinistic bull-spit out your pie hole."

His brow furrowed as if she were the one who needed a mental-wellness check. "I'm going to take all my chauvinistic bull*shit* and keep you safe. Like it or not."

He hustled away and left Chelsea with her head spinning.

So much had changed the day Mac gave her the news. Chelsea had fought for a new normal, searching for a way to live life without the best friend who had been close enough to be her sister. But now, with a pile of photos and anonymous redacted reports, questions shredded her healing.

If Liam had information about a *second* shooter, then nothing would keep Chelsea from inserting herself into the manhunt—whether he liked it or not.

CHAPTER FIVE

WAKING IN THE Nymans' guest bedroom felt like a chore, but Liam couldn't say no when Linda and Frank had asked him and Chelsea to stay late and look through pictures. Eventually, the evening ended, and he was glad he'd stayed. The conversation had taken his mind off the envelope.

Though not for long. After Linda and Frank went to bed and Chelsea took the guest room, Liam bedded down on the couch. Sleep didn't come, and he'd spent most of the night envisioning the CCTV pictures and wondering where they came from.

Somehow, he'd fallen asleep. Chirping birds warned him that morning had arrived.

Bacon and coffee scented the air, and he scrubbed his eyes. His first thought was the manila envelope and its contents. He had to make calls. Someone would know who delivered the information.

But he didn't know whom to call first.

Damn. His mind raced and tripped at once, and he dropped his head back. The living room ceiling held no answers, but staring into nothing reminded him that he needed coffee, so he threw off the afghan blanket and stood.

Muffled conversation and happiness trailed from the kitchens as if it was another ordinary day. Maybe it was. Perhaps that was what he'd been struggling to understand over the last twelve months.

Liam rubbed the back of his neck, and laughter rang out again.

Chelsea knew what he knew, or at least what he'd guessed what the pictures and report meant, but he could hear her laughing up a storm with Frank and Linda. It wasn't that he wanted the world to mourn without end, but they didn't have to sound so damn happy. He didn't know how to move forward the way everyone else had seemed able.

He replayed yesterday's back-and-forth with Chelsea, and his need for coffee doubled. Breakfast might be awkward, but his need for caffeine trumped the need to avoid her.

Liam ran a hand over his chest. Frank loaned him a shirt and jogging pants, and the clothes fit too tight. He adjusted the waistband and pulled at the sleeves, then headed into the kitchen. "Morning."

Frank, still laughing quietly, let the paper drop. "Fresh pot just finished."

Chelsea twirled a pen between her fingers, offering nothing more than a polite-but-not-really smile, then turned far too much attention to a fruit smoothie before she jotted a note along the margin of an oversized piece of paper.

The kitchen door that led outside opened and Linda dusted her hands and shut the door with her hip. "Good morning." Opening a cabinet under the sink and removing a new trash bag, she said, "Your plate is in the oven."

"Thanks," Liam mumbled then poured coffee and retrieved the still-warm plate, wondering how long everyone had been awake and how he slept through their noise.

Linda relined the kitchen can. "Did you sleep okay?"

On the couch, next to mystery documents? Not a chance. "I survived."

Linda gave him a warm smile but then turned to the dishwasher.

He took a seat at the kitchen table and studied the room. Each person acted as though yesterday hadn't occurred. Their easy chit-chat and normal morning activities rolled along as though it wasn't the first time they'd been together since the funeral.

Linda leaned against the counter and paged through a cooking magazine. Every few pages, she'd mention how a picture made her hungry. Frank would say something about how he couldn't wait to try whatever she suggested, then he'd page through the town paper, remarking about the high school team or a new transportation plan, and Linda would agree.

High school football games and a new traffic light? Liam didn't understand why no one felt like him—out of sorts and lost. Maybe because they weren't at fault. Realizing that stabbed him in the chest.

"How's the book going?" Linda asked Chelsea.

"It's just a mock-up but..." She twirled the pen. "Not good."

Frank folded the paper and laid it down. "Why?"

She shrugged. "Something's not right, and no matter what I jot down, it doesn't help."

Liam wanted to point out the obvious. Julia wasn't there—*that* was the problem. He didn't know what the shit Chelsea was doing with their book mock-up thing, but the answer glared like a neon sign.

"You'll figure it out." Linda turned a page in the magazine.

"I thought..." Liam placed his mug on the table loudly enough to grab the room's attention. "Today would be different."

"Different how, sweetie?" Linda asked.

"Just different." He shook his head, frustrated. "But you are doing everything the same."

"What do you mean?" Linda studied him curiously but then her features softened as she understood. "Nothing will ever be like it was."

He understood that. It wasn't as if he'd spent the year moping under a dark cloud. At least not all the time. But he needed something to change. Hell if he knew what it was or how to do it.

"Are you okay?" Chelsea asked softly.

"Never mind. Forget I said anything."

Chelsea rolled her lips into her mouth then offered a pitying smile. "Okay."

Damn, he didn't want to feel guilty for snapping at her on top of everything.

Linda closed her magazine and moved to the table. "Maybe it shouldn't have taken us a year to get everyone together. I couldn't have managed what we did yesterday after the funeral... But hearing from her friends and sharing our stories made my heart fuller."

He shoved a piece of bacon into his mouth, having no idea when would be the right time.

Chelsea laid her pen on the oversized page. "It's going to be okay."

"Forget I said anything." Liam chomped on another piece of bacon, ignoring the eggs and muffin. He sensed Frank and Linda staring and could feel Chelsea study him. She could still be upset about last night. They hadn't traded a word when Linda and Frank forced them to sit together and look at pictures. He bet she was silently cursing him out with her ridiculous name-calling. Donut brain. Sprinkle ass.

"I think," Linda said, "this year has been hard, and we've all had to find a new normal. That doesn't mean we don't hurt."

He rubbed the back of his neck, not sure what to say.

Frank offered him the paper as though the mundane activity might help.

"No, thanks."

And with that, Linda reopened her magazine. Frank stood and headed to the coffee pot for a refill, and Chelsea twirled her pen as if she were headlining a marching band.

The dryer signal chimed, and Linda pushed back from the table. Frank wandered from the kitchen with his refill.

Liam scowled at his eggs then dug in and tapped his bare foot. Chelsea's pen dropped onto the table, and he looked up. Her dark pink-lips were pressed into a tight line that made them lose their color. Her eyebrows arched, and she stared as though she were waiting.

"What?"

"Don't be like that to them," she scolded.

He smirked. "Don't act like it's party central—"

"Oh, give me a break. No one's acting like that."

Liam shoveled another mouthful of eggs into his mouth.

"You're not the only one who has had a hard time since she died."

"Then act like it," he snapped.

Her lips parted—then she slapped her mouth shut. Tears formed in her eyes, and she dropped her chin. Shit, he didn't mean to do that. His throat knotted, and a lonely emptiness washed away his hostility, no matter how hard he tried to hang on to its protective armor.

"Sorry," he finally muttered, though she'd hid her face with an intense study of her notes. "That was a dick move."

Chelsea shrugged, not glancing up.

"And about last night." He stabbed the eggs, moving them around. "I shouldn't have been a dick then, either."

She made angry marks across the page. "Don't worry about it."

"Why doesn't this feel weird to anyone else?" He gestured toward the living room then the bacon.

Her pen hovered over the paper, then finally, she lifted her head. "It does. It feels terrible."

He didn't know what to say.

"You know what I miss?" she asked, twisting the pen between her fingers.

He wasn't sure he wanted to know. "Hmm?"

She smiled, glancing to the side, then laughed. "This morning has been so quiet."

He froze and realized that even with the buzz of conversation, the kitchen was quieter than it would've been with Julia's laughter. Then he smiled too. "You two were loud." He laughed. "Even when you *thought* you were being quiet."

Feigning surprise, she said, "You act like we were obnoxious."

"And you act like I never received a drunk-dialed pick-up request from a bar."

She laughed again. "*Never.*"

He snorted.

"But if we ever did, we couldn't have been obnoxious."

They laughed, and he relaxed as they reminisced. Each recalled story brought on another one until he realized that this was what everyone else did yesterday. He leaned back in his chair, feeling not as empty, but he sobered.

Chelsea offered an understanding nod as though she could read his mind. She inhaled and finally let it go when she picked her pen back up and returned to her work.

"What are you doing?"

Her face scrunched. "I'm making edits. Or at least trying. But they're not working."

"Why aren't they?" He leaned over the table to eye the page. It was mostly filled with pictures. A large amount of the text had been crossed out. Tiny notes filled the margins with arrows and lines, and several photos were marred with question marks and slashes.

"Because she was always the photographer and the one with the artistic eye. I don't know why something isn't working. I just know it isn't, and—" Chelsea pushed back from the table and retrieved another print from under her purse then laid the regular-sized page in front of him. "And because my pictures are awful compared to hers."

He eyed the pages but didn't see any difference. "Eye of the beholder, maybe?"

Shifting her weight, she frowned. "Probably not."

He couldn't see a problem with any of the pictures. Hell, he couldn't distinguish between Julia's work and Chelsea's. He eased back in his chair and focused on his coffee, trying to remember the last time he'd asked Julia about the book, but came up blank. "I didn't pay enough attention, did I?"

Chelsea cocked her head. "To the books?"

He nodded. "Yeah."

"You did," she promised and made a cross over her heart. "I would've heard otherwise." She paused with a knowing look. "Actually, we *both* would've heard otherwise."

He chuckled, then leaned back, arms crossed, and realized that he had been moving through the motions for the last year, not living life, wishing each day would start and end differently. Yesterday's celebration and today's coffee with Chelsea had seemed like torture, but maybe those were the two things he needed.

Needed for what? The past wouldn't change. The future waited. All he had to do was live. But hell, he'd forgotten how.

CHAPTER SIX

THE CONVERSATION DIED, and Chelsea couldn't read Liam's expression. His attitude had swung from caveman-like to understandably quiet. He'd wrapped his hands around his coffee mug and stared in a way that she thought it best to leave him with his thoughts. Then the doorbell rang.

"Liam," Frank called from the living room, "you have a visitor."

Liam arched his eyebrows. "Wonder who."

Her nerves tingled, and they both had to be thinking about the package he received the day before. Liam pushed out of the chair and left the kitchen.

Nosey, she couldn't sit still and carefully padded to the edge of the kitchen but couldn't hear anything.

She bit her lip, wondering about the authenticity of the report and pictures. She didn't know why they'd be fake but didn't have an answer to why Liam had received them anonymously.

Frank walked into the kitchen, eyeing her as he eased by, and her cheeks flushed. She wasn't spying, per se, but more questions compiled with each word of the hushed conversation she couldn't hear, and maybe, if she heard Liam's conversation, everything would make sense.

"You won't be able to hear unless you scoot closer," Frank pointed out as he refilled his coffee mug.

"I'm not trying to listen." Except, obviously she was, and Chelsea edged around the corner, still unable to see whom Liam was speaking with. They stood on the front porch, and the glass storm door showed their backs. Then Liam turned.

Chelsea jumped back. As fast as he'd gone outside, he strode back in, but he diverted upstairs instead of the kitchen.

She inched into the living room. The large man on the front porch faced away from the house. His shoulders reminded her of Liam's. Both were broad and tall, but the man outside had darker hair, and without seeing his face, she sensed he was older.

A minute later, Liam hustled down the stairs. He wore his dress pants from the day before and the button-down shirt, haphazardly tucked and unbuttoned at the collar. When he turned to look over his shoulder, he had more color in his face than Chelsea could recall seeing in quite some time. "Tell Linda thanks for breakfast, and I don't know when I'll be back."

The glass storm door slapped shut as he rushed out.

"Yeah, sure."

She walked to the front porch in time to see both men, equal in height and bulk when side-by-side, beeline for a large black SUV with tinted windows. A third man stepped out of the back. He had dark hair like the man who had come to the door, and while he was not as muscular as Liam or the man by his side, Chelsea could tell he wasn't a lightweight.

Linda stepped to Chelsea's side, surprising her.

"Who was that?"

Shaking her head, Chelsea said, "I don't know."

They watched as Liam disappeared into the back of the SUV. The man who had knocked closed the back door then moved to the driver's side.

"Huh," Linda said.

The SUV's engine roared when it turned over, then the vehicle raced away. Chelsea watched until it turned.

"I hope everything is okay," Linda said, sounding as uncertain as Chelsea felt.

Between the vehicle and the manila envelope, Chelsea was confident everything was *not* okay, but she didn't know why.

CHAPTER SEVEN

AFTER ONE LONG-ASS drive with the two men from the Department of Homeland Security in the armored SUV, Liam and his silent companions parked at what had to be a DHS black site, though neither man would confirm where they'd taken him.

They'd moved him like a prisoner with the added bonus of covering his eyes and ears and binding his hands with plastic zip-tie restraints. Restraining and hooding civilians was a step beyond anything that he'd seen stateside in the military or while contracting.

It wasn't until their journey took them to a freight elevator in a cold building that Liam believed they might have come to their final destination. The elevator descended many floors until his escorts led him out. They paused for locks and doors, but still blindfolded, Liam had only vague guesses to rely on until one of the men removed his restraints and unwrapped his head.

White lights blinded him. Liam blinked and held out his hands until his equilibrium balanced. *Where are we?* The holding room—or maybe a better description would be a cage—had glass walls. The metal ceiling gleamed with razor wire curled in tight circles.

A three-stories-tall fence, threaded with razor-wire ribbons and with high-voltage signs posted, enclosed the glass cage.

"They're not messing around." Whoever *they* were. Liam rubbed his wrists and stepped up to a metal table. Four chairs waited, one on each side. He took a seat to face the door and continued to study the peculiar holding cell.

The two men who'd brought him there disappeared through a glass door that didn't have handles. Hinges and a rectangle outline were the only visible sign the glass had an opening.

A cold, sterile-scented draft pushed through the wire ceiling, and though he was alone, he felt as if he were under a microscope.

"If this is how you treat your friends…" He scooted his chair in, noting the lack of vibrations as he slid across the glass-like material. "I'd hate to be your—"

An alarm beeped like the sound of a delivery truck in reverse, and the metal-and-glass doors opened noiselessly. Two different men entered the outer perimeter then stepped into the glass room. Their tactical pants and dark shirts differed from suits of the men who'd knocked on the Nymans' door, but they were still the same type of person—large and commanding.

Splitting apart to take their seats, they revealed a much smaller, much older woman in a bloodred skirt suit. Liam thought she was vaguely familiar, but he couldn't place the beady dark eyes or her lipsticked scowl. Her high heels gave her added height, but even as Liam stood to greet them all, he towered over her.

The men had a look that Liam appreciated—assholes with a side of get-the-job-done. He respected that. But the lady… she distinctly did not give off a military vibe, though she seemed as though she'd seen the worst the world had to give.

Liam extended his hand to her, unsure if that made her an ally or a problem. "Ma'am."

Her firm grip belied her petite stature, and Liam then greeted the men who flanked her, standing like two columns of security.

The woman nodded, and they moved to the table. She pulled out a chair and took a seat. "I'm glad you've arrived."

Her voice tickled a memory, but he still couldn't place her—not that remembering names and faces was his strong suit. "Arrived where?"

"You're not at liberty to know." Brushing her well-sprayed hair behind an ear and folding her hands on the table, she said, "But here you are, nonetheless."

"It wasn't an invitation I would say no to." The man at the Nymans' door had announced himself as an agent from the Department of Homeland Security, produced a DHS badge, referenced the manila envelope, and asked him to go for a drive. Liam couldn't have dressed faster than he had.

The corners of her eyes crinkled. "Liam Adrian Brosnan. Army reconnaissance captain, retired. Currently freelance contracting."

"Correct." He pursed his lips. "Forgive me, but I'm not sure who you are."

She held his eyes for a second longer than was comfortable. "Senator Samantha Sorenson."

Shit! She chaired the Senate Intelligence Committee. "Ma'am, forgive me—"

She waved his apology away with a toss of her hand that made her gold bracelets clink against her slender watch. "While time had gone by, first, on behalf the president and my Senate colleagues, please accept my condolences."

Apprehension and anticipation of whatever was *second* felt like heavy, wet cement in his chest. "Thank you."

"I trust you've reviewed the package we had delivered," she said.

He had to concentrate to keep a sudden restlessness from bouncing in his feet. "I did."

"Good. Because that leads to our second point of discussion."

Every question and conspiracy theory he'd twisted in his mind overnight again spread through his thoughts like an unchecked wildfire. The anxiety mixed with the guilt and loss that Julia's remembrance event had conjured. Liam swallowed hard, vowing to remain unaffected by whatever came next.

"It's our conclusion that Julia Nyman's death was premeditated and expertly planned."

The room tilted. Premeditated murder hadn't crossed his mind during his extensive guesswork. "I'm sorry, but what?"

The senator repeated the exact same words in the same tone, this time adding on *murder*, but Sorenson could have just as easily been reading a stock market report for how factual and emotionless her tone was.

He shook his head. "It couldn't have been."

Sorenson didn't respond.

Memories of the date night made sweat break out on the back of his neck. "No one knew where we were going. Not even Julia knew where I was taking her." He didn't understand. "Who would want to hurt her?" A true-crime journalist might make a few enemies, but he couldn't fathom her reports leading to murder.

"Her? No one," Sorenson said.

Liam's eyes bulged as if she had proven his point.

"It wasn't her they wanted to hurt."

"Then who?" Exasperation colored his question more than he wanted to show.

"*You.*"

CHAPTER EIGHT

EVERY MUSCLE IN Liam stilled. His thoughts stalled, leaving him to contend with the thudding pound of his pulse until he spat, "*What?*"

Her bracelets jangled again. "You were part of Operation Red Gold."

Several years had passed since Red Gold, but Liam didn't confirm her statement. As far as he knew, Red Gold was classified as top secret. He didn't plan to take a single fucking breath until someone volunteered what the hell was going on.

"For God's sake." Sorenson huffed. "I chair the Senate Intel Committee. Even the goddamn president has to update me."

Liam's eyebrows arched. The two men who sat on either side of her didn't react, and he decided to take his cue from them and ignore the bravado. He'd keep his answer concise and pray this conversation was sanctioned. "Yes. I was a part of Red Gold."

"Were you aware of casualties?" she asked.

"There were no friendlies on the casualty list." Of that, he was certain. As for the details, specifics were fuzzy. He hadn't thought about that in years.

"That's not what I asked."

"Ma'am, with all due respect..." Liam glanced at the other men. Their faces held no information. For all he knew, this could be some convoluted masquerade to extract intel, and suddenly, he couldn't be sure of the men who'd transported him or who controlled the location they were in. He wondered if the salacious documents about Julia were a lure that had trounced his better judgement. "We debriefed years ago. There's likely a report better suited to provide you an update than I could."

"I provided *you* an update on your girlfriend," she said pointedly then moderated her tone. "This is related."

Liam couldn't make any connection between Red Gold, Julia, and Sorenson. His temples ached. "There were casualties of enemy combatants, but I don't recall the exact count."

"What did you do with the bodies?" she asked.

The question unnerved him. "What does that—"

"*The bodies?*" she said again.

His jaw twitched. "Our instructions were specific. Bag and tag 'em."

"Then?"

Then? What does she think we did? "I don't know their final destination. My job was done."

Sorenson's sharp chin jutted toward the man at her right. "Mr. Westin, care to elaborate?"

"The dead count included," he said, not missing a beat, "a young woman named Quy Long."

Shaking his head, Liam said, "We had confirmed intelligence. No women. No children. None were within a desert mile of that place."

"That was the best intel available at the time," Mr. Westin added vaguely.

Liam's nerves danced, and he doubled down on his words. "And we didn't see any."

"You wouldn't have," Mr. Westin said.

Tension built in Liam's shoulders. "We only interacted with tangos who engaged us with weapons first."

"Quy Long engaged with you first."

"A woman was fighting?" Liam reassessed what he could remember about the mission. "Their patriarchy wouldn't allow it."

"There's always an exception to the rule," Westin continued. "Her father, Tran Pham, has had his fingers in every domestic and international terrorist attack in the last two decades. He's the exception to almost every rule you can think of."

"I haven't heard of him before." Though Liam wasn't sure he was the best candidate to make a list of terrorist protocol. His job had never been to dabble in the intelligence community's tedious work, only to follow orders based on their findings.

"Most people haven't," Sorenson said. "Pham stays in the shadows."

"I'd assume everything the IC works on is in the shadows." Liam wondered what they thought his experience with the intel community was.

The senator repositioned, and her jewelry clinked. "Think of him as a fundraiser."

"All right..." If that was the case, they'd brought the wrong man in to discuss terrorism financing. Military contracting had many facets, and Liam's didn't reach to fundraising. Hell, the first fundraising images that came to mind were Linda's kindergarten brownie bake sales.

Westin cracked his knuckles. "He's the money man behind several terrorist states, yet only a few dozen agencies worldwide focus on Tran Pham."

"Why?" Liam asked.

"Some in the IC believe he's a myth."

"But he's not."

"Not one bit," Mr. Westin confirmed.

"And we killed his daughter?" Liam asked.

"Bravo, Ace. Now it's clear?"

As clear as mud. Liam focused on Westin. "Are you searching for him?"

"Not personally."

"I am," Sorenson interrupted.

Liam glanced around the table, unsure how that connected his participation in Red Gold and Julia's *premeditated* murder. "Why are you telling me?"

Mr. Westin lifted his chin to the second man. "Mr. Black?"

Mr. Black eased his elbows onto the table. "Julia's death initially piqued the interest of the feds because of her work on Zee Zee Mars."

Liam's mind reeled. "You think Zee Zee Mars is mixed up in this too?"

"No," Mr. Black corrected. "It's not Mars's MO, but Julia's work with someone on the Marshal's Most Wanted Fugitive List caused the government to take a closer look. That wasn't a fast process, but when they did that, her death provided the missing lynchpin to connect a much larger, unnoticed problem."

Liam clenched his molars. "And what was that?"

"Other victims that were connected to Red Gold."

"Connected how? My old platoon?"

Mr. Black nodded. "Yes, but indirectly. They weren't victims. You weren't the victim. Yet each of you was victimized."

Liam inhaled and held it. If what Mr. Black said was true, Liam hadn't only failed to protect Julia from the shooting, he'd also brought the gunman to her. A wave of guilt made him queasy. "This is my fault—why?"

"Pham required his daughter to train like those he funded so she could have respect when she took over his work," Westin said. "That included live-action combat training."

"Field training would have protected her from their naysayers," Mr. Black further explained Pham's rationale.

Naysayers seemed an understatement for a group that didn't believe women could hold leadership roles, but then again, he didn't understand the logic of terrorism. "And Red Gold killed her?"

"Red Gold killed her *and* took her body," Westin said.

"In Pham's mind," Sorenson interrupted, "*you*, personally, stole her body."

"Me?"

"You led your platoon."

Liam processed the information. "It's been years."

"Pham is patient, meticulous, and vengeful."

An eye for an eye. "Who else did he attack?"

"In the last few years…" Mr. Black produced a tablet and gestured to the screen. "Parents, in-laws, wives, a girlfriend, and a daughter died. Some families were hit more than once."

"We believe Pham's focusing on connections that would be classified as loved ones," Westin added.

Liam pictured their faces as if years hadn't passed. Pain bubbled in his chest. "How?"

"Explosions in the home made to look like accidents."

He remembered the night of the Red Gold operation and the brilliant fires that tore through the night sky with detonations and gunfire. The mission had been deemed a success, but if his commanding officers knew then what he'd just learned… His stomach roiled, and he jerked his head toward Westin. "But Julia was shot."

"She's the outlier," Mr. Black answered instead.

"But you're sure this is related?"

"Without a doubt," Sorenson answered.

"How do you know—"

"We're aware of a related situation." The senator pursed her lips. "And between your team, you, and the situation—"

"It's an abduction," Westin said, shedding light on the mystery.

"Which adds nothing to our current discussion," Sorenson snapped.

"Agree to disagree, Samantha." Westin smoothed a hand over his dark beard as if he needed to focus his hands on something other than the senator. "Questions?"

So many… Liam balled his fists. "Why did it take this long to figure out?"

"Pham spent years planning this hit job," Mr. Black said. "Your team has been split up for years. Different states, different jurisdictions. It doesn't appear many of you stayed in touch."

The blame weighed heavily on Liam. It was true. They'd mostly moved on to new lives. It wasn't as if any of them were dropping in on one another online or in person.

"If it hadn't been for Julia…" The senator's jewelry clinked. "The deaths would've gone unnoticed."

"Unnoticed," he repeated numbly.

"Unnoticed and chalked up to faulty electrical work, gas line breaks, or appliance malfunctions," she continued. "But when you can tie each explosion together, the revelations are quite stunning."

The woman simplified their tragedies to data points in a word problem. His jaw clenched.

Westin's eyes narrowed. Other than the reference to the senator by her first name, his reaction was the first time that either man had shown a flicker of emotion. Westin's glare silently shouted a giant *Shut the fuck up* in Sorenson's direction, and as heartsick as Liam was, he fully supported Westin's sentiment.

"You should know," Black said, breaking the tension, "you are one of the few people to have seen Tran Pham in the flesh."

Raising his eyebrows, Liam thought back. *The man with the questions on the Metro, the one who made me uncomfortable—he knew Julia's name.* Culpability and regret pounded. "The second shooter. That was the man who exited the tunnel."

Westin nodded. "Tran Pham."

"He talked to her. Small talk."

"He identified her," Westin clarified.

"Then why not just..." A lump in his throat cut him off. "Why not just shoot her? Right then and there? Without the elaborate charade."

"He deems you responsible." Westin stroked his beard. "Just like he holds himself responsible. You fucked with his head. Now he's here to fuck with yours."

Westin was correct. A mind fuck had Liam by the balls. Every question, every memory that he replayed every day for more than a year. *How would the outcome have changed if I hadn't tried to be a hero?* That bravado had forced him to lose the greater battle.

"Look, Brosnan." Westin planted his fists on the table. "We need your help to end this."

He blinked, surprised by the quick turn in the conversation. "What kind of help?"

"It's simple," Sorenson said. "Give us a list of your loved ones."

They wanted him to name a potential hit list. But he didn't have anyone anymore.

Black produced a paper and pen. "Write it down. That's easier."

Numbness stiffened his hand as he picked up the pen. Its cool black metal weighted his fingers down as if he'd grasped a cinder block. "I'm not close to anyone but the Nymans." He scrawled out their names—Frank and Linda.

"The kindergarten teacher and the banker?" Black asked.

Liam straightened. "The Nymans are in danger?"

They didn't answer.

"Your father?" Black asked.

Liam shook his head. "We're not close. We haven't talked in years. I couldn't tell you where he is."

Black took back the paper and didn't ask about his mother. Liam guessed that meant they'd done their research beyond the Nymans, but reassurance didn't come. "Are Linda and Frank in danger?" Obviously, they were. "What are we going to do?"

"Nothing," Sorenson said.

Liam balked. "What?"

"What the senator means," Westin snarled, "is we are in a unique position."

"*We* aren't in a position. *I am.*"

"With only one target, we know who Pham will likely hit next."

Their cavalier wording hit him like an avalanche. "Let's be clear. If the Nymans are in danger—"

"*Let's be clear,*" Sorenson snipped. "You are the best opportunity our country has had to apprehend an international terrorist. The greater good is most important. Above our personal concerns."

Westin's jaw ticked, and if Liam didn't need to know more, the meeting would end right then.

Westin glared at the senator then added, "Look, Brosnan. Pham doesn't know we're on to him. The Nymans cannot deviate from their normal schedules."

He resisted. "You want to use them as bait? They're civilians."

"They're targets," Sorenson corrected. "Whether you like the truth or not."

"No way." He'd hide the Nymans himself then patrol the streets if it kept them safe.

Sorenson steepled her fingers. The glittering bracelets dropped down onto the cuff of her suit jacket and twinkled under the bright light. Each sparkle stood out of place in the sterile glass room. "No one wants the Nymans to be in danger, and everyone knows we have a duty to protect our country."

Her condescension only pressed salt into a wound. "They need a protective detail."

"No," she said firmly. "With the exception that you can keep an eye on them from a distance—*if* you can do so without tipping Pham off."

No problem, if wrapping their yard in razor wire and bunking on the front porch with artillery meant he wouldn't tip off Pham. "I'll talk to them."

"Not an option," Sorenson responded. "*They* will tip off Pham."

"*They* won't."

"Of course they will," she said. "They'll watch over their shoulders and skit around like the boogie man is behind every mailbox."

He frowned then looked at Westin and Black. Both waited, expressionless.

"I'm not asking for your help," Sorenson continued. "I'm telling you this is your duty."

"I don't work for you."

"You have an allegiance to this country, and if you don't, I'll keep you locked up where you can't interfere."

Indecision wrecked his thoughts, but he didn't have a choice. "How long will it take to catch Pham?"

"However long it takes," she said. "He's a virtual ghost."

"Who was abducted? When?"

"Quite some time has passed, which is why we're focused on Pham, rather than finding the victim."

There had to be a better way to do it. He couldn't protect the Nymans indefinitely. "I don't see how this would work."

"Officially," the senator said, "DHS will sign a contract with you."

"For what?"

She shrugged a padded shoulder. "It doesn't matter. But it will afford you an income, allow you to keep an eye out for the Nymans while staying in contact with me."

There wasn't another option. Some involvement was better than none. Still, short of staking out the Nyman's street, he didn't how to keep them safe with the senator's restrictions. Liam tried again. "There has to be another way."

"There's not." Senator Sorenson straightened. "We want him, and he wants to hurt you. It doesn't get any simpler than that."

CHAPTER NINE

MORNING SUN BLED through the gauzy white curtains, and Chelsea thought the day was starting far too early. She hadn't expected to spend another night but Linda had wanted to break out the pictures and home movies again. Chelsea couldn't deny her that, and after a quick run back to her condo to pick-up an overnight bag, they stayed up late and reminisced.

"It's too early," she told the birds that chirped from their perches in the Nymans' pine trees. She was an early bird herself, but even the sleepy, crack-of-dawn tweets were too early.

She rubbed her eyes, and still wearing her comfy sweatpants and old college tee, she stretched to begin her day with a fresh start, thankful that dreamland had coaxed her to a magical place where Julia was a phone call away, Liam didn't seem stuck, Chelsea's photography didn't stink, and her self-analysis didn't abound.

She'd fallen asleep re-reading her handwritten notes in the margins of the pictorial layouts. Chelsea lifted the closest one and cringed. "Sleep didn't help. I still suck."

The photos she'd snapped could've been taken by a child—a distracted one who didn't know how to focus or when to use a flash, and Chelsea tossed the papers away. Self-pity and frustration bubbled again. No matter which versions of the same picture she studied, no matter if the shots were lightened, darkened, or cropped, they wouldn't work.

Chelsea fell onto her pillow. "One of the many reasons I still wish you were here."

But whispering to a nonexistent Julia wouldn't change Chelsea's lack of photographing talent. Maybe she had taken the celebration of life as hard as Liam, but in a different way.

She rolled out of bed with all the grace of a linebacker and caught a glimpse of herself in the dresser mirror. She even looked like a football player with dark mascara smudges under her eyes.

Swiping the makeup with her fingers didn't help, so she grabbed the makeup remover from her overnight bag and a tissue off the dresser. Then, *presto*—the football-player eye-black wiped clean.

Adorably horrible picture frames decorated the top of the dresser, and Chelsea twisted the makeup remover bottle closed. She wasn't sure why Linda insisted on keeping the picture frames that she and Julia had made years ago. The preschool *gifts* looked like Pinterest fails with painted acorn-and-macaroni embellishments. Yet Linda displayed them as if the girls were the second coming of Monet. The guest room was a museum to their arts and crafts.

Chelsea snorted. One of the frames didn't even have a picture. The silly thing would probably fall apart if anyone tried to add one. She carefully lifted the fragile frame and ran her thumb along the finger-painted edge.

Maybe her work photographs were similar to their childhood frames. Maybe *someone* wouldn't think the pictures she took were delete-worthy. Maybe all Chelsea had to do was give herself a semblance of grace and take another look.

Or, maybe not. A blue-and-yellow acorn dropped from the frame. "Oh, coconuts," she muttered and set the frame down before she could do more damage.

She hoped a cup of coffee and a smoothie would turn her mood around. Smoothie first. Those were always better than caffeine.

Then perhaps her pictures deserved another look. She grabbed her pages, slipped out of the guest room, and padded toward the kitchen. The coffee hadn't been brewed yet. It was still too early for even Frank and Linda.

Chelsea eased around the corner, yawning—and jumped. "What," she hissed, "are you doing?"

Liam sat alone. The oversized stuffed chair had been angled to face the front hallway and door. "Nothing."

The erratic racing of her pulse had barely settled. "Do you have any idea how badly you scared me?" *Do you have any idea how awful you look?* Dark shadows hollowed his eyes, and his hair pointed in odd directions, as though he'd run his hand over his forehead and through his hair a hundred times.

She assessed the facial scruff and the exhaustion in his barely focusing eyes. He looked as though he were on a night-shift bender. "Have you gone to sleep?"

"Since when?"

Oh, there was an answer that said precisely what she needed to know. She eased onto the couch and put her printouts on the coffee table. "Liam?"

His forehead furrowed. "What?"

"I really think you need to sleep."

"I will."

"Like, now," she insisted.

He barely shook his head as if she couldn't understand where he was coming from. "I can't. Not right now."

Chelsea chewed her bottom lip, unsure of how to convince a trained operative who was confident he could handle sleep deprivation that the time had come to wave the white flag at the Sandman. She came up empty but asked, "Nightmares?"

His brows knit. "I'm not having nightmares."

"Linda has a couple sleeping pills," she pressed. "I can get you one."

He snorted then cocked his head, staring as if she couldn't be more oblivious. "I don't need a damn pill, Chelsea."

She matched his scowl. "Well, you need something."

"Yeah." He softened. "I do."

Like sleep! But she bit her tongue—then she recalled how he'd rushed out the door. "Where did you go?"

His dark-green eyes shot to hers. The color intensified, almost as if he had so much to tell but couldn't. "Nowhere."

Lying eyes—that was what they were called. "All right then. You don't need anything. You'll sleep later, and you can't recall where you went." She pushed up from the couch. "Everything is obviously perfectly okay."

He cracked his neck then returned to his vigilant study of the hallway and front door. "Obviously."

She snatched her printouts and turned. "When you finally go to sleep, try to be a nicer person when you wake up. To you and everyone else."

She stalked to the kitchen, frustrated that someone who seemed smart and acted tough couldn't see that she wanted to help—and how she genuinely hurt for him.

"I can't," he muttered before she made it to the kitchen.

Chelsea stopped, surprised by his worried tone. She pivoted and leaned against the wall. "Why not?"

Liam looked like the poster boy for sleep deprivation. Cloudy eyes and a pallor that set off her internal alarm. "Tell me why."

Remorse flickered across his face, though it was only a hint and was mostly hidden by shadows that fogged his eyes and cheeks. As much as she wished he'd share, she couldn't make him. Trying would fail. She had enough of that right now. "Never mind. Don't worry about it."

"Good."

Irritation pricked. She'd given up too quickly. She didn't move. He didn't acknowledge she remained, simply watching the door and hallway. What if he'd come up with some butternut bananas idea that he has to patrol the Nymans' house?

The more she studied his alert-yet-exhausted stare, the more convinced she became that he was on a self-imposed patrol. She couldn't understand his rationale, but she knew he desperately needed to sleep. "Liam, I can stay here," she quietly offered.

His chin jerked up, and the greenness of his eyes reminded her of a dark forest hidden by a foreboding storm. Perhaps he'd think she was the crazy one. What she offered made no sense unless she'd guessed correctly. In a long silence, the semi-ridiculous offer remained on the table.

"I can watch," she continued. "If you're making sure they're okay." Chelsea gestured in the direction that led to Linda and Frank's bedroom. "I'll watch if you promise to sleep. Go take the guest room. Just throw my stuff to the side."

Two small lines deepened between his eyebrows. "You think I'm cracking up?"

"Does it matter?"

He scrubbed his face with his hands, pushing his fingers into his thick hair. "You're armed?"

His question worried her, and she would much rather be the one with a gun in the room. "Should I be?"

"If you want me to get some sleep," he said.

"Give me a minute." Even when she was off-duty, her service weapon wasn't far away.

With his agreeing nod, Chelsea collected her gun, which was safely tucked in the guest bedroom, then thought about how long he would need to sleep. No fruit smoothies for her. Her icy-fruit jones would have to wait, and one day, Liam would owe her big time.

She snagged a granola bar from her purse to go along with the Glock 9mm handgun and wondered when Linda or Frank would wake up. "A gun and granola." She headed back toward the living. "Not how I thought this day would go."

CHAPTER TEN

"NO!" LIAM KICKED, and his fists flew up. Blinking, he tried to make sense of what was happening, but the suffocating cloud disappeared. His heartbeat drummed. Sweat dampened his chest, and he blinked again, making sense of his surroundings. The guest room. He'd been sleeping. "Damn."

His fists fell limp, and he kicked away the tangled sheets. He hadn't had a nightmare since… well, never. He didn't often dream.

But that nightmare could've been real. Linda and Frank and even Chelsea had called for help. They'd begged for a savior. The closer he came, the farther they slipped away.

He walked to a window overlooking pine trees lining the backyard and pressed his forehead against the cool glass as afternoon sun poured over him. He hated the orange glow of the late day. It made rooms too hot and promised time was slipping away.

Liam rubbed his eyes and checked the alarm clock. He hadn't meant to nap for this long. Though his sluggish mind had cleared, he had a duty to Linda and Frank. He walked to the bathroom, only allowing a few minutes to pull himself together, and hustled downstairs, uncomfortable that he'd burdened Chelsea.

Protecting the Nymans was his duty. The situation was his fault, and Chelsea couldn't understand the gravity of the threat. At least, not when he couldn't share information. Senator Sorenson would have his ass thrown in a black hole so fast, he wouldn't even see the black helicopters swooping in to take him away.

★ ★ ★

"WELL, WELL, WELL." Chelsea straightened in the oversized chair. "Good afternoon, Sleeping Beauty."

Liam slowed, taking her in as though she were the one who needed a psych consult. Perhaps no one had ever called him a Disney princess before.

"I didn't mean to sleep that long," he said gruffly. "Sorry."

Chelsea stretched. Other than quick trips to the bathroom or to snag fast meals from the fridge, she hadn't moved. "Not a single hiccup to report."

Rest had brought color back to his face, but his eyes danced around. "Thanks—" He walked to the window and glanced toward the driveway. "*They left?*"

"Uh, yes."

"You let them leave?"

She chewed the inside of her mouth, trying to remember that Liam was losing his mind and that swiftly kicking him in the 'nads wouldn't be kind. "I did."

He paced and muttered. Chelsea could've sworn she heard something about reckless irresponsibility.

"Sorry," she snipped, all her do-gooder sentiments gone as he continued to grumble. "I forgot my bags of chains and restraints at home."

He stopped cold and gawked as if she'd thrown off her shirt.

The weird comparison made heat skirt up her neck, but she brushed the awkward thought away. "You should try asking what day it is after you say hello."

His face pinched. "Excuse me?"

"Or even how long you slept..." She tried to control the snark, but given that the alternative was shouting, Chelsea didn't fault herself too much.

He hesitated. "How long did I sleep?"

"You walked upstairs yesterday morning."

His lips parted, but he smacked them together. "Damn it."

"*You're welcome, Chelsea,*" she offered. "Thank you, Chelsea, for taking part in this elaborate charade—"

"You stayed there?" He gestured toward the oversized chair in disbelief.

"The whole time? Yup. Don't ask me why," she answered.

Liam cast a self-conscious look her way. "You didn't sleep."

"I'm exhausted like I've never been. And hungry."

"You didn't eat?" He straightened.

"Of course I did. And I peed too. If you want to know every little detail." Perhaps now he was piecing together how her offer had turned from a minor inconvenience into a marathon of boredom. This entire pantomime was ludicrous.

He staggered to the couch, dropped, and buried his face in his hands.

That might've been the right moment to slip out. With all of the bickering, she was going to need a smoothie. One with extra protein for strength and whatever could be added for sanity—a miracle drug all blended up. It might be the only thing that could keep her from wringing his ungrateful neck.

But he didn't pick his head up, and worry got the best of her again. "What is going on with you?"

"Nothing."

Nothing, of course. Why should I expect him to clarify his erratic behavior? Still, Chelsea waited for him to provide a real answer and tidied the mess of work papers, magazines, and books she'd piled around the chair. But she couldn't ignore how the end of the world pressed on his shoulders. "Look, Liam."

He didn't unbury his face.

"I'm worried about you."

"Don't be," he mumbled. "I'm the one person you *don't* have to worry about."

"Would you stop talking in code?"

But he didn't explain. She never should have volunteered to sit watch over a living room. Enabling him had made the situation worse. Her aggravation surpassed a level which a smoothie could salvage.

In need of something much more potent, she stomped toward the kitchen pantry, on the hunt for feel-good food, and came face-to-face with a beautiful jar of queso.

Times like these called for fake cheese. The unnaturally orange container beckoned for her to drown her exasperations in junk food. She grabbed the jar and a bag of tortilla chips.

His footsteps approached.

She stepped away from the pantry, armed with her snacks. "What? Your special lookout post can be unmanned now?"

Liam stepped in front of her path to the kitchen table. "Real nice."

Chelsea elbowed by him. If ever a time existed to throw a temper tantrum and demand to be alone, the present moment seemed right. But she couldn't. Instead, Chelsea held the queso in one hand and the chips in the other and shook them. "This is the only thing I want to deal with right now. Go away."

"There are so many things going on right now," he said, explaining nothing.

She shook the jar and bag again for emphasis then sidestepped him. "I'm tired and angry—" Suddenly, the loss and how their lives had changed over twelve months hit Chelsea like a ton of coffee cake. Overwhelmed, she wanted to cry. But that sure as SpaghettiOs wasn't going to happen in front of him. "I don't have to explain anything to you."

"You should go home." His jaw ticked. "Really, you shouldn't stay here anymore."

She choked off a scream. *Who died and made you king?* Her throat seized. Julia had died. Everything had changed. A tear threatened to spill down her cheek. He would *not* make her cry.

"You can take the chips and cheese with you," he offered.

The junk food wasn't the problem! A fat tear spilled down her cheek. His sharp green eyes narrowed, and his scrutiny was as draining as it was infuriating. She wanted to make him understand but couldn't, and she slammed her fists down.

The chips crunched on the stone floor. The queso jar shattered. Orange cheese splattered around her bare feet. The glass jar lay broken, shards strewn around the point of impact. Her breath shook, but even as she stood like an island surrounded by cheese and glass, letting loose provided relief. Even if it were just for that second.

"Shit, Chelsea." Liam stepped forward.

She put her arms up to keep him at bay. All she'd wanted was queso and now she had to escape. She pushed onto her bare tiptoes and spun, wishing she could disappear.

"Hang on," he ordered. "I can help you."

No way.

"Dammit, Chelsea." He reached for her and wrapped an arm around her waist. Despite her protests, Liam swooped her from the mess.

The next thing she knew, her butt was on the cold granite counter, and he'd positioned her feet to drop into the sink.

"Do you mind?" She slapped his hands away. "Stop."

Ignoring her, Liam blasted cold water from the faucet, and Chelsea jumped, twisting from the basin. He clamped a hand on her knee. His fingers flexed to hold her leg in place. "Stay put."

She froze. He'd never touched her before. Not like that. Not with that kind of voice. She didn't move a muscle. Water rushed over her feet, and he took a step back, folding his muscled arms against his chest.

Though his hand had moved, he pinned her with a look, and finally asked, "Are you okay?"

She tore her gaze back to the sink. "I'm okay—I don't know why I did that."

"Sure you do."

Chelsea chuckled and cocked an eyebrow his direction. "Why?"

He half laughed. "Let's just say that I'm grateful the floor took the beating and not my head."

She tried not to laugh. "I wouldn't have slugged you with the cheese."

Liam bobbed his eyebrows in a weird way that made her wonder if he'd found another person to be bananas with.

"I would never intentionally harm a jar of queso," she quickly followed up.

The corners of his lips quirked. "I don't know."

"I have too much respect for the healing properties of food."

He snickered and stepped closer, giving her feet a cursory inspection under the running water. The cheese had washed away, and after they both took an uncomfortable moment to glance at her toes, Liam turned the faucet off. He handed her a towel. "I think you're going to make it."

When she finished drying off her feet, she folded the hand towel and braved a quick glance at Liam busying himself around the kitchen. She found no judgment etched onto his face, which was more than she could say for herself earlier.

He paused and leaned against the edge of the counter. His stance reminded her of a mountain, resolute and unmoving. The silence didn't feel awkward, but she couldn't define the thick air or how the kitchen seemed smaller. Finally, he said, "Thanks."

She adjusted on the edge of the counter. "What for?"

His jaw ticked. "For staying in the living room. Even if you think I'm nuts."

"Bananas."

He grinned, mouthing, *Bananas.* "I needed sleep."

"You did." She unfolded the damp towel and wound it around her hands, drew in a long breath, then glanced at the cheesy mess. "Maybe I do too."

"Maybe so." He eyeballed the floor, shaking his head with a small grin. "That was perfectly innocent queso."

She snorted then laughed. "I'm sorry. I just lost it—And I can't believe I cried."

She *never* cried.

"It was more like a single tear." He moved next to the sink where her legs dangled over the counter. "I didn't know you had it in you."

What kind of person does he think I am? Her brow furrowed and lips rolled together.

"I didn't mean that," he retracted. "However you took it."

She waved the apology away but stayed mum. Emotion had lodged itself in her throat.

His hand touched her forearm. "Seriously, Chelsea. It's been a charged couple of days after a hard year."

She stared at the ceiling. Tears wanted to fall again. Everything she'd kept pent up inside her fought to be free. Her shoulders tightened, and she squeezed her eyes closed.

Liam draped his arm around her shoulder as though he wasn't sure how to hug. "Maybe you should just… cry."

"I don't want to."

His hand gripped the opposite shoulder, hugging. "If it keeps you from hurling queso…"

She choked on laughter, then inexplicably, tears fell. Chelsea tried to hold them in. If she cried, she felt as if she'd somehow failed, and couldn't fail right then. Someone in the kitchen had to be strong.

Then again, she couldn't remember anyone ever hugging her when she cried. Against his shoulder, Chelsea let go and sobbed for everything she'd held in for a year until she could take a deep, tearless breath.

"Better?" he asked.

She draped her head back onto his shoulder. "Don't tell anyone."

"Wouldn't dare."

He held tight until she finished, and she prayed that she'd never lose control like that again.

CHAPTER ELEVEN

WITH ANOTHER LONG workday done, Chelsea let her weary eyes slide shut the moment she'd shifted into park in her condo's parking space. All she had to do was make it through the next day, and the weekend would open its arm and save her.

Daily tasks in the office had never been so exhausting, and she'd never had such a bad day.

The bad luck started before she walked in the front door and had crashed into a maintenance man and his bottle of paint stripper. The noxious odor made her sick to her stomach all day. Calhoun gave her the worst looks, as if she wanted to smell like a toxic waste dump. *Don't fumes like that give people cancer? Brain tumors? Nosebleeds?*

Chelsea hadn't been able to change into a backup pair of sweats because she'd had to make a court appearance late in the afternoon.

When she returned to the office, Calhoun had *made adjustments.* She could work on Zee Zee Mars as long as Mac was looped in on every single angle.

One look at Mac, and she knew he didn't want anything to do with Mars. She could see his resentment, and lectures would inevitably stem from the change in their partnership.

At Calhoun's direction, she and Mac stepped into a conference room, and Chelsea wasted their time explaining what Mac didn't seem to give two hoots about. His eyes glazed over when she pinpointed her hunches and mentioned assumptions.

When Mac couldn't have seemed any more disinterested, she'd asked, "Why didn't you tell Calhoun I had this handled?"

He'd shrugged and responded that Mars was a good investigation to tie his name to.

His admission had shattered a large slice of respect she held for him. That coupled with how she never understood his aversion to this investigation's reliance on gut reaction. Zee Zee Mars would be found no other way.

Chelsea rubbed her hands into the hollows of her eyes and summoned enough motivation to get out of her vehicle and go to her condo.

Knock. Knock. "Hey."

Chelsea jerked, earning a small laugh from Liam, then a quick wave.

She opened the door. "You wouldn't be grinning if you realized how close you came to becoming acquainted with my door."

His lips curled up, and he moved to the side, allowing her to step out. "You wouldn't have."

"I would've if I didn't recognize you."

"But you did." He waited for her to pull out her purse then shut the driver's door. "Catlike reflexes."

She scowled. "I might still, just because."

"Because you like breaking stuff?" He chuckled, taking a playful defensive step back.

The queso incident would never be forgotten. Volcanic embarrassment rocketed up her spine.

Her cell phone rang, and she used the phone call to change the subject. *Unknown number.* She silenced the call and turned back to Liam. "Why are you hanging out in my parking lot?"

"I wanted to check on you." He gave her an undecipherable look. "Did you know that glass shards can travel inside your body?"

Her face puckered.

"It could take years for a sliver to come out."

"That's why you're here?"

"It sounds problematic—and gross."

She wrinkled her nose. "I don't have glass shards coursing through my body."

"Would you know?" he asked.

Chelsea rolled her eyes even if somewhat amused. "That's why you're here?"

Ignoring her question, he said, "Sometimes they pop out. Like a pimple."

"Ew, Liam." But that shouldn't embarrass her after the queso-throwing incident. "I'll keep an eye out for unexpected blemishes." She turned toward her condo building, and he fell into step with her, so she stopped. "Do you have other first-aid fun facts?"

"I had a shitty day."

Oh. Chelsea offered a sympathetic nod. "I can relate."

He ambled forward, and she caught up as they crossed the parking lot and stepped onto the sidewalk.

"And I did some Googling." Glancing down, he gave a wry smile. "Glass jar wounds. Cheese sauce poisonings—"

Chelsea elbowed him.

"*Oofh.*" He covered his ribs, sidestepping out of striking zone. "Easy there, killer."

"Watch out, or someone'll be able to Google death by funny bone."

Unafraid, Liam slid back to her side. "Ha, ha."

They hit the stairs to the second-floor walkup and stopped at her condo door. She pulled out her keys. "Why'd you have a shitty day?"

He sobered. "I had a meeting with this... lady."

Twisting the key in the door, she said, "I hear those are scary."

He quietly chuckled. "She has an ice chest instead of a heart."

They stepped inside. Chelsea dropped her purse and tossed her keys on a small table. "Ah, that makes more sense."

"Nothing about her makes sense." Looking around the room, Liam said, "I expected you to be more organized."

"You've never been in here?" She tried to think of a time he had been, but with Julia's unit in the same complex and so close, that was where he'd met them if they were going out. Occasionally, he'd picked Julia up from her unit, but he never came upstairs. "Huh." She extended her hand, exaggerating the gesture. "Then welcome."

He eyed her pile of junk mail next to the keys.

Chelsea shrugged. "I don't check voicemails, and I don't do junk mail either."

"You're just a regular rebel, huh?" Liam walked across the small entryway to the living room and fell onto the couch.

"Make yourself at home."

He stretched his arms out. "How was your day?"

She snorted.

"That good, huh?"

"I'd classify mine as awful also."

"Mean ice-chest ladies?"

She smiled. "Nope. Overbearing men."

"I've heard that type exists."

She laughed and realized it was the first time all day she enjoyed a conversation. That said a lot about how her partnership with Mac was deteriorating and how she appreciated Liam's unannounced drop-by.

They weren't friends. Liam could be classified more like an associate or maybe an acquaintance, though that seemed too impersonal.

Wait! Liam was at her condo and not patrolling the Nymans. Had he let go of the depressing and impossible need to fix the past? She wanted to ask but didn't want to rehash what had happened.

"You know what?" he asked.

"If you tell me another glass-shard-pimple fact, I'm going to throw you out."

His wide chest lifted with a stifled laugh. "We need to get drunk."

Her eyebrow arched. "I'm sorry. *What?*"

"We need a drink. Preferably a shitload of them."

"We don't."

"*I* do."

Well, she wasn't going to tell him to go drink alone. But maybe she was too practical for weekday drinking. "I could make you a smoothie."

His eyebrow arched.

"They've been known to do the trick."

"Unless your smoothies include tequila, triple sec, a couple limes—"

"I'm not making you a margarita!"

"I'm more of a bourbon or beer guy, anyway." He narrowed his eyes.

"And you're what? Gumdrops? Lemon drops? Whatever they're called?"

She dropped on the couch next to him, cocking her head.

"I know you drink." He faced her. "You might not curse, but I know you drink."

"I curse."

"Yeah, what the Scooby Snacks did that snickerdoodle do isn't—"

Chelsea smacked his arm. "Oh, excuse me that I employ a little creativity to liven up the day."

"If you think calling out fudge berries is great, you have to let me introduce you to my good friend tequila." He leaned close and whispered, "That asshole really knows how to liven up a day."

"I know tequila," she insisted.

"Do you?" He tilted his chiseled jaw.

"Promise. But I'm not going anywhere tonight."

"All right." Liam clucked and pushed off the couch. "Your loss."

Disappointment swelled in her chest. She wanted their laughter to linger. "Some other time?"

"Sure." His shot-down grin mirrored how her chest felt, but he headed to the door. "Whenever. Let me know."

Chelsea stood. Remorse pushed her to rush. With quick steps to catch up, they bumped when he slowed and turned.

"Whoops." Flustered, she took a step back. "Sorry."

The slight space separating them was still too close, and Liam had to look down.

Chelsea inched back again, flush and offering another apology.

Hope brightened his emerald eyes. "Change your mind?"

Had she? Her heartbeat drummed. Chelsea swallowed, not sure why she'd hurried to the door. "Well, um—Are you going home?"

He pursed his lips, not as though he were thinking over his options, but maybe as if he wasn't sure what he wanted to say.

Chelsea wrapped her hand around his arm. Instantaneous warmth spark under her palm, and she drew back, not anticipating the hard-cut bulk of his muscles. She tucked her hands away, safe and hidden, under her crossed arms.

The front door was an arm's length away, and despite the cool night, her condo seemed as if it had warmed. The air felt fuzzy.

"No," he finally said in a low, rumbling tone. "I'm not going home."

A zing tingled up her neck, and she stepped away from the source she didn't understand. "Don't drink alone." She rocked back onto her heels. "Okay?"

The corners of his lips tightened, not quite smiling, then he backed away. "Have a good night, Chelsea."

CHAPTER TWELVE

COLD FALL AIR slapped Liam's face, and he hustled down the flight of stairs, unsure what the hell had happened. For a moment—or maybe longer, he didn't know, but for that slip of time, humor and happiness had found him, and he almost felt normal again.

But the feeling was fleeting as his phone vibrated in his pocket and Chance's name popped up on the caller ID.

After a long week of keeping an eye on the Nymans, Liam had made the executive decision to ask a contracting buddy for help. If he didn't, he might crack up without sleep. Chance also eased his concern when Sorenson had wanted to meet with him.

His buddy had agreed to his vague terms with few questions. But a call from Chance was a reality check, a reminder of the burden of uncontrollable problems. Liam answered. "What's wrong?"

"Dude." Chance chuckled. "Take it easy and know if there's a problem, I've got it handled."

Liam had a minuscule list of people he would entrust Linda and Frank with, and Chance held court at the top. He rubbed a hand over his face and muttered, "Sorry. What's up?"

"You know the Nymans' next-door neighbors with the for-sale sign in the front yard?"

Liam's interest perked up. "Yeah."

"They had a moving van here today."

"Really?"

"They haven't sold and don't have a contract."

A vacant house next door to the Nymans was excellent news. He had run out of excuses to hang around their house, and if he and Chance intended to keep an eye on their property, an empty house next door provided a slew of surveillance possibilities.

That didn't help him when Linda and Frank left the house, but Sorenson seemed convinced that if an incident were to occur, it would be at the Nymans' home. Liam wasn't so sure since Julia had been an *outlier,* but what other intel did he have to rely on?

Frank and Linda kept usual routines. Frank spent time at the bank, which offered some degree of protection, but Linda, surrounded by children at an elementary school, not so much. Liam had no idea how to keep an eye on them without equipment or assistance.

"Sounds like a good opportunity."

"And," Chance added, "I asked around—"

"We're trying to stay on the down low—"

"We are."

Liam grumbled.

"Anyway, I think I've found a beneficial hookup for all of us. In the next week or so, you'll be able to get your hands on some *toys* that'll make this a lot easier."

Toys meaning surveillance equipment, he hoped. "Yeah?"

"Yeah," Chance confirmed.

Liam nodded, working his jaw. He could handle a week or two without the type of military-grade equipment that he'd used during his army recon days, and he tried to take comfort in working with a good friend like Chance, who, after a conversation of *I can't explain but trust me*, armed himself to the teeth and took Liam's request like an order.

"Appreciate it."

"Good. Wasn't easy," Chance added. "Go get some sleep. You sound like shit."

Earlier that night, Liam wouldn't have been able to deny his depleted level of functioning. But leaving Chelsea's condo, he'd had unexpected pep—even if he was leaving to grab a drink alone. "Eventually."

"Liam?" Chelsea called from the second floor.

He spun and didn't wait to wrap up the call with Chance. "Talk to you later, bro." Then Liam met her as she rushed down the stairs. "Hey—

everything okay?"

She stopped abruptly and clung to the railing. "I didn't realize you were..." She pressed her lips together. "So close."

He shook the cell in his hand then pocketed it. "I took a call."

"Oh, right." She still hadn't let go of the railing.

He shifted his weight, not stepping closer but damn sure not moving away. Chelsea edged back up a stair.

Tension pricked in his chest. His mouth felt dry, as if he'd trucked across the Sahara, not down a simple flight of stairs. "Decided you needed a drink?" he asked, then relished the opportunity for company—*her* company.

As she nodded slightly, a cool breeze picked up. She shivered and let go of her death grip on the railing. "Guess it was that kind of day."

CHAPTER THIRTEEN

THE GUSTY NIGHT whirled, promising thunderstorms, and Chelsea tucked the wayward strands of hair behind her ear. Nervously, she smoothed the rest of it down as she tried to read his face.

His unbreaking focus made her stomach clench. It would be insane to believe he could read her mind, but he seemed to accept her sudden arrival as though he also felt the surge of overwhelming, unexplainable loneliness.

Thirty minutes earlier, she would've begged for solitude. After Liam left, her condo's silence made it impossible to stay alone.

"Let's go to Smokey's." He nodded in the direction of the neighborhood shopping center within walking distance.

A drink and company would be nice—no matter the unusual stiffness in her shoulders. "Sounds good."

He sauntered the way she and Julia had journeyed many times before when they'd wound through her condo park and across the street to grab groceries from the Bag N Go, pick up a piping-hot pizza at Papa Pizzas, or relax at Smokey's with an IPA or summer-inspired cocktail.

But the night didn't seem to call for highbrow beers or pink umbrellaed drinks.

Chelsea and Liam fell into an easy stride down the sidewalk. Small talk didn't come, but then again, she didn't feel as though she had to speak.

They came to the narrow footpath.

"After you." Liam gestured.

Chelsea wasn't self-conscious—or she shouldn't have been. She didn't know why, but her gait felt awkward, as though she didn't know whether she walked too fast or too slowly, and her arms felt gangly. Keeping her hands and fingers straight, she clamped her arms to her side.

"Left... left... left, right, left." He chuckled and stepped out of line. "Are you marching?"

"Are you watching me march?" she shot back with an anxious *I told you so* ringing loudly in her ears.

"Hard not to."

What does that mean? But she bit her tongue.

Liam stayed on the grass while she walked on the worn path until they came to another sidewalk and needed to cross the street.

Traffic was never busy that time of night. The flow of commuters had died down from a low roar to the occasional car, and they waited to cross.

At the first break, he rested his hand high on her back. She straightened, overthinking a simple, protective habit. Liam was chivalrous, and she appreciated the manners. What she couldn't explain was, as they crossed the pavement, she could still feel where his palm had rested before his hand dropped away.

Maybe she hadn't spent enough time around gentlemen lately. She had no other way of explaining why she noticed.

They made their way to the shopping complex. Restaurants and a grocery store lined one side. Her favorite smoothie place stood out like a neon pastel oddity, but they turned for the complex's lone bar.

The bell over Smokey's door jingled as they stepped through, and she headed to the bar stools. He threw his credit card down as if to say it was going to be one of those nights, and the bartender, who knew them separately but well, nodded hello.

"What'll it be tonight?"

"What'll it be?" Liam leaned against the bar top, looking at Chelsea.

Tonight didn't feel like a beer night. It felt like a night to take a few shots until her cheeks tingled and her mind let go of the last year. The kind of night when she could laugh without reminiscing and didn't have to offer an apology for wanting a night out to forget a bad day. "Bourbon."

Liam gave an approving laugh. "Two shots of Makers. Make 'em doubles."

Two doubles quickly became four, and the evening was exactly what she needed. They complained about work and people watched, guessing the whos and whys of the bar patrons around them. Their laughter boiled, and the fun from hysterical to heartbroken, was a cathartic release that she couldn't have imagined. Chelsea clung to his stories and jokes, letting the liquor's burn take responsibility for how her cheeks flushed.

A man came up behind Liam and clapped him on the back. "How you doing?"

Liam turned, and Chelsea caught how the night's merriment fell from his expression. "Hey, Buzz."

Buzz glanced to her and said hello, then turned back to Liam. "Sorry I missed the thing for Julia last week."

The real world crashed onto her shoulders, and she zoned out as Liam and Buzz made small talk. A paralyzing realization struck. The two people closest to Julia, the friends who carried a silent darkness, had been enjoying life with raucous, unrepentant indulgence.

Liam turned back to the bar as Buzz left and fell silent. For a year, they'd both been riding the highs and lows of a roller coaster. The conversation with Buzz had thrown them an unexpected loop-de-loop.

"You know what I feel bad about?" she finally asked.

He rubbed the back of his neck. "This."

"And that I don't hurt as much I did that first day. Or the first month."

"Or during the first year," he said.

Chelsea paused. "I know time heals, and I don't miss her any less. But the smothering pain is gone."

He gave a silent, stoic nod again.

"I feel guilty that I feel better, because I'm not letting her go," Chelsea whispered, unable to stop talking.

Liam rested his hand on her back as though he knew she couldn't stop, and she deflated, taking a haggard breath.

"You okay?" It sounded as if he'd aged a hundred years. Liam rubbed a small circle in the middle of her back, and she leaned toward him, unsure of the answer.

He waited and inhaled deeply, somehow seeming as though he were growing bigger and wider, broadening his shoulders to take on the weight of the world. Then he let it out, and with it, he settled like a calm mountain in the poorly lit bar.

"What's something you've never done?" he asked, changing the subject.

Chelsea stared at the dingy ceiling and tried to think of all the things she'd never done. Nothing came to mind. All she could think about was how he watched her. "No idea."

Liam chortled. "Come on."

"I don't know!" Heck, right then, she couldn't see beyond the confines of the bar, much less string together a dream activity in the real world. "Besides, that's a personal question."

His dark green eyes sparkled, even as his eyelids narrowed. "You two were so different."

"True." She twisted on the bar stool to evade his analysis. "*Darts.*"

"What?"

She was almost confused by what she'd said. Her tongue was several steps ahead of her bourbon-soaked thoughts. "I've never played darts."

Cracking a smile, he asked, "That's on your bucket list?"

"Well… no." It had simply popped into her head. "But I've never played darts."

He leaned toward the bar and asked for a couple of beers. The long necks quickly came, and he took them both and stood. "Let's go."

CHAPTER FOURTEEN

L*ET'S GO? GO where?* They couldn't leave with their drinks, and confused, she asked, "What?"

Beers in hand, Liam side-eyed her. "Darts?"

"*Now?*"

He laughed as if her poor bourbon-soaked brain was much slower than even he thought. "Yeah, sunshine. *Now.*"

Goosebumps surprised her, but she had more pressing problems to figure out like how to get out of darts. "I can't. I don't know what I'm doing."

"You'll figure it out." He turned toward the back of the bar.

"I like to know how to do things before I get myself into a pickle," she said then pushed off the barstool.

Whoa, boy. Maybe she should've stood slower. The bar room teeter-tottered, and she squeezed her eyes closed. His steady hand met her arm, and Chelsea peeked one eye open, then the next. "See? I shouldn't be allowed to handle sharp objects."

Liam wrapped her beer in her hand then pulled her toward the game area. "It's not hard. What you don't know, I'll teach you."

Her stomach fluttered even as she rolled her eyes hard enough to fall over. "I didn't say it was, and I don't want to learn in public." Still, she trudged behind him, sipping her beer.

They stood by the darts, and he commanded in a loud voice, "Excuse me, everyone? Please look away."

"Liam!"

No one glanced their way. She scowled, and he grinned with triumph.

"Just watch the master." He took a long pull of his beer and set it on an empty table. In less than a minute, Liam had snagged the darts and hit the bullseye. Then he did it again and again, one after another.

"Show-off," she muttered.

"Your turn." He winked.

How did she get herself into this position? She couldn't do this.

"Want me to show you again?" he teased.

Her eyebrows arched. "No, I'm good."

But she wasn't, especially under his unwavering attention. Then she smiled and knew exactly what to do. Chelsea swaggered and strutted toward the dartboard, giving her best Liam impersonation.

"What the hell is that?"

She pulled the darts from the board with decidedly less smoothness than he'd managed, but she turned and tossed her hair back. "*The master.*"

Smirking, he said, "I didn't throw my hair."

"Didn't you?" She tried her Liam-strut again and positioned on a line.

What the cupcakes am I supposed to do now? She'd only been able to sink a basketball shot after she'd studied the physics behind a good throw.

Chelsea wasn't even sure if her vision was blurry. She tried closing one eye. Her balance shifted.

"Hey, there," Liam said, quickly stepping to her side. "Both eyes open."

"I can do it however I want."

"Obviously." He snickered.

This is going to be so ugly. After another ridiculous hair toss to set his expectations, she aimed and pegged the dart toward her goal.

Crash and burn. The little thing didn't even hit the board.

"Would you like some help?"

Of course she would. But instead, she pointed the next dart at him. "I already watched *the master.*" Then with more flourish than she meant, Chelsea turned toward the dartboard, ignoring how the bar room tilted, and made a plan. *Focus on more oomph and forward trajectory.* That had to be the meal ticket. She threw the dart.

Again, crash and burn. Chelsea blew out a strong breath, exasperated. Liam howled.

She wagged the hand that held the remaining darts, stepping closer. "Who knew you were such a bully?"

"Who knew"—he disarmed her and held the darts away from her—"you didn't do everything perfect the first time."

Perfect? Ha! "You don't know me."

"I'm learning." His fingers drifted along her lower back, then he gripped her side and redirected her back to the line.

Her stilted steps suddenly seemed sober and robotic. She wasn't used to his touch—not that there was anything inappropriate about Liam's friendliness.

She was what was wrong.

Or the bourbon could be blamed.

Something, somehow, made his fingertips mark the very spots that he'd touched, and she hated how wonderful it had felt.

As directed, she stood on the line, stiff and certain that the ability to hear her own heart palpitations meant that she needed to go home. But she didn't want to.

"First…" Liam stepped behind her, placing his hands on her hips. "Loosen up. You're snapping like a trap."

Her mouth dried. An overwhelming urge to flee gripped her thoughts, but her feet cemented themselves on the line.

"Take this foot." He moved to her side and tapped her right thigh. "And put it forward and turn a little."

An ocean of awareness crashed through her, and she blindly tried to follow directions and breathe simultaneously.

"Good, good. But lean your weight onto it." Liam pressed on the small of her back. "Perfect. Just like that."

"Okay," she said so quietly he couldn't have heard. Blood rushed in her ears, and confusion stole her focus.

"Your left leg will keep you balanced." He moved in front of her, and his piercing green eyes made her heart leap. "Make sense?"

Chelsea needed to leave. He remained in place far too long then gave an uneasy nod and moved behind the line—behind *her*—close enough that she smelled the scent of soap she'd noticed earlier.

Liam slipped a dart into her hand and lifted her arm. As he drew back, his fingers breezed along her exposed skin until her shirtsleeve offered protection. Then he corrected her grip. His torso pressed against her back. "Real loose. Like that. Keep the dart's nose up, and… aim."

"Aiming." Her voice sounded distant and scratchy, and cold electricity shivered down her back when he stepped away, leaving her cocked and ready.

"Fire at will."

She threw the dart, and after it launched, squeezed her eyes shut more for the need to compose herself than to worry about the shot.

"Beautiful."

Chelsea opened her eyes. The dart hung on the lower left outer ring of the board. Her jaw fell, and shock cleared every other worry away. Throwing her arms out, she gave a celebratory cheer. "Yes!"

He clapped slowly, boasting a proud smile. "You did it."

"I did!" She twirled, spinning too close to his chest, and his arm caught her side.

"Careful," he said, low and disconcertingly.

She faltered, half tripping, half falling, still laughing and cheering as she hugged him in celebration. The spinning bar lights and dark shadows slowed the instant that he balanced her against his chest.

A heaviness over took her eyes, sliding them closed, and she inhaled a woodsy scent that mixed with a clean soapy smell that she was quickly identifying as specifically Liam.

His arms swallowed her, and if his shoulders were as broad as a mountain range, his stomach was solid as a chiseled boulder. She relaxed into his hold and clasped her hands around his back. The strong band of his arms tightened, and dipping his chin, Liam nestled his mouth dangerously close to her temple. Only the sparse shield of her hair separated his lips from her skin.

She tensed. He froze, and they scrambled apart filled with awareness that she would never admit to. Chelsea turned away, embarrassed and questioning what on earth she'd just done.

It was a hug. That was all. Perfectly harmless except for the unacceptable and overpowering rush of lust. Her stomach turned, but this wasn't the kind of problem she could ignore, and she faced him. "I'm so sorry."

He was almost too much to take. The green in his eyes had darkened. His forehead was etched with perplexed worry. "Don't be." He pivoted and threw the last dart. It hit dead center, and without so much as a second glance, he headed toward his beer.

Oh, sugar snaps. She'd messed up. Chelsea didn't know what she could say, because it was how she'd reacted on the inside that required an apology. Simply hugging someone was, in and of itself, not a big deal. Admitting to how their hug felt? She didn't want to ever think about her reaction again.

Liam slung back his beer then set it down. He stared at it so long that mortification crisscrossed her back. When he turned, his emerald eyes connected with hers in such a way that she cringed.

With that, he crossed back to her. Her stomach flipped, and she couldn't identify his reaction. *Anger? Disgust?* Whatever emotion was painted on his face, it had a hold on him as she'd never seen on a person.

Gosh, she shouldn't have gone to the bar tonight. Her hands covered her face, and when she glanced up, he stood close. She took a step back, but Liam stepped closer, breaking the distance she'd made.

"Look..." he began.

Oh no. Tears burned her eyes. She couldn't listen to a pitiful explanation about how she shouldn't hit on him, how he couldn't be interested, how terrible she really, truly was, even if she had no idea before. "Please don't be mad at me."

He squinted then laughed. And not a basic, pitying laugh or a worried-for-her-sanity one, either. His head tipped back, and with a ginormous smile, he belly-laughed.

"Liam!"

He straightened, and his eyes watered.

"Liam! Do *not* laugh at me."

Finally, his hysterics slowed, leaving him shaking his head.

Chelsea whacked his chest. "I am *mortified*. You need to stop!"

"Things happen," he finally said, whatever those unnamed, undefined things were.

"I climbed you like a celebrating monkey. That's not a thing—"

"Oh shit." The fierce laughter returned.

"Liam!" She stomped her foot like a pissed-off toddler. "Stop laughing."

"A celebrating monkey."

Gah! She couldn't take another excruciating second of embarrassment and spun away.

His strong hand caught her arm, spinning her to face him, then both his hands rested on her shoulders. "Thanks."

"*What?*"

"I forgot what it feels like to live, and in one night, you gave that back to me."

CHAPTER FIFTEEN

L*EFT… LEFT… LEFT, right, left.*

Liam didn't know why his old drill instructor's monotone bark came back to mind as thunder rumbled in the distance. Maybe because he'd teased Chelsea earlier while they walked down the same path. Or maybe he needed a simple way to keep his head clear. The night was over, and despite a few moments of unsettling clarity, it had been a good time, exactly what he needed to blow off tension.

With the marching words playing in his head, he put one foot in front of the other on the worn path as they returned to Julia's—or rather, *Chelsea's*—condominium complex.

He swallowed hard, uneasy about the raw past and the new interest that had caught him unaware. What was going on?

Hell if he knew. But those few seconds he'd had Chelsea wrapped in his arm were the only sane ones he could remember recently.

His eyes drifted down Chelsea's back as they marched along the path. Her butt swayed, not as if she were swaggering or shaking it, but just the hypnotic cadence of her hips and the enticing curve of her ass.

His mind flashed, and he wondered what was under her pants. He pictured dark lace underwear that stretched across a backside he could hold onto. A hot sweat broke out on his chest despite the cool, windy night that promised storms later that night.

Liam tried to ignore thoughts about Chelsea's ass. He didn't need to picture her—not naked, not clothed, and not in lacy undergarments that gave a tease about what was beneath.

"Shit," he muttered and focused on the comfort of boot-camp ditties.

Don't stop. Don't ask. Don't think. He would keep moving no matter the questions or discomfort. If he could do that in boot camp, he could do that walking across a damn path.

Her dark hair hung below her shoulders. It swayed in the same rhythm as her ass, and he pinched his eyes shut. It wasn't as if she were wearing anything new or different. Any time he'd seen her after work, she wore the exact same thing, a dark jacket over a blouse and pants, almost like a uniform.

"Why do you wear the same clothes every day?" he asked, wanting to focus on anything but how everything on her swayed.

She turned abruptly, and he bumped into her.

"Shit, sorry," he said.

Chelsea balanced, bracing on his forearm, then jumped back as if she'd touched fire. "I don't."

He eyed her clothes, unable to see detail in the dark but recalled every time he could. "It looks the same."

She shifted uncomfortably and shrugged. "You're now a fashionista to boot?"

His eyebrows pinched. "To boot, what?"

"Military something or another." She ticked off a finger. "Dart master and, now, fashionista."

He chuckled. "Fair enough. And I'm a contractor."

"Whatever that means."

Chelsea turned back to the path, and he fell into stride next to her. She had a point. His job was hard to define. He was more like a military freelancer for special teams, and he liked it that way.

"Is your Glock part of your uniform?" he asked.

She glanced at him and shook her head. "Not necessarily."

"You didn't change before you went out tonight, but no gun?"

"How would you know?"

"Because I'm a military something or another."

Chelsea chuckled. "Interesting job talent."

"I'm known for a variety of skills."

"How do you know my gun is not safely tucked somewhere within reach?"

"Because…"

He stopped, and she did too. His gaze swept from neck to ankles, inspecting what he already knew. Not once, not twice, not any specific number of times that he could recall, Liam had watched how she moved, the way her pants fit over her thighs, and how they tapered down her leg. He'd studied her shoulders, her posture, her chest. Even if he hadn't realized what he'd done, Liam knew that he could recall a three-hundred-sixty-degree memory of how she looked.

But on top of that, he'd been close enough to smell the lemon in her shampoo and had touched her, learning that she had power under her layered uniform.

"I would've felt it."

Chelsea's lips parted.

Maybe he shouldn't have said that. Appropriate conversation had never been his strong point, and when bourbon and beer were thrown in, sometimes the truth came out.

And maybe he also shouldn't have thought about her body, but he had, to the point of distraction, and he didn't know why he'd never noticed a hundred things about her that he'd noticed that night.

The recall of their every connection filtered through his thoughts with such intensity that it made him crave their closeness again. Instead, he stepped back.

"My service weapon is locked in a small gun safe in my condo." Her eyes darted around and finally landed on his shoulder, settling for a moment before she turned, walking again.

They stepped onto the sidewalk and wound through the complex. Thunder rumbled again, and he noted that the weather report had been wrong by about half a day. Friday's thunderstorms had arrived early.

Lightning cracked far off in the sky, and the amber light of the neighborhood lampposts illuminated their familiar walk.

The sidewalk came to a T intersection, and Liam turned right—alone.

Momentarily confused, he pivoted. "Hey—"

Chelsea faced him on the opposite side, each a step away from where the sidewalk split. Julia's condo had been to the right, and Chelsea's was to the left. Turning had been a habit, even if it had been a while since he made the journey.

"Shit." Memories splintered him from the inside out.

"Are you okay?" Chelsea asked with genuine concern.

His throat ached, and he inhaled and rubbed his hands into his hair. *What am I supposed to say?* A year had gone by, and he still hadn't learned the words that could explain the void.

Chelsea waited, and he shrugged. Neither moved, as though there were an invisible line between them.

Finally, she said, "Call your Lyft from here. I'll wait with you."

He stepped to her side of the T, and they walked toward her parking lot, where their night had started. She angled them toward a bench.

"I'm going to sit out here for a bit," he offered. "Until I'm okay to drive."

Thunder cracked, as if God were laughing at him.

Tipping her chin up, she said, "That's not going to happen."

His forehead pinched. "I want to go home."

"Want to or need to?"

"What I don't want to do is split hairs."

"Fine." She crossed her arms. "Lyft. Uber. Whatever else is out there. A taxi. I don't care. But you're not driving."

He bristled, knowing he was wrong and stubborn but that his mind wouldn't change. "I'll sleep in my vehicle."

She rolled her eyes. "Yeah, I believe that."

Liam scowled, swaying at the most inconvenient moment. *Shit.*

Chelsea raised an eyebrow. "I'm not in the mood to bury two of my friends."

Friends stuck out to him. They weren't friends before, but maybe they were now, because of tonight. He liked that, in a possessive way, he could lump himself into her tightly guarded group of friends.

"So," Chelsea continued, "be stubborn all you want, but I'm not going to let you drive drunk."

His jaw set, and he wanted to explain he wasn't drunk but didn't want to lie.

Fat rain drops splatted, and she turned her face toward the sky. "As if I didn't need another reason to let you drive."

He silently lamented and pulled out his phone. The heavy *plip plop* of raindrops was few and far between, almost as if the storm were spitting at them. But begrudgingly, he cued up a ride-sharing app.

The first one reported that the closest ride was forty-three minutes away. The second nearly doubled that—definitely a con of living far out in suburbia on a work night. He sighed, scrolling for another option, then admitted, "I'm not keen on public transportation."

Why was it so hard to admit that? He had never taken an Uber or Lyft and only had them on his phone to help a friend out. It wasn't that he had a fear of an unknown driver—more as if he'd seen too much random tragedy and couldn't get comfortable with the idea of another person having that much control.

She stared as if he needed to explain, but he shut down. His lips flattened, and he crossed his arms. "Don't worry about it. Never mind."

He didn't want to explain that, logically, he knew ride sharing was much safer than driving himself home. But he hated the lack of control the night Julia died on the Metro, when he couldn't control who was around and where they went.

"Order your ride, and I'll tell you something to take your mind off it," she offered.

He wanted to protest again and explain there was nothing to ignore, but instead, curiosity got the best of him, and he wanted to hear her talk. Liam glanced at his options, choosing the one that let him have more time to listen to Chelsea. "Done."

She stared at the low clouds. "My mother didn't want me to work with the feds."

That wasn't what he'd expected her to say.

Liam watched her knot her fingers and study them with vexatious intensity. "I was supposed to be a lawyer."

He grinned and could see her as a balls-busting attorney. "You're tough and good at getting your way. A lawyer would be a good fit."

Her self-deprecating laughter was almost inaudible. "Being a lawyer sounded awful after years of dreaming about a job I couldn't have."

"What was that?"

"Law enforcement."

He lifted an eyebrow but kept his bevy of questions to himself.

"It wasn't what my mom thought of as picture perfect, and after a lifetime under her regime, I broke free." She snorted. "I'm so wild, huh? Rebelling against my mother, I jumped head first into law enforcement."

"Admirable, if you ask me."

Chelsea lifted a shoulder. "When the strongest force in your life tells you one thing—be a lawyer and you will matter—and then you don't? It's terrifying not to matter."

"Of course you matter."

She hesitated. "Not to her. Not as much as I could have."

He didn't know what to say, other than knowing how Chelsea followed her heart through that tough of a barrier elevated her even higher in his opinion.

Liam checked the app. Thirty-nine minutes to go. As the heavy raindrops picked up speed, he leaned back. "Why did you share that?"

Chewing the inside of her cheek, she shrugged. "I don't know. I've never told anyone that before."

He mulled that over. "Why me?"

Chelsea gave a sweet but uncomfortable grin. "Because I think you told me something tonight that made you feel vulnerable."

His eyes shot to her as he wondered how in the hell she'd pulled out the truth from his passing remarks.

"I just thought it'd be easier if you weren't the only one on this bench who felt exposed."

She'd done him a solid, and it had worked. "Do you like your job?"

"Mostly. The paperwork and transport is boring but important. But I love when I'm able to focus on Zee Zee Mars. Though my boss and partner wish I'd let the FBI handle it."

He shifted. "You know what?"

"Hm?"

"I say let it go. If you're happy, then the naysayers can go screw off."

"Hear! Hear!" Chelsea raised an imaginary glass as the rain began to fall hard enough to be annoying.

He checked the app—and shit—now the time showed an additional fifteen minutes.

She glanced at his phone. "We'll drown by then."

"You should go upstairs." *Why did I let her sit here in the rain, anyway?* His mind wasn't clear. "I promise I'll wait for my ride."

She wiped rain off her forehead and stood. "Come on. Crash on the couch."

His heartbeat escalated, and the desire to stay closer to her far surpassed the benefit of not taking a ride with a stranger. He didn't know what to do with that and couldn't answer.

"Liam." She touched his wrist. "Come on. The couch is calling for you."

Chelsea left him, as if the only answer were to agree with her. She didn't look back when she reached the stairs. Liam caught up. A minute later, they were inside her condo, and he'd been ordered to sit in a dining room chair as she turned the couch into a guest bed, piling blankets and pillows onto it.

He watched her re-fluff a pillow. "You know I've slept on a cement plat in a war-torn country before?"

"Oooh." She feigned amazement. "You are such a tough cookie."

He laughed. "I'm just saying…"

"You've also slept in a bed," she said matter-of-factly. "If I can make the couch comfortable, I'm going to make it comfortable."

When she was done, Chelsea stepped away from the couch, and he stayed in his chair. They exchanged looks of gratitude for the night out—and awkwardly ignored what had happened between them.

After too long of a silence, she offered, "Good night, Liam," and disappeared down the hall with a wave.

He stared at the couch-turned-bed and the empty hallway then finally whispered, "Good night, Sunshine."

CHAPTER SIXTEEN

S*UNSHINE…*

Liam didn't know where that nickname had come from. If he'd been pressed, he would've assumed that someone called "sunshine" would have blond hair or was overly friendly.

But that wasn't Chelsea—dark hair, dark eyes—and her disposition wasn't necessarily sunny. More like radiant with a vivid mix of mystery.

She could turn a shitty day around, kick him in the ass if need be, or give him a look that did very good things to his bad thoughts. Each had happened tonight, and that made her shine like the sun, as far as Liam was concerned.

He kicked off his shoes, fumbled to turn out the light then toppled onto the couch made up as if he were a king. Liam stretched, and it took a toss and a turn until he found the right spot, despite, or maybe because of, the fluffy layers.

Alcohol and exhaustion pulled at his tired eyes. He hooked an arm around the pillow, breathing in lemons and lavender, but jerked away, shocked at how vivid Chelsea became in his mind. He was suddenly wide-awake. His blood rushed, and no matter how he eased against the couch again, all he could smell was the memory of her.

Fucking hell. If he needed to get laid, he needed to think about it some other time than when he was near Chelsea. Finding her suddenly attractive made him feel a kaleidoscope of guilt and anxiety that ran through him like lava.

As carefully as he could, Liam laid his head on the pillow. Citrus and sweetness made his mouth water. He closed his eyes and remembered how it felt to innocently curve his hands around her body.

Liam's breathing became irregular. Arousal rushed from his chest to his cock, and he wanted to ignore his judgmental thoughts as he stared at the ceiling. But his erection thickened, much to his excitement and disappointment. Even his lips tingled at the idea of stroking to thoughts of Chelsea—her hair, her flushed cheeks, and how she claimed to have climbed him like a monkey. He laughed even as he palmed the bulge in his pants.

Breathless and shaky, he shut his eyes and pressed his lips tight, pinching them between his teeth. Because fuck it, he was painfully erect.

Liam carefully loosened his pants and stroked himself. A full-body shiver cascaded from the top down. Erotic thoughts tumbled in his mind—Chelsea clinging to him, the scent of her hair, and the softness of her skin. The small details he'd somehow remembered now danced as his grip tightened and he jerked harder and faster—her laugh, her stubbornness, and the way her lips curved, plump and full.

What would it take to touch her? To feel her?

God, he was on the brink of orgasm, dreaming about how her tongue might torture him and what it would be like to slide his hands between her legs and find her—so unbreakable and unstoppable—wet.

His hips rocked. Chelsea's name hung on his lips as he teetered on the edge of an insane climax. Then he yanked his shirt up and came, muttering her name like a prayer to god for sanity.

Under the protective shield of Chelsea's blanket, Liam sucked air until he could open his eyes again. His heart slammed in his chest, and he needed to clean up. But first, he lay there, wondering how the night had done nothing short of leaving him blindsided.

CHAPTER SEVENTEEN

CHELSEA'S FRUIT-AND-YOGURT SMOOTHIE would have to wait. *Or does it?* She paced the kitchen, itching to flip the switch on her blender. But waking a sometimes-snoring Liam up with the high-pitched whirl of her smoothie maker wouldn't be the nicest move.

Then again, she wasn't sure how long he planned to sprawl on her couch. Maybe a guy like him needed an alarm clock like a blender because trouncing around her condo hadn't made him stir.

She leaned against the fridge. Pacing a small circle hadn't done wonders for the slight hangover she'd woken up to, and honestly, she dreaded flipping the switch, as it would make her temples pulse.

But a smoothie addiction was a smoothie addiction, so she called out, "Liam? Wake up!"

The guy didn't even stir.

She peeked around the corner then yanked back to the safe confines of her kitchen. He was still in the same state that she'd seen him in on the couch—sans shirt, with one bare leg dangling free from the protection of a blanket.

His long legs had muscles that still seemed thick with strength even while he slept. Jeez Louise, a quick look at her couch was more of a jolt than she could've manufactured with a protein-packed, vitamin-C-boosted smoothie.

"Wake up," she called again.

He snored.

Maybe she needed to abandon him there, get a smoothie across the street, and hope to the heavens that, when he woke, he said something like *Pass the Pepto* and not *Please don't use me like a jungle gym again.*

If he were wearing a shirt, it would be easier to wake him, and she became aware that if the previous day hadn't happened, she wouldn't have cared if he were shirtless. A little bit of clothing, or total lack thereof, wouldn't have stopped her. Nothing ever did—except, apparently, a shirtless Liam who showed a little bit of leg.

A warm flush curled up her back.

Her phone rang, and since she didn't recognize the number, she let it ring without sending it to her full voicemail box on the minuscule chance he'd react to the phone call.

Which he didn't.

Chelsea pushed from the wall, annoyed in a hundred ways, and made the noisiest steps she could muster. He snored and turned over.

She cleared her throat.

Another snore.

Gritting her teeth, Chelsea changed her stomps to tiptoe steps, acutely aware that there were only six feet between her and his naked chest. If he didn't wake up soon, she'd have to chuck kitchen goods at him. No one wanted to wake up with a whisk smacking their face.

"Liam!"

He shot up. "What—?" Then he scowled. "Damn, Sunshine."

"I thought I'd have to throw something at you."

"Huh?" Confusion creased his forehead. "Why are you yelling?"

What was she supposed to do? Shake his broad, bare shoulder? "You don't have a shirt on." Or pants. But that seemed incredibly awkward to point out.

The blanket covered his mid-section as Liam swung his legs off the couch and buried his head in his hands. "You didn't yell last year when I passed out on the beach."

"Two years ago." And that didn't matter after the previous night with its semi-flirting and weird connection. *Or has he forgotten?* Hope surged. "Not the same. Never mind."

His grouchy expression broke, and he dropped his head back against the cushion, seemingly amused as she gawked. "Do you have coffee?"

"I wanted to make a smoothie."

"There's a rule against both?"

She turned and headed for the kitchen, refusing to react when she heard the quiet pad of his footsteps behind her. She reached into the freezer for the waiting scoop of ice cubes. After she'd dumped the ice cubes in the blender and turned it on, she stared at the wall, scared to find out if he'd put a shirt and pants on.

Or, rather, hadn't.

She couldn't trust herself not to turn pink. She'd had a hard time looking away from the definition in his frame even while he slept. Pathetic. But that was the truth.

"Are you making enough to share?"

"Sure." She studied the blender, watching the swirl of fruit color rise as it mixed with the yogurt, then turned it off. An air bubble popped as the smoothie came to a rest, and she added another heap of ingredients and ice.

The ice sank into the mixture, and in her peripheral vision, she saw Liam come closer. She flipped the blender to high speed for no reason other than she'd confirmed he had donned pants but no shirt.

The smoothie was in danger of turning into a frappe if she didn't turn off the blender, but she couldn't move with him standing so close.

"I think it's good." Liam reached in front of her and turned the knob. The screaming whirl became a whining rumble as it came to stop, but she didn't take her eyes off the raspberry-pink drink.

An air bubble popped to the top, leaving the drink more than ready to be served, but she couldn't grab the glasses without turning toward him. Her blood rushed in her neck.

"Everything okay?" he asked with a low, pebbled coarseness that held an edge of concern.

She didn't know the answer, as much as she didn't remember how to breathe without reminding herself—in, out, in, out. But she painted on a professionally nondescript smile and turned. "Why wouldn't it be?"

He snickered, cocking an eyebrow.

Oh yeah. He remembers last night. Then why the Fudgsicles hasn't he put on a shirt? Chelsea pressed her fingertips to the edge of the counter and used every minute of federal agent training she'd ever endured to mask her thoughts. "Can you hand me two glasses?"

His jaw ticked. The emerald green in his eyes was liable to set a fire—or maybe it had, deep below her stomach. She twisted away from his stare. "Cabinet to your left."

Liam retrieved two glasses and returned too close to her and set them down. His hip leaned against the counter, mere inches from her hand. Chelsea licked her lips, unnerved by his nonchalance. Standing seemed awkward, and she didn't know where to rest her eyes.

"Thanks for last night," he said.

His gratitude shattered the last slip of resolve she had left, and as heat suffused her cheeks, she jerked the blender up and poured their smoothies. Finally, with a task to do, she handed him his drink and offered a benign nod. "That's what friends are for."

Friends were for lending a shoulder and for keeping each other from drinking and driving, and that was it, not for flirting with her best friend's boyfriend, even if he wasn't anymore. She tripped through the mental gymnastics needed to understand that complication and focused an unneeded amount of attention on her smoothie glass.

He took a sip and gave an approving nod. Chelsea sipped also, vowing not to stop until she'd found her composure, but when her throat froze and an icy chill shivered along her shoulders, she gave up the idea of poise.

Liam had a way of watching her that belied the casualness in his stance. He drank his smoothie with ease and watched as she most certainly didn't. "Do you have to go to work?"

She could've kissed him for changing the subject—but she could've kicked herself for thinking about kissing him. "I have to brief Mac on a couple things..."

"He's your partner?"

"He's a lot of things. Partner would be the best title."

His head cocked. An eyebrow arched as if he wanted her to keep explaining.

"Not personally," she quickly added. "We're close. In that way that you are if someone's got your back."

He hummed as though he understood, straightening, but his lips remained pressed thin.

"Mac's a good guy," she continued needlessly. "A little, or a lot, overbearing. But dagger sharp and smart."

Liam's jaw barely relaxed. He held up his glass. "Let me finish this, and I'll be out of your hair."

"Don't rush."

But he gulped the rest of the smoothie down and washed out his glass in the sink. He strode away, and she put down her glass on the counter, noticing how her hands vibrated almost as if she needed to come down from a burst of adrenaline.

When Chelsea was certain she could act like a normal human being or even a so-called friend, she tossed the empty yogurt container into the recycling bin and refilled her ice trays. Shutting the freezer door, she sighed and closed her eyes in a last-ditch effort to calm herself before walking out to say goodbye to Liam.

And she could. *Nothing* had happened with Liam. She didn't *want* anything to happen. The previous night with him had been some weird, alcohol-to-blame type of mourning.

Chelsea forced her eyes open and came eye-to-eye with a photo of her and Julia. The selfie was one of Chelsea's favorites where they'd wrapped their arms around one another. A magnetic frame held the picture. Its all-caps lettering arched above their heads—Best Friends *Forever*.

CHAPTER EIGHTEEN

THE WORK DAY kicked off with a small meeting. Mac had sat next to Chelsea as Calhoun discussed an upcoming partnership with the CDC to transport materials for a bioweapon project. The shipments were important to national security, and the Marshals were tasked with ensuring a smooth shipment.

As soon as the meeting had wrapped, Mac beelined for Calhoun, and they fell into a quiet discussion. When she'd joined them, the conversation died. It'd been spectacularly uncomfortable, and she begged off with a self-conscious wave.

Which was how she ended up staring at her laptop screen. The room's fluorescent lights had mocked her firm belief that smoothies could act as a hangover wonder drug, because after the morning meeting and reading an email from Mac, Calhoun CC'ed, filled with questions and noting missing forms, a dull ache formed above her right eye.

Heat blasted from the air vent above. The stifling temperature didn't help her headache. It had to be seventy degrees outside, but with Fall officially kicked into high gear with pumpkin-scented lattes and football chatter, the building's maintenance department had decided to kick on the heat.

Chelsea tugged at her collar. She rolled her shoulders and opened a link to another form that Mac said she'd missed. *Was he still with Calhoun? Why hadn't he mentioned the paperwork if it's so important?*

She bet Mac and Calhoun were holed up somewhere with a fan or even a window that opened. Her jealousy knew no bounds at the thought of a fall breeze.

Maybe Chelsea could convince Calhoun to relocate her desk so that she and Mac could converse instead of shooting emails to one another. They weren't even on the same floor.

Again, she tugged at the collar of her starched button-down blouse and wished she'd worn a thinner, less abrasive fabric. Taking off her suit jacket hadn't helped much, and worse, despite the fact that she'd showered and readied as she did every morning, she could have sworn she could smell the slightest hint of bourbon hanging in the air, making her stomach turn.

A hard rap knocked on the doorjamb, and Chelsea jumped.

Calhoun stepped into her dungeon office. "How's it going?"

She searched for Mac behind Calhoun's large frame, but he was nowhere to be seen. She gestured to the screen and the printer. "About as can be expected."

He gave a good-natured chuckle then settled on the edge of a short filing cabinet. "Mac mentioned there was some missing paperwork."

She ground her molars. Mac was going to find himself dealing with a peeved partner if he had too much to say.

Calhoun waved his hand. "No one's tattling, Kilpatrick." But he crossed his arms and looked down his nose as if that weren't true. "I asked if he was getting caught up."

"I think he is."

"There's a big difference between providing backup and working this angle alongside you. I have the feeling that Mars is about to strike again. If we could find her before she does…"

She bit her lip, finding no reason to explain about Mac's abysmal interest in Zee Zee Mars.

"He's worried about you." Calhoun's gaze tightened. "And after talking to him, I'd be lying if I didn't say I was too."

Her eyes widened. "I'm not sure how comfortable I am that he went to you instead of me." For the life of her, she didn't know why their relationship had grown rocky.

Calhoun sniffed. "And I'm more comfortable with Mac involved on the day-today when it comes to Mars."

"I am *this* close to homing in on Zee Zee."

He nodded like he'd heard it before—because he had. "And Mac will be by your side when you do."

"He *will* be," she promised.

"Good. It'll look great for all of to be able to earn that credit."

Credit for what she'd been doing for years? The idea was infuriating. "He hates everything about Zee Zee," she reminded Calhoun. Couldn't her boss recall how often Mac had mentioned that Zee Zee had taken up important real estate on the most wanted list. Privately, he acted as though her obsession with Zee Zee Mars would hold him back from gaining leadership positions.

Calhoun moved to the window. He used his fingers to pull apart the blinds then yanked the cord. Sunlight flooded the already warm office, not helping her hangover. She tried not to wince.

"Not much of a view, huh?" Calhoun asked of the back alley lined with a row of dumpsters.

"I was never in this for the view."

Fortunately, he dropped the shades. The blinds' clatter echoed in her ears.

Calhoun paced to the other side of her desk. "Have you checked in with Dr. Casper lately?"

The department shrink? "No."

He frowned.

"Was I supposed to?"

"I understand there was recently an event for Julia."

Chelsea's eyebrows arched. "A bit ago."

"It's been a long year," he said expectantly. When she didn't respond, he continued, "How are you handling that?"

"Is that why you asked me about Dr. Casper?" They had protocol, and she'd followed it, which was to say, she didn't do anything. If she'd shot someone, if her partner had been shot, or if she'd been shot, she would have gone to see Dr. Casper, but none of those events had occurred.

When she'd felt the need to discuss Julia, Chelsea turned to Linda and Frank, or a few close friends. And... most recently, Liam.

"It wouldn't be mandatory," he suggested vaguely.

"Sir, it's been more than a year."

Then Calhoun pinged her with a rapid slew of questions about her clarity and focus, all of which Chelsea answered with unease.

Calhoun paused. She apparently hadn't said the right words to abate his concern. Though she hadn't known he *was* concerned. *What had Mac said?*

Chelsea bit away a tart retort as Calhoun pursed his lips.

"Have you taken time off for yourself?" he finally asked. "A vacation? Time with family?"

"Last year, around the funeral."

He pursed his lips again as though he had to think over her uncomplicated answer.

"And, honestly, I don't need a vacation," Chelsea added.

He hummed. "Maybe you should take the afternoon."

Stunned, she blinked. "What? Why?"

He propped an elbow on a crossed arm and rested his chin in his hand, stroking it.

"Sir?" Chelsea pressed.

Calhoun turned, giving the office door a quick shove so that it clicked shut, and he stepped back to her desk.

"Have you been drinking today?"

Chelsea reeled. "What? No."

"I smell alcohol."

Her eyes bulged, and her mouth gaped. Dumbfounded, she could barely string thoughts together. "*No*, I haven't been drinking."

"Have you been," Calhoun continued, "drinking more than normal?"

"*No,*" she said through clenched teeth.

He took a deep, long sniff. "I smell alcohol."

Her cheeks heated. "This is absurd—"

"Chelsea, you smell like booze."

She couldn't find the words. The explanation was simple enough. The previous night, one single, solitary night, she'd hit a happy hour and drunk too much. But a couple shots and beer were hardly a problem that required her boss to show up.

"Sir," she tried, swallowing over the sudden dry mouth and pounding headache. "Last night, I went out with a friend. Maybe we hit the liquor harder than usual—"

Calhoun's forehead pinched.

"Considering I don't drink often," she amended. "Harder as compared to not usually."

"Just a regular Thursday night except for with liquor," he summarized. "Go see Dr. Casper."

Incredulous, she felt her jaw drop. "Because I went out last night?" *Is this a double standard?* She couldn't count how many times the men in her office had gone out for drinks for no reason or because some sports team was on television, just as they were every week.

"Because I said so."

His reasoning wasn't flawed. It was nonexistent. "Sir, this isn't necessary."

"Consider it a requirement." Calhoun dropped his chin as if to declare the conversation over then added, "And go home."

She blanched, and he gave a curt nod.

"This is ridiculous."

"Go home, Kilpatrick. Make an appointment with Dr. Casper next week." He turned to leave but stopped with his hand on the doorknob. He gave her a once-over assessment. "Take some time off, and I'll check in with you in a couple weeks."

The door opened and closed, and Calhoun was gone. Exasperated, Chelsea grabbed her phone, knowing the last person she should call was Mac, and scrolled for Julia. But reality hit. Julia would never answer again. That had been a mistake she'd made a few times over the last year, and Chelsea let the phone slip from her hand. Tears burned at the back of her throat, and even though she was alone, she refused to let them slide free.

Her phone buzzed with a text message. The screen faced up. Liam's name showed on the notification. Chelsea took a deep breath, understanding his bad day more than she had the day before, and picked up her phone.

LIAM: *I thanked you for last night. But I didn't for breakfast.*

Her phone buzzed again with a second text.

LIAM: *Thanks.*

A small grin curled on her face despite what had transpired in her office. She didn't want him to make her smile, especially not when she'd been upset and ready to call her best friend. Yet she really, *really* did.

CHAPTER NINETEEN

LIAM'S TO-DO LIST that morning had been a short one, consisting of one action item—check in with Chance—but now that Liam had parked his Explorer, he hadn't been able to get out. At least not before sending Chelsea a text.

Their dynamic was complicated. He saw no reason to muddy the morning. They hadn't done anything wrong. No matter how he replayed the night before, they hadn't crossed a line. But then again, maybe that was his problem. *Is there a line?* Of course there was, but he didn't understand it.

Nothing about Chelsea was taboo. She did not have a partner—even her partner wasn't her *actual* partner. And well, Liam was the complication—or rather, *Julia* was.

No two ways about it, he missed her as he would miss the sun if it didn't rise one day. He'd loved her and would always.

But the urge to be near Chelsea the previous night had caught him off guard. Liam twisted his hands on the steering wheel, gripping it tighter until the plastic hurt his calloused skin.

If he wanted someone to fuck, he should find someone to fuck. End of story.

But his eyes hadn't roamed a single day that he'd been with Julia. Nor had they a single day after her death. Until the previous night. They had roamed and meandered over every inch of Chelsea. The bar had been filled with other women Liam could've studied, women with less or with decidedly feminine clothes on.

But he'd been stuck on Chelsea in her simple pantsuit and sensible shoes. He almost laughed at how unflattering her clothes could've been.

But Liam didn't care.

He still found her ass irresistible and paused to appreciate the swell of her breasts. The thought of lemons nearly gave him an erection, and he tightened his grip on the steering wheel all over again.

His phone chimed. The text message notification appeared, and he swiped the screen. She'd replied with a smiley face and a thumbs-up.

Liam laughed, and he could picture how she methodically calculated her answer when she had no idea how to respond.

Two taps came at his window. His adrenaline kicked into high gear as he jolted.

It's just Chance. Not a Tran Pham soldier announcing himself with a resounding hello. Chance leaned against the hood with his fist resting on the fender.

Liam needed to chill out. He jumped out and shoved his cell phone into his back pocket.

"All's quiet on Mount Ida Ave," Chance proclaimed as though narrating a World War II documentary. "Nary a minivan broke the speed limit, nor a squirrel buried more than their share of nuts."

Scowling, Liam said, "Thanks, jackass."

"You sure you're working on solid intel?"

Liam nodded. He was about as sure as he could be, given that he couldn't double-check the information from Sorenson and Westin. But Liam couldn't explain that to Chance. Hell, he'd already said far too much.

If he had to defend himself for bringing in another person, Liam would argue that Chance had the same clearances he did. Even if they hadn't been on Red Gold together, Chance easily could've been. Luck of the draw didn't care who she screwed.

"All right." Chance shrugged. "Your equipment will be here in a week, plus or minus."

That was better than Liam could've hoped for. "Thanks."

"But I've got to roll out right now. I think a job's come up, and I have to check in."

Liam understood. He couldn't expect Chance to help unconditionally without more information or compensation. "I appreciate everything."

"You'd have done the same thing if I asked."

True.

Chance crossed his arms, and worry creased his forehead. "Hey, look. I have a guy I trust. I could call him up to help out."

"Nah."

If Sorenson learned Liam had looped in Chance, his ass was grass. But if he were caught with Chance and others… Liam didn't care if he never saw daylight again. His concern would be Sorenson calling off the whole operation. He would never be able to wrap his hands around Tran's throat, which was the sweet hope that coaxed him to sleep every night—the belief that one day he would slowly drain Pham's life, as Pham had done to Julia.

"You sure?" Chance asked.

"Sure enough," Liam mumbled.

They leaned against his Explorer and stared down the block toward the Nymans' house.

"What's your plan? Be everywhere at once? Never sleep?"

"Something like that," Liam muttered.

"Brother, you can't stay awake twenty-four hours a day, and even if you continue to try, you'll be slow on the draw if something happens."

Liam grumbled. Chance's logic made too much sense. He needed another person.

"I don't have to list your strengths and weaknesses." Chance slapped him on the back. "But I never thought stubbornness would be one of yours."

My strengths? He got shit done, like staying awake until he knew a better way to help the Nymans. His weaknesses were planning and fucking contradictions.

His stubbornness was a byproduct of black-site prison threats and knowing he didn't have the right plan to do his best work. "I'll work on that."

An impossible task… Liam dropped his head back and stared at the cloudy sky. Success depended on how he balanced his expertise and the circumstances Sorenson defined. That seesaw had to level out, or the Nymans would die. But the truth was, the seesaw would never level out. Balance didn't exist.

CHAPTER TWENTY

WHEN CHELSEA HAD tracked down Mac, she could tell that Calhoun already looped him in. Maybe the entire floor knew that their boss thought she was drinking while doing paperwork in the basement.

Chelsea had swung by Dr. Casper's office, also, crossing her fingers that the doctor would relay to Calhoun the pointlessness of her forced time off, but Calhoun had headed her off there too. The doctor was waiting and ready for her, making the trip futile—unless you counted Dr. Casper repeating her now *required* time off and handing her a filled bottle of Xanax.

The anxiety medicine made Chelsea incrementally more anxious. *Should I take it? Why would I? Or do I now have a reason to?* The bottle was more anxiety inducing than she could've imagined, and it took Chelsea all of two minutes at home to dump the pills down the toilet.

The moment the pills whooshed down the drain, her worries melted away. But she would go nuts without anything to do. She even had strict instructions not to *think* about Zee Zee until she came back. Mac seemed positively gleeful, and she didn't know if that was because Chelsea had, technically, never taken a vacation, or maybe Mac hoped Calhoun would release him from their partnership.

Boredom had already planted its claws into her shoulders, and she didn't know what to do other than clean. That finished quickly, so Chelsea paced. First, she walked laps around her condo, then she moved outside, striding through the parking lot, and the open grass area that the condo complex centered around.

Finally, she gave up and lay on a park bench, staring at the bright-blue sky, which swirled with big cotton-ball clouds.

Another storm would come in later, most likely much like the thunderstorm from the night before, but for now, she would wait until something besides Zee Zee Mars inspired her.

"What are you doing down there?"

Chelsea turned toward the voice, and the condo's maintenance manager ambled down the path. Something safe and knowledgeable always shined in Raul's face. He knew how to fix every problem, many of them having nothing to do with the condo's physical property.

Raul tilted his head as though she were a curious subject lying on the park bench in the middle of a workday.

To be fair, she probably *was* curious-looking. "I'm… getting some exercise."

Chelsea stretched as if she'd recently finished a workout.

"Is that what Marshals call 'pacing'? Exercising?"

Busted! She sat up. "Maybe. But today, I'm officially on vacation."

His nose crinkled as though the air stank. "Sounds awful."

"I'm bored," she replied.

"I can tell." He gestured across the street. "Go work out. It'll clear your head."

The neighborhood gym, Muscled Up, suddenly called to her despite the fact that she felt like a half-dunked muffin. Hours ago, a workout would've been torture, but now she needed to push herself. Calhoun could allude to her lack of fitness for duty, but she could prove otherwise, even if it was only to herself.

"Go on." Raul shooed her. "Before you pace again, and I have to seed the lawn."

They shared a laugh, and she waved goodbye to go change into workout clothes. After she'd finished a protein bar and an apple, she grabbed her bottle of water and headed out the door.

Gone was the pure-azure sky, and thunder echoed distantly as dark clouds churned. Just as quickly as her day had changed, the sky had, too, and Chelsea opted to drive to Muscled Up, even if it was close.

She parked in front of the gym. A large Popeye arm served as their logo, and a young couple stepped out as she waited to go in.

The sign for Smokey's caught her eye. The bar was only a few storefronts down. She stared, letting the door to Muscled Up close.

The previous night, with its memories of hands brushing, looks lingering, and the warmth of their close proximity, held her spellbound. Goose bumps burst down her bare arms, making her shiver. A two-second-recall of their unrestrained hug looped through her brain.

When the door to Muscled Up opened again and jarred Chelsea, she snapped from the delicious moment where Liam's thick arms wrapped around her.

She shuffled in and swiped her plastic key chain card.

"Is the temperature dropping again?" the desk girl asked.

Chelsea paused, realizing that shiver bumps covered her arms. "Maybe so." Then she rushed away.

Reacting to Liam was shaking everything she fundamentally understood about herself—her loyalty, her likes and interests, and her ability to control the most basic of responses.

Another round of shivers danced down her spine. *Whoo boy. That had to stop.* A run or maybe pull-ups could clear her mind of the vivid, visceral, highly inappropriate recollections.

Otherwise, Chelsea was nothing except traitorous and horny. Nothing good would come of that combination.

CHAPTER TWENTY-ONE

ONLY TWO MORE. Two more pull-ups would be impossible, but that was how many Chelsea had assigned to forget about *all* the men in her life—Mac, Calhoun, *and* Liam. Two more pull-ups could erase her thoughts, including how she'd tried to call her dead best friend.

Her lungs burned, and her arms faltered. "Two—" So close, but she didn't let go. She growled, gritting her teeth and cursing with the wrath of cupcakes and coconuts until she inched her chin over the bar then dropped.

One left.

At that point, she would rather die on a pull-up bar than fail. Fire bit her grip, and burnout shook her muscles, but she ignored the stars threatening to form in her eyes and refused to give up.

"You've got this." Liam stepped into her peripheral vision.

If Chelsea had the strength to order him away with the grinding of clamped molars and pure determination, he would've disappeared in a poof of transporting magic.

Instead, she clung to his encouragement and rose above the bar, huffing. "*One.*"

She lowered, retaining as much control as she had left, then let go.

Stars danced, her limp arm muscles dangled, and the blood rushed in her head. A dizzy spell jeopardized her ability to remain upright. But she turned toward Liam, wanting to know if he was starring in her epic hallucinations or if he was really there.

He extended a hand as if she might topple over. "Overdoing it a bit?"

She tried to steady her breathing. Offering a simple *no* seemed harder than her oxygen-deprived mind would allow. But she wouldn't let him gawk as if she were near respiratory arrest. Chelsea shook out her arms and reached for her water, semi-sure she'd remain standing. "What are you doing here?"

"I left my card at the bar last night."

She cut a questioning glance. The gym was most definitely not the bar.

He gestured in the direction of Smokey's. "But they're not open yet."

Still, that didn't explain why he was in the gym.

"And I saw your Jeep." He ran a hand over the stubble on his jaw. It was a shade darker than his hair, and it added an unmistakable edge that she'd never noticed before. His intense eyes settled on her as if he'd said all the explanation he had to give.

The look pinned her in place, but not in an uncomfortable way. More in a way where she consciously had to remind her lungs to work. *Inhale, exhale. Don't, for all that was good and holy, pass out under his scrutiny.*

He rubbed the back of his neck. "Decided on a sick day?"

"No. I..." Well, she didn't want to explain what had transpired earlier.

"Am I supposed to guess?"

She focused on her water bottle. "My boss sent me home." Then Chelsea snuck a quick peek at him.

Liam remained like a statue, silent and waiting for her to continue.

The idea of sharing Calhoun's ridiculous accusation was irritating. She huffed. "Apparently, I might have a drinking problem."

Liam pressed his lips together trying to stifle his laughter.

"Hey!" It wasn't funny.

But he chuckled.

Chelsea smacked his shoulder. "It's not funny."

He snickered. "Yeah, well, it kind of is."

"*How?*"

"You? You're like a gun-toting cupcake."

Her jaw fell then snapped shut. "*First off,* cupcakes could have a drinking problem."

"If cupcakes could drink." His amusement knew no bounds.

"You just said—" Her brows pinched. "*And second,* I don't have a drinking problem!" Chelsea cringed, positive that anyone within a twenty-foot radius could've heard her. "*I don't*, and you know it. I know it."

He didn't stop laughing.

"This will go in my file!"

Eyes watering, Liam gasped with mock horror.

"This is your fault."

"Totally." He crossed his arms, nodding sarcastically. "Absolutely."

"I would've gone to bed if you hadn't shown up," she pointed out. "And arrived at work bright-eyed and bushy-tailed."

"You're always bright-eyed." He cocked a half-grin. "Maybe even bushy-tailed too, if I knew what that meant."

Her stomach flipped even if she wanted to strangle him. "It means eager."

"Like a beaver?"

"What? No!"

"I didn't think so." Liam stepped under the pull-up bar next to hers.

"What does that mean, anyway?"

"Who knows, sunshine." He stretched then grabbed a hold of the overhead bar, effortlessly lifting his chin high.

She watched the indentations of his muscles flex and the rest of the gym, with the clang of weights and the whirl of exercise machines, faded.

With smooth finesse, Liam eased down. His sinewy muscles straightened. He wasn't dressed for the gym. The dark jeans and cotton shirt alone would be cause for him to stand out.

But his T-shirt clung to his sculpted back and powerful shoulders. As he continued, each steady flex and pull over the bar belied its difficulty, and Chelsea couldn't ignore his physique. His shoulders tapered. His backside rounded. For the quickest moment, she pictured his backside, bare. She could imagine how his buttocks would flex when he thrust. She could almost feel the delicious friction between her thighs if he lay over her.

She staggered back, scared how much more she wanted beyond their drunken hug. She wanted him on her, *in* her, caging her to his chest.

"Excuse me," a voice pulled her back to the loud gym. "Are you using that still?"

A woman motioned to the pull-up bar next to the one Liam was using.

Chelsea didn't move. "Yeah, sorry."

But she wasn't sorry one iota. Liam held himself over the bar for a beat then eased down and dropped. He clapped his hands together then worked his shoulders back.

Fidgeting with her water bottle, Chelsea couldn't look him in the face after her imagination had gone on a tear. "Are you done?"

"Not sure. Are you?"

She clenched the bottle, finally glancing up. Exertion colored his face, but he didn't breathe hard—barely broke a sweat—and he held her in place with only a long, undecipherable look.

"What are you doing?" she asked.

"Working out with you." His eyebrows barely arched. "What did it look like I was doing?"

She glanced away again, unable to explain his actions any more than she could her thoughts. "Because *that* makes sense."

"Trust me," he mumbled. "Nothing makes sense anymore."

CHAPTER TWENTY-TWO

CHELSEA DID A double take, in absolute agreement. She could have sworn Liam's green eyes darkened. But she played it safe, as though she hadn't heard what he said.

Because he was right. Nothing made sense any more, and if they weren't careful, they'd misstep.

Faux naivete was pointless. His jaw flexed, and time passed slowly.

"What's wrong?" he asked.

What a question... She gulped. "Nothing. I just thought a workout would help with my frustration."

"Did it?"

She didn't want to answer because she didn't know.

"Chelsea." His tone gave no indication what would come after the lingering, lazy way he said her name. "There are more constructive ways to let go of frustration."

Heaven help her. A thousand unacceptable ways came to mind. Sparks and shivers exploded across her skin. But, she couldn't look away.

"Now are you done?" The woman from before broke their trance.

Relieved and annoyed, Chelsea shook free from the daze. "One more set."

Because, if she didn't burn off her *frustration,* she'd combust.

Chelsea jumped for the bar, finding the right position for her hands. It wasn't easy, and, shifting weight from one hand to the other, her sore fingers lamented that her grip was as good as it would get. Then she pulled herself up.

"One." She could feel his stare as surely as she felt the skin burning on her palms.

"Well, hell." Liam jumped for the bar next to her. "If this is how it's going to go..."

He pulled up, and she eased down, repositioning her hands again. Her arms ached. Her shoulders hurt, too, and tomorrow she'd feel it, but right now, she refused to drop and continue their conversation, which teetered on the edge of admitting interest.

Liam lowered. "I could think of better ways than this."

What the double marshmallows does he mean by that? She growled and pulled herself up, gritting her teeth over the bar. "Then go hit the heavy bag."

He pulled up, and she trembled, holding the position. Then with ease, he lowered again. She did so without the fluid dynamic.

Again, Chelsea had to readjust her grip. Her arms and hands were tiring exponentially faster than her last sets. She wouldn't be able to continue at this pace.

He moved up and down again, and his casualness suddenly struck a competitive nerve in her. She hated to lose—not that they were in a competition. But maybe they were. She pulled up *again*.

Their pull-up seesaw moved in tandem until she stopped, unable to lift herself one more time. Sweat tickled her upper lip and slid between her breasts. Then she dropped, pins and needles pricking her fingers. Too tired to shake out her arms, she muttered, "I hate to lose."

His shoes slapped on the mat when he came down. "I didn't realize this was a competition."

The pins in her palms transitioned into a burning sensation, but she was finally able to feel blood coursing in her arms. Chelsea shook them out then stretched.

"Are you ready to talk?" He stretched as she did.

Oh, heck no! About this? Us? Last night? Or does he have some magical way of reading my mind, where he saw his naked butt all but dancing on display? "Nope."

"Should've guessed."

Without a strong rebuttal, Chelsea spun away, retrieved the sanitizing spray bottle, and wiped down the bar. He didn't say a word when she decided a second cleaning might be in order, and Liam took the bottle and towel from her hands and cleaned his bar with far less diligence, then returned the bottle and tossed the towel.

Running away was the only possible answer for their situation, but she had nowhere to go.

He returned and asked, "Where to next?"

A light triangle of sweat dampened the front of his tight shirt. The shirt sleeves squeezed his biceps, and the workout had made the definition of his muscles and veins stand out.

He scanned the gym since she opted to mentally stutter and stay silent, then based on where his gaze hovered, she knew he would pick the treadmills.

She turned to eye the wall. The row of treadmills, mostly unused, lined the far corner. Running without the possibility of escape didn't seem like the best idea.

"Or we can go grab my card from Smokey's," he offered.

No way would Chelsea walk into last night's ground zero. But running? She tried not to groan and gave herself a pep talk. Her arms and hands were dead-dog tired. Not her legs. She could handle a treadmill. "Let's run."

He snorted but led the way to the last machines in the corner. How quiet and intimate… the perfect place for Liam to tell her how flattered he might be, but that he wasn't interested. Or maybe, he could explain why this sudden crush was ten kinds of wrong. Whatever she sensed from him, it was unequivocally *not* attraction. It couldn't be. He'd said as much! Nothing made sense. She'd created problems where there were none before.

Liam punched buttons on the treadmill's screen and jogged. She eyed his machine and punched buttons until their inclines were at the same angle. The treadmills quietly purred as they ran side by side.

The lack of conversation was good. Things couldn't be awkward if they weren't discussed… right?

He checked her screen, and her eyebrow arched. Liam punched the green arrow, striding faster.

Chelsea tried to ignore his adjustment, but he'd run then look her way, run again, look again.

Maybe, perhaps, she *was* competitive. Chelsea jabbed the green arrow to match his speed.

He laughed, and she ignored him. Finally, she hit that place where endorphins pumped, and each stride made her feel as if she could fly—

Liam punched his stop button, and not waiting for the machine to slow, he stepped on the edges. "What the hell are you doing?"

She punched the stop button also and scowled. "What does it look like?"

"I'm not your mother, your boss, or your partner."

She had no idea what he meant by that. "No kidding."

"What are you trying to prove?"

"What?" She wasn't trying to prove anything. She was hiding! That was all and far easier to understand than unwanted chemistry.

"If you need to prove yourself to some jackass boss…" He bunched his shoulders. "Then you have to do that. I can't say shit about the expectations you deal with—"

Her brow furrowed. "I'm sorry?"

Liam gestured at the pull-up bars. "Sending you home because you were hungover? I can't imagine the shit you put up with as a woman."

Her jaw fell. They were very much *not* thinking about the same problems.

"We're all frustrated," he continued. "I'm frustrated. You're frustrated. Everyone in this goddamn gym is probably frustrated."

She closed her mouth. Her heart was racing faster than when she was running, and she didn't know where he was going with their conversation.

He stepped down. "I need to talk to you. Even if I'm not supposed to."

Or maybe they *were* thinking about the same thing. She didn't know.

He dropped his head back and ran his hands into his hair. Sweat made it stay where he pushed it. "I don't know how much I should say."

Say nothing. Please, don't say a word!

"I should say nothing," he snapped. "There are rules. Spoken and unspoken. I get that. But shit…"

If she could erase last night, how she'd held on to him, how she'd reacted when he positioned her legs and arms… Chelsea bit the inside of her mouth.

"What I'm trying to say is…" He pulled her off the edge of her treadmill.

She didn't have the mental or physical strength to cover his mouth.

"I need your help."

Wait—what? Chelsea had amped herself up to a dangerous level of panic. *He wants help?* She hadn't only read the change in their conversation wrong. She'd misread the entire time in the gym. "What are you talking about?"

He glanced toward the ceiling then eyed the light crowd in the cardio section. "I can't talk about it here."

"Talk about *what*?"

His eyes narrowed as if he couldn't describe the topic. "Sort of a work problem."

That was his frustration? He'd been commiserating about work, while she'd ogled and fantasized. Her cheeks flamed.

"Actually." Liam shifted. "That wasn't the only reason I came in here."

Holy mixed signals, her panic screeched back into place.

"But the pull-ups helped me work something out."

She was glad it had helped one of them. "That's good."

Too bad her workout had the opposite effect and left her with more questions than when she showed up.

"So." He tossed a thumb over his shoulder. "I'm going to grab my card from Smokey's, then, if you had a few minutes to listen, I could meet you at your place?"

Chelsea bit her lip. Saying no could draw his attention to her concerns. Saying yes would put her in a small space with a man that seemed either totally aware or completely oblivious to their chemistry. "Yeah, sure."

He pulled in a deep breath then said, "I hope you'll still talk to me when I've said everything that needs saying."

CHAPTER TWENTY-THREE

LIAM WAITED FOR the daytime bartender to find his credit card and close him out, but the minutes ticked by. He wanted to hurry. A strange sensation pressed on his chest when they split outside the gym.

Nerves would've been the easiest description. Telling Chelsea that he was to blame for Julia's death would be a harsh blow. His fingers drummed on the bar top. He was drawn to the electric hum that flowed with Chelsea. But would that change when he confirmed what had always been his worst fear?

Finally, his card appeared, and he quickly added a generous tip as an offer of apology for not cashing out the evening before, then he hustled to his Explorer.

As he fumbled the keys into the ignition, he noticed his hurry, and he dropped his head against the seat. "What are you doing?"

Nothing. They'd done absolutely nothing because he wasn't jackass enough to rebound into the world of women by wanting to fuck Julia's best friend.

If more than a year had gone by, did that make Chelsea a rebound?

He turned the key, wanting regret to wreck him, but it never came.

Liam blew out his cheeks then secured his seatbelt and ignored his newfound attraction. He needed her help and had to concentrate if he wanted to tiptoe around a conversation with her that Sorenson said he wasn't allowed to have.

The drive to the condominium parking lot was short. He skipped stairs as he summited the second floor and knocked.

No answer.

He knocked again, and after a short wait, heard her call through the door, "One second."

Finally, the knob twisted, and Chelsea threw the door open. "Hey. Give me a second to finish changing."

Wet hair draped over her shoulders. She'd changed into jeans and an extra-large T-shirt. Her breasts swayed under the soft fabric, and all he could think was *braless*.

"Sure thing." He signaled that he'd be on the couch because if he said anything else, who knew how it would sound.

Liam settled in the living room but couldn't ignore a mental replay of her nipples pressing into the shirt. She could hide behind baggy clothing, but nothing she did could stop his imagination.

Would her breasts feel firm? Do her nipples match the deep pink of her lips? He repositioned on the couch, giving in to one last wonder of how Chelsea might sound. *What makes her hum? How would she sigh?*

"If you need anything from the kitchen," she called, "just grab it."

He exhaled, feeling the tightness course his body, and pushed a hand across his face. "Yeah, will do."

But he wasn't about to stand and put his arousal on display. Again, Liam repositioned, grabbing the closest magazine from the coffee table, and tried to kick back as though he gave a damn what the page he turned to said.

Chelsea returned. She wore a new shirt, bra clearly in place, and a flowing sweater that dangled to her thighs. He noted, without meaning to, how it failed to hide her curves.

"You need help." She sat on a chair adjacent to the couch and perched her bare feet on the edge.

Yeah, he sure as hell did, but he stared blankly.

Her arms wrapped around her shins, and she hugged her legs. "At work?"

At work... "Right." Damn, he needed to focus. But there she was, shower fresh, and he probably stank like the gym and had an erection to hide.

She bounced up and angled her chair, then wrapped herself into a ball again.

"Do I smell bad or something?" He turned his head from side to side, smelling his armpits and nervously laughing.

"No!"

"You backed away," he pointed out.

"No," she insisted. "I thought… maybe you wanted space."

His eyebrows arched. "Either way, I didn't expect to work out in jeans."

She waited, eyes wide, for him to explain what he needed. Here went nothing. He hoped she didn't try to gut him when the conversation was done.

"A few years ago, I worked a job where someone's loved one, his daughter, died."

Liam had likely already said too much. That was more than he'd shared with Chance. But, he hoped, Chelsea had to have at least some level of security clearance.

"After a few years," he continued, "the person who was hurt—" He was being too vague. "For conversation's sake, we can call him…"

"Fred," she offered.

Random, but he'd take it. "Fred," Liam repeated. "A few years after Fred's daughter died—"

"How'd she die?"

"During an op." He wouldn't give specifics. She needed distance and deniability.

"She was killed," Chelsea confirmed.

He nodded.

"Friendly or enemy?"

He thought about the lines that they were already going to cross if she helped him. "Enemy."

Chelsea took that in then unhooked her arms from her legs to sit cross-legged in the chair.

"Fred gained access to a list of people involved in the operation where his daughter died. For the last few years, Fred has planned and carried out his revenge."

Liam paused for a question, but she didn't ask any.

"He's targeting the loved ones of the people on that list," he continued.

"Are you on that list?" she asked quietly.

He nodded. "Yeah."

Chelsea pressed her lips together then tilted her head. "Julia?"

Again, he nodded. His chest ached as if an anvil were pinning him to the couch. "Yeah. She was killed to hurt me."

Her dark eyes grew glassy, but she took a deep breath and pinched the bridge of her nose. Finally, Chelsea asked, "That's why you think I won't talk to you again?"

"Why would you?" he asked.

She didn't dispel his concern, but the color faded from her face and her head angled toward her lap. Damp hair curtained from the side of her cheeks, masking what little her expression might show.

Julia had died because of him, and now Chelsea knew the ugly truth. She knew how unfair her death had been, knew that because of his actions, everyone had suffered. Their loss was because of him—as simple as that.

She stood, emotion tight on her face. Her fists hung limply by her side as she stalked to the couch and towered a foot away.

Liam held his breath. Whatever she had to say, whatever blame she forced him to hold, he deserved it.

Chelsea dropped, nearly sitting on her ankles, and hovered in front of him. "Are you okay?"

"Me?" He didn't understand and jerked back.

She wobbled, off balance by his quick move, and slapped her hand on his knee to steady herself. He covered her hand with his. His other one caught her shoulder.

"Shit," he offered. "Sorry."

She eased onto the couch and laid a hand on his forearm. "Are you okay?"

Why did she ask that? "Julia *died* because of me."

Chelsea bit her lip, studying.

"Why aren't you yelling?" he demanded. "Cursing—or whatever it is that you do."

She rubbed his forearm as if to promise one day he wouldn't hurt. It made him angrier. Liam snagged his arm away.

"I'm so sorry," she said.

"What? Stop that," he snapped. "Why the hell—"

"Neither of you deserves that—"

"No shit. But I'm to blame!"

Chelsea wrapped her arm around his shoulders, holding tight when he yanked back. Her other arm locked around his chest. He couldn't breathe. He *shouldn't* breathe. If someone had to die because of Red Gold, he should have been the one.

His molars gnashed. He'd come to Chelsea to ask for help, to tell her the truth, not for her to comfort and console him.

She let him go, and Liam hated how cold the room grew without her close as much as he hated her pity. "I'm not here to feel better."

She held his gaze. "Consider it an added bonus."

"Chelsea, *I caused her death.* What don't you understand?"

"You'll never be able to move forward until you realize you aren't to blame."

Who said he wanted to? Liam didn't know right from wrong, up from down. He sure as hell didn't know what moving forward even meant. But he knew Chelsea wanted him to feel better. "Fine. I'm not to blame."

Chelsea's pink lips thinned into a stubborn line. "I was trying to help."

They'd spiraled away from the point, and he had to focus. Otherwise, who knew where they would end up. *Like her bed.* Shit, what was wrong with him? He cleared his throat. "I'm worried about Linda and Frank."

Her eyes flashed. "Wait—are they in danger?"

"I think so, yeah." He couldn't lie as worry clouded her face, and admitted, "Yes, they are."

"What are you doing about it?" she asked incredulously.

"Talking to you."

Chelsea's brow pinched. "Liam—"

"This is a thousand layers of complicated and classified."

"So?"

"I have orders."

"To what?"

"To stand down."

Her jaw fell. "*Why?*"

Her reaction mirrored his initial one. "If I said, I think you'd be in danger."

"That's *horseshit,*" she snapped.

Liam froze.

"Don't look at me like that. Tell me why."

Chelsea could curse. That was a level of pissed he didn't know existed, but her rage didn't change the situation. "There's a level of government interest and involvement that I can't understand. The kind where if you know too much, if I share too much, if we get caught doing what I'm about to ask you to do, we'll end up in some unmarked dungeon at a nonexistent black site."

"Liam," she finally whispered, "what have you gotten yourself into?"

CHAPTER TWENTY-FOUR

ANGER, SKEPTICISM, HEARTACHE, and fatigue cycled through Chelsea's thoughts. What was this madness? *Black ops gone bad?*

"Well?" she pushed. But she wasn't sure what she wanted him to explain.

He pushed a hand into his hair. "This is why I need your help."

She couldn't tell if he was nuts or up creek, without a paddle, and then she remembered the mysterious package and the man on the porch who Liam had left with. Chelsea nodded, urging him to continue.

"I know this sounds…"

"We both know how this sounds," she said, mentally pulling herself into a Marshal mind frame. "Forget that, and tell me what you need in order to keep Linda and Frank safe." She'd figure next steps, like lovingly securing him a psych hold or biting the bullet to loop in Mac, later.

"I don't have the manpower to keep an eye on the Nymans twenty-four hours a day."

Worry needled. "Who's watching them now?"

"Someone I contract with."

That wasn't good enough. She narrowed her eyes.

"His name is Chance." Liam's lips flattened. "That's about all I can share—that, and he hooked me up with some equipment. I'll have my hands on it in a few days."

She still wasn't convinced and crossed her arms.

"Look—" He shifted uncomfortably. "If you help me with the Nymans, we'll catch Julia's murderer. It's all tied together."

"Why didn't you just say that?" That is, if what he said was credible.

"Because I *can't.*"

And if there was truth to his beliefs… "I can help with—" *With what?* She didn't know any details.

"Recon and surveillance isn't the same thing."

"I know."

"Surveillance isn't my forte." Liam seemed disappointed. "I'm good at what I do, and I'm smart enough to know this can't be my first surveillance-planning job."

"That's *my* forte."

"I thought so."

She inched forward. "I have paid time off, at least for now, I'll give you that."

"I can't answer much more than I shared already."

Chelsea gripped his forearm. "No more questions asked. As long as we keep the Nymans safe and help facilitate an arrest."

"Deal." Liam covered her hand with his and squeezed.

She flushed. His lingering touch brought to light the problem that she'd forgotten for only a few minutes: Liam electrified her.

She jerked her hand back then chanced a quick glance up. Liam knew why she'd pulled away. He had to. But he didn't say a word about the obvious.

They were still far too close together. His body heat made her nervous, but she didn't move away. His eyes dropped to her mouth, and her heart jumped.

Apparently though, heart palpitations were enough to make her move. Chelsea scooted, and he chuckled.

"What?" Why would he call her out like that!

He pressed his lips together as though her leap across the couch were funny and not necessary. Maybe Liam was someone who laughed under pressure.

"Maybe I do smell funky, huh?"

Yeah, that was it. Her mental eye roll nearly somersaulted. But maybe she should thank him for giving her a graceful exit from additional bumbling antics.

She wrinkled her nose and waved her fingers to ward off a nonexistent stench. "The funkiest."

"We can—" He thumbed toward her dining area table. "Sit on opposite sides?"

Her eyebrows arched. "For?"

"While we whittle down a plan?" he reminded her.

Oh, cheese and crackers. She needed time to pull herself together. "Why don't you just go grab a shower?"

He hesitated, and she thought about him in her shower. *Cheese and crackers, again!* A wave of heat rushed over Chelsea.

"Either way, I need a smoothie." She popped up, content to take the mental image of Liam naked and showering to a deep grave—or at the very least, her kitchen.

CHAPTER TWENTY-FIVE

LIAM MADE HIS way to the bathroom with a small smile he couldn't shake off his face. Chelsea had jumped, and he'd never pictured her as… cute.

And that she was. Very cute, in a jumpy, sweet, sexy kind of way that he should ignore since it made her uncomfortable. Hell, it did him too, but in a way he hadn't felt in a long time. Maybe in a way he wasn't supposed to feel again.

He squinted, not having thought about dating since Julia. Was a year long enough? Who set the rules when it came to next steps?

He entered into the bathroom and breathed in the citrus-warmed air. Humidity hung from Chelsea's shower, and while the fog on the mirror had faded, moisture shadowed the glass with iridescent patches.

Liam stared at his reflection. Maybe *he* was the one to make up the rules.

Or maybe he should chill out. He was only there to enlist Chelsea's help.

"Focus," he said, then flipped the hot water on in the shower.

Three bottles were decorated with lemons and flowers, each with a slightly different label—shampoo, conditioner, and body wash. They were the source of the lemons and lavender scent that had driven him to distraction. Now they gave him the mental image of Chelsea rinsing suds from her body.

He'd never make it through the day if he didn't stop the explicit thoughts. He stripped and pulled the curtain back then caught himself because there was no way he could use her lemon-colored plastic poof. A washcloth would do fine.

After a quick inspection in a cabinet and under the sink came up empty, he checked a tall, skinny closet to the side of the shower. A quick perusal showed towels, which he grabbed, *hand* towels, and more poofs. *How many poofs does a woman need?* But no washcloths.

A plastic closet organizer with drawers sat on a shelf, and he pulled the top one open—*hair crap*—then shut it, checking the bottom one—"Oh, damn!"

A bottle of lube and a thin pink vibrator. He slammed them away. The plastic drawer organizer pushed far into the closet.

Cringing, he tried to move it back. The last damn thing he needed was for Chelsea to think he'd snooped.

To hell with the washcloth. But he couldn't let go of the image of the vibrator. He entered the shower as his erection thickened and let the water spray his face. Closing his eyes didn't help.

What does she think about?

He puffed out his cheeks and blew into the water. Why couldn't he let it go?

Liam adjusted the temperature until the water was nearly too hot, and he gritted his teeth. He shouldn't have looked, shouldn't have imagined. But God help him if he didn't wonder how soft the insides of her thighs might be.

"What the fuck is wrong with you?" He pulled out of the scalding water and pressed against the cool tile, unable to tone down his arousal.

Why is Chelsea different now?

She'd always been attractive with a heavy curtain of dark hair that hung around her face, but he'd never wondered how the strands would feel.

Her lips had always been the same shade of pink. But now he wanted to feel them against his own.

Nothing had changed about Chelsea overnight.

Not in the last week or over the last year.

He was the one who had changed.

Hell. Liam growled and grasped the bottle of shampoo, needing to do his business then escape the bathroom. He shampooed as quickly as he could manage then used her soap to wash, praying that if he was the one to smell like a bowl of lemons and flowers, his reaction to Chelsea's scent would wane.

He showered off then turned the water to cold, holding himself there until he had to get out. Liam took the added step of reciting the names of every ugly, hairy, dirty, and disgusting dude he'd ever had the misfortune to smell, whether in boot camp or a cramped plane, so he could finish the afternoon without a hard-on.

Still, that wasn't enough to calm down his curious, horny mind.

Liam wiped a streak through the steam-covered mirror and told himself, "Everything will be fine."

It had to be. If he couldn't concentrate while they planned, the closest thing he'd ever had to a family would be at risk.

Liam closed his eyes, aggravated that he needed a pep talk to keep himself in line. But like it or not, the lecture was needed, and the voice of his boot camp instructor barked for him to focus.

He took a deep breath and… glanced at the pile of his dirty clothes. No change of clean clothes. *Awesome.*

He scowled. If ever was there a screaming example of how distracted he was, then a lack of clean clothes was it. How could he I protect anyone if he couldn't manage to dress his self?

He considered donning the dirty ones but they were soaked after dripping all over them.

Liam wrapped the towel around his waist and cracked the door. "Hey, Chelsea?"

Nothing.

He stepped into the hallway and called again.

No answer. Again. *Where is she?*

"Hey." He slicked water off his hair then walked toward the living room when the front door opened. "Hey—"

"Liam!" Chelsea put a hand over her eyes and spun away. "What are you doing?"

He tried not to laugh. "I was looking for you."

"You're naked!"

"You didn't get a good look then." He snickered as she continued to cover her eyes while facing away. "I'm more covered than I'd be at the pool."

"I went to take out the trash." She waved her arm behind her back. "Go put on your clothes."

"*Clothes* are the problem and why I was looking for you."

"What does that mean?" She stopped waving but didn't turn.

"Mine are dirty and wet. Do you have something I can throw on?"

She waited, maybe working that over in her mind. "Hang on a second."

Then she sped down the hall.

He stared and smiled. "I'll be in the bathroom."

"Sure," she called. "Sounds good. Shut the door."

He chuckled and wandered back to the bathroom.

A minute passed until she knocked. "Incoming."

He cracked the door, and Chelsea blindly tossed clothing his direction then rushed away. "Thanks." He picked up the sweats and held them out. They seemed far too large to fit her. "Whose are these?"

"What?"

He pulled on the sweatpants. Not his size, but definitely closer to his than hers. He opened the door. "Whose clothing did you give me?"

"Does it matter?" she called.

"Just curious." Or something. He pulled the sweatshirt over his head. Was she dating someone? Did these belong to an ex? Liam pulled at the tight sleeves, making his way to the living room and spied her on the couch. "Snug fit."

Chelsea's eyebrow arched. "Better than a towel."

"I appreciate the clothes," he said. "Even if they're small."

Her other eyebrow arched, and she cocked her head. "What's that supposed to mean?"

He shrugged. "I don't know. I'm bigger than whoever is missing their clothes."

Her lips parted, then Chelsea rolled her eyes. "I can't believe men sometimes."

"What?" he asked.

"*Bigger than?* Are you trying to one-up someone you don't know?"

He balked. "No, I'm not."

She jumped off the couch and re-enacted his entrance, strutting, and then flexed. "It's a little tight around all these big, manly muscles."

"You like pretending to be me, huh?"

"Who wouldn't?" She flexed again. "With guns like these."

He laughed. "I don't sound like that."

She shrugged and slid back onto the couch. "Maybe you're wearing my dad's clothes."

"Then your dad's a little skinny."

She chucked a pillow at him.

The unknown bothered him more than it should. "You're not going to tell me?"

She ignored him then led the way to the table. "I worked while you played in the shower. Take a look at what I've put together."

He might've done a lot of things in the bathroom, but playing wasn't on the list—even if he'd wanted to.

A notepad with a hand-sketched layout waited, and Liam picked it up. She'd marked the drawing with a few *X*s and arrows.

He flipped through the pages and read detailed notes. Chelsea notated the Nymans' routines—their jobs, habits, commutes, and usual errands. Basically, she'd nailed everything about how the Nymans lived. "You did all that when I was in the shower?"

"Yeah."

"Wow." All he'd accomplished was finding her vibe and managing not to jerk off again. "Good work, Sunshine."

She sat down at the table and twirled a pen. "Thanks."

Liam pulled out a chair. The condo seemed darker than it had been, as if on cue, thunder boomed and shook the condo. "Here it comes again."

A knock on the door made him jump.

"Easy, gunslinger," Chelsea joked and shooed him back into his chair. "I ordered pizza."

"Good thinking." But he couldn't settle back into his seat. The unexpected made him edgy, and everything about today had an element of surprise. As she settled up, he walked into the kitchen, needing something to do like plates or napkins.

Liam grabbed a cabinet handle but paused. Would he stumble upon a sinfully sexy belonging? Hopefully not in the kitchen. Still, he nervously swung the door open and stole an uncertain glance. Nothing but plates. Hallelujah.

For the next few hours, they ate pizza and made plans. He marveled at how her mind worked and congratulated himself for asking her for a helping hand. This was very much her bailiwick.

By the time the pizza was gone and evening had come, they had three operational objectives, and Liam was semi-comfortable they could assure the Nymans' safety. Though, he was less than semi-sure they could do so while avoiding Senator Sorenson's intrusive eye.

But if they ran into a problem with the senator, he'd figure out how to cover his ass. It might even mean sharing the truth with Chelsea. He wondered how she'd react to Sorenson's use of civilians to capture a terrorist.

Right now, that wasn't the intel he wanted to burden her with. The repercussions could be ugly.

If only he'd had more time with Westin and Black. Liam was certain that they would see the situation from his side and would assist in detailed planning with firepower.

He flicked a pencil and watched it roll over the papers. Then he glanced at her.

Chelsea pulled a band off her wrist and knotted her hair into a messy bun. Strands fell loose, but she didn't touch them. Maybe she didn't notice. But he had.

It'd been hours since they first started working. While they were busy, his mind didn't wander. Now that they were finished…? His mind was on a roll. He pushed his chair to balance on its back legs.

Thunder clapped again, and Chelsea startled. The earlier storm had been all bluster with only a few raindrops.

Now, another boom vibrated the condo, promising far more intensity than the earlier sprinkle. Just as soon as the thunder hit, thick splats of water pelted the windows.

Liam eased his chair onto the front legs. Lightning lit the darkening sky. The overhead lights flickered and turned off.

A shiver rolled down his back. He always enjoyed power outages and couldn't explain why. Maybe it was the silence, shadows, and stillness that came with hiding in the dark.

"Guess this one is for real." Chelsea pushed from the table and left the room.

She returned with a small plastic tub, set it on the table, and extracted a bag of small candles. "If I go through the fuss of lighting a few candles, the lights will turn back on like magic."

He laughed. "Is that so?"

"It's a proven fact." Chelsea struck a match and lit two small candles then shuffled their paperwork into a pile. She gathered it in her arm and handed him the matchbook. "Maybe we need a couple more lit. There are some by the couch."

His eyes were adjusting well in the dark, and Liam watched her store their plan in a kitchen cabinet that held a small, paper-sized safe. He chuckled quietly. So the unexpected did exist behind cabinet doors in her kitchen. But a safe wasn't likely to do anything for his arousal like imagining Chelsea's orgasm.

She returned to the living room as he struck a match and lit two candles in glass jars. They cast a warm, waving light. Chelsea eased by, taking the lit candles, and placed one on a side table and the other on the coffee table.

Lemons and lavender hung in the air.

"The quiet's my favorite part," he said. Gone were the hum of the circulating HVAC unit, the slow spin of a fan, and the gentle sound of the refrigerator. Their movements were the only thing that could be heard.

They stood by the coffee table, and she didn't say anything. The small candles barely lit the room, and with each second of quiet, pressure tightened in his chest.

Liam licked his lips. His breaths slowed, and he couldn't ignore the wonder and hunger—but he had to.

How he reacted toward her, with her, because of her… he needed to leave. He gestured toward the door. "I'll head out."

She gave a quiet "Oh" marred by a slip of disappointment.

Shit, that wasn't what he needed to hear. *How about a high five? A kick in the ass?* Anything that would show his interest was one-sided. He didn't want to go. *That* was the problem.

"Are you sure?" she asked.

Not at all. He stepped closer. Her beautiful eyes watched warily. They couldn't do this. Because of the past. Because they had a job to do. Those were catastrophic problems.

Touching Chelsea would change everything.

CHAPTER TWENTY-SIX

LIGHTNING STREAKED. THUNDER cracked. It was almost as if Mother Nature was shouting for Liam's attention. But he wasn't sure what she was saying.

Rain pelted sideways. The intensity drummed, roaring against the windows.

Several cracks of thunder rolled, and the lights blinked on for a flash, then stayed dark again. It was enough to break the tension.

"On that note." The corners of his lips turned. "I'll head out before it gets worse."

"Liam." Chelsea shook her head. "Don't be ridiculous. You can't go out in that."

He probably should. The cold water and crashes would keep his mind clear. The wind howled. All he had to do was walk out the door. "Promise I won't melt."

Warily, she glanced at the windows. Again, thunder and lightning exploded loudly enough to make Chelsea jump. "Melting isn't my worry."

He walked across the living room to the windows and pressed his forehead to the cold glass. The rain hit with such power that he could feel them beat against the window.

Her footsteps quietly came close, and her arm grazed his when she stopped to stare into the dark.

Electricity skipped to his neck and somersaulted down his spine. The palm of his hands tingled. Hell. He had to go. But he didn't move a damn muscle.

"The worst will be over soon," she whispered.

Liam closed his eyes. He prayed that was true. Not the storm—who cared about the lightning—but the deep, intense need that had him trapped, where he couldn't pull away and didn't want to.

Another slice of lighting followed by a thunderclap that shook the windows. It made Chelsea jump, and she laughed quietly. "I swear, I'm not scared of storms."

He turned. "I didn't think you were."

Lightning struck and thunder rumbled again. "See?" She tilted her head toward the rain. "I didn't jump that time…" Chelsea wouldn't look him in his eyes. "Is the thunder farther apart?"

He didn't say anything.

"The storm's lessening."

"Maybe so." Time to go. But he didn't want to leave. Liam studied her soft hair and her strong shoulders in the candlelight. He let his gaze drift down and stopped at the base of the window. Her fingers clung to the windowsill with such pressure her nails might leave marks. "What's wrong, Chelsea?"

Stupid question. They both knew what was wrong.

"I'm not sure," she whispered.

"What would happen if…" His chest ached, and Liam moved close behind her and stared out her window. "*We told the truth?*"

Rain rolled. The howl of wind picked up and faded again. "I don't know."

Liam removed the slip of distance between them. She stayed still as if he weren't there and the swell of her ass didn't rest against his body.

The scent of lemons and lavender teased. Her warmth ran through his blood like a rich, caramel shot of whiskey, and he broke the stranglehold that uncertainty had on him and brushed her hair to the side.

She quietly gasped but remained still.

His fingers skimmed across the nape of her neck. "Tell me to leave. Tell me to get the hell out."

Then he prayed, for her, for him, that he hadn't fucked up their new-found friendship because of the carnal daydreams he imagined about their slick naked bodies wrapped together.

"Tell me to go." And he prayed that she'd say no.

Her uneven breaths mirrored the cadence of his, and still she said nothing—which was answer enough. She didn't say go but hadn't said stay.

He took a step back, deflated but with his unsaid marching orders. An apology was in order, but hell if he knew how to word it.

Chelsea's hand dropped from the windowsill, reaching behind, and she gripped the side of his thigh. Her fingers clung to his pants like she couldn't move, but he couldn't leave. "Wait."

He understood her internal war but didn't know what she wanted.

She shivered, and the faint tremble made his eyelids drift shut. Maybe they'd stay shut until reason or sanity showed up.

Chelsea pivoted, and her upturned face held questions he couldn't answer.

Liam leaned a forearm over her head, pressing against the cold window. His fingers brushed over her cheek. Her eyelashes fluttered as his knuckles traced to her chin then fell away.

Lightning lit the sky. Thunder rumbled. The window shook, and she whispered, "Don't leave tonight."

CHAPTER TWENTY-SEVEN

"There's nowhere else I want to be." Liam searched for doubt, and when Chelsea didn't give him any, he brushed a wayward hair off her cheek again.

The careful touch made her eyelids lower, and she trembled as his fingers touched her chin and traced from her jawline down the slope of her neck.

Her erratic breaths matched the wild race in her heart. Arousal coursed through her curves, and she shivered when Liam leaned close enough to kiss her—but didn't.

He didn't rush, and she didn't know why. But Chelsea savored the slow-burning seconds that made her ready to explode.

Finally, he brushed his lips to hers. The softness made her moan. The tease left her humming for more. If she'd had any last-minute hesitations, they'd disappeared as his tongue pushed into her mouth.

The lighting-swept sky raged, and she needed more. Shrouded in the dark, painted in candlelight, she clung to him.

The storm howled and shook. Cold glass pressed against her back as Liam pinned her against the window. She wrapped her arms around his neck. His erection pressed against her body as his strength surrounded her. Glittering desire rushed, and she couldn't get enough of his touch.

He nipped and kissed and groaned. The world spun around them, and she snaked her legs up his powerful thighs, moaning his name.

He lifted her up, and his groin flexed against her mound. "Shit, Chelsea." Thunder and lightning crashed. Liam whipped his tongue down her neck. "Killing me."

She writhed, urging him for more—but Liam jerked away.

"*What?*" she cried as her legs fell down.

Their breaths raced. His deep blazing emerald eyes wouldn't let her go.

"Liam, what?" Though that time she whispered.

In their panting silence, the rain storm wailed. She shivered against the cold window and studied his rugged features, etched with concern.

He swept her into his arms and carried her to the couch then lowered her to the cushions, half holding, half pinning her in a delicious, possessive clinch.

Liam let the weight of his body blanket her until she couldn't move and didn't want to.

This was that moment where they could walk away, no harm, no foul. Or at least without paradigm-shifting damage. But she didn't want to hold back. "Even before this, storms were my favorite weather."

He grinned. "I'd hate to ruin one of your favorite things."

He was one of her favorite things. She didn't know when or how that'd happened. They still teetered on the line where all could be turned around, where they could walk away and maybe survive. But she didn't care if they saw the line again. Something raw and rabid, without clothes and regrets, needed to happen.

"Tell me what you want."

Everything! Didn't he know? Her cheeks blazed. "You can't ask me that!"

"I can do whatever I want," he teased.

Yes, he could. Except leave. If Liam walked out the door, she was positive she wouldn't survive the night.

He pushed onto the couch and lay on his side. They were face to face, and vivid, visceral ideas of his corded legs nudging her softer ones apart caused her to whimper.

"Tell me," he said.

"I can't," she admitted. "I'm not sure about anything when it comes to you."

He squeezed her to his chest, wrapping her safely in his strength. She imagined how Liam would press himself inside her body, how her fingernails would dig into his back, and the soul-claiming way he'd make her stretch to his length and girth. A needling arousal pulsed.

He gently swayed his palm from her side, over her hip. "Do you like this?" His fingers danced along her waistband, dipping to tease her bare stomach. "Or like that?"

Her breath caught in her lungs. *Both!* Need sparked along her stomach. Her breasts hurt, painfully aware they'd been ignored. Her tight nipples beaded against her bra, and she couldn't think.

"What else makes you moan?" Liam dipped his hand under the waistband of her yoga pants. He didn't slide under her panties but curled his fingers over her mound. Her wet arousal had dampened the fabric, and he licked his lips the second he realized how very turned on she must be.

"I want this." His voice rumbled as he pressed against her apex—then drew away.

The movement was slow, but the touch was gone, and she mewed in protest, making him smile.

"And…" He feathered the tips of his fingers across the softness of her belly. Back and forth, until Liam brushed the underside of her breast.

She purred, unable to keep quiet as he caressed her. "Liam…"

"And…" he said again, cupping her breast just as he did to her sex. "This."

"Yes," she murmured as the massaging pressure increased. "That feels so good."

His touch grew bolder. He thumbed her nipple, plucking to gage her reaction, then he nuzzled her neck once he seemed sure to have found the pressure they liked.

He flicked open the front enclosure of her bra, cursing when her breasts released. "Sweet Jesus, your tits."

Shocked, she jerked back to read his face.

"What?" he asked.

No one in their right mind thought she had a great chest. They were a little too small compared to her bottom, which was a little too large. She was ill-proportioned. But nothing she could see indicated he offered an unfounded compliment. He *liked* her chest.

She shook her head. "Nothing."

Liam dipped his mouth and sucked. The hot wetness of his tongue, how he nibbled and released, made her delirious.

Chelsea clawed at his sweatshirt. She needed his skin on hers. "Take this off."

Liam tore it away then swiftly shed her shirt and tossed it aside. She had a brief worry that it had landed on the candle, and he laughed when she grabbed a quick look.

"Do you ever let go?" he asked.

"Of?"

"Everything but what's in front of you?"

She didn't answer.

"I won't burn your condo down," he promised then eased onto his knees for a neck-kissing angle that made her want to scream.

This was primal, unlike any pleasure she'd ever experienced, and they hadn't even started down that actual road.

Chelsea squirmed. Her hips rocked to find an immaculate pressure as his hand cupped over her pants.

"Please."

"Don't rush me," he chided but slid his hand into her panties.

"Liam," she moaned.

Her sensitive skin tingled. Wet and swollen, she throbbed. His gentle caresses and strong strokes made her cry. He strummed and teased, playing with her clitoris one moment and toying at her entrance seconds later.

"You're evil, and so very, very good." She squeezed her eyes shut, and she might kill him soon if he didn't—

A finger pressed carefully inside, and a low rumble of approval growled from deep in his chest. A dangerous desire ricocheted deep from within her as his finger eased in and out.

"More."

He added a second finger on the next thrust.

She arched, and her thighs trembled. "Yes."

Her lips parted, and she let out a shaky gasp.

"Watching you…" He gave her more pressure, a deeper intrusion. "Is better than I could've dreamed."

Self-consciousness heated her face. But the pleasure he gave her swept away the shock.

Each stroke drew faster. Every time, he curled his fingertips just enough, faster and faster.

Chelsea gripped his forearm, begging for harder, harsher, more.

A possessive guttural kiss burned onto her lips, and that was everything she needed. She exploded against his hand, succumbing to a kiss so satisfying that he sent her flying high into the stormy sky.

CHAPTER TWENTY-EIGHT

"HOLY HELL." LIAM craved Chelsea more in her moment of pleasure than he knew possible. Her bliss was intoxicating. The way she smiled and sighed and kissed him was different from anything he had ever experienced.

And if he thought the magnitude of her climax might require rest, he was wrong. Even as she quivered with carnal aftershocks, she'd still kissed with enough heat to make the devil sweat.

Lust burned inside his chest, and Chelsea fueled their explosive fire with an exploring touch. Her fingernails lightly teased, but then they'd dig into his biceps. She'd sweep her lips across his skin and catch him off guard with nips and licks. Each touch stoked him higher, made him harder, and longing nearly blinded him until he'd eased to her side.

She slipped off her yoga pants and lay naked by his side. Her dark hair piled on a pillow, and her dark eyes were hidden by a relaxed lazy flutter of her lashes.

Liam let his gaze roam from her lips down.

"Your turn," she whispered, reminding him with a sweet, sultry request that once again, he'd only seen the tip of the iceberg. This woman was the real Chelsea, the one who helped without question—or too many questions—and followed her passions. She lay bare for him, and he wanted to strip away her defenses, to learn every reason her guard went up or her trust went down. Liam wanted to discover her secrets, in bed and out.

And it didn't hurt that she wanted him to come as hard as she just had.

Chelsea covered the bulge straining in his pants. Over the cotton fabric, she stroked him and gaged his face. Her hand stilled. "Do you want to get naked with me?" Her touch pulled away. "Or not. No big deal."

He stilled her retreat, gripping her fingers. A flash of excitement crashed over him at their touch. He didn't breathe and wasn't sure she did, either. She never blinked as Liam pressed her palm against his dick.

"Sunshine, I want..." His hand covered hers, and her lips parted as if she were taken aback by the stiffness. "To be naked with you."

The pink tip of her tongue darted out and licked her lips, and the quiet shake of her breath made him gulp. But her fingers didn't move.

Liam held back, not wanting to push, but the lengths he'd go to for her stroke again damn near scared him.

A small concerned line pinched between her eyebrows. "Are you sure—"

He was as sure as he'd ever been. Liam rolled away and stripped. His length hung heavily for her, and he pressed his lips together, inhaling so deeply his chest nearly burst.

He gripped his cock and slid his hand down the shaft. The smooth heat was heavy in his palm, and he couldn't tear his gaze from her.

Her hair spread over a pillow, and she waited, eyes wide and wondering. He gripped himself tighter, fondling in a way that left nothing to her imagination—what he wanted and what she did to him. Liam took a painstakingly slow pause to make sure she was aware.

"Do you understand?" he asked, his low voice vibrating. "I want you."

Chelsea pushed onto her elbow, pivoting onto her side. "I've never been with anyone like you."

"Like what?"

She sat up, pulling her legs in front of him until he played with himself inches away from her lips. "Sexually confident."

He paused, realizing what he'd said and how he put himself on display—it wasn't confidence. It was an unrealized trust—that she'd gone through a hell that no one could imagine but him—and pure, testosterone-driven desire.

He stepped closer. Her hands replaced his. She eased both her palms together, mirroring around his cock and sliding up and down. At the crown, her thumbs parted, following the thick ridge of his head, then she eased her hold down to the base of his shaft again. His head dropped back.

The way she touched him, curious but greedy, made his eyes roll back.

Warm, wet heat encircled the blunt head. He jerked and looked down. Plump pink lips encircled his cock. Her eyes shut, and she hummed, hungry and needy as she slipped her mouth down.

"God, Chelsea," he breathed.

The tight hug of her lips made his balls tighten. When the back of her throat hit his dick, he ached, holding himself back, needing to be inside her more than he could fathom.

Liam ran his fingers into her hair, memorizing the wicked way she took his cock. He would dream about this again one day. He would need it when the world seemed too bleak.

She gripped his ass with one hand. The other bobbed with her mouth, and the edge of pleasure was near—so close, too close.

He pulled back, gasping at what he'd done, and angled over her, taking her swollen lips in a kiss, tangling their tongues.

She nodded, urging him on, reassuring him that she craved him as much as he needed to be inside her.

But the truth was, he didn't understand.

Nothing about them made sense. None of their chemistry, the fire-sparking connection, had been a hint of an interest. Until now.

Chelsea lifted her hips and offered herself.

Her body made sense—those eyes that held him hostage, and the way she came. *That* made sense. He understood the need to hear her come again as well as he knew he needed oxygen to breathe.

And in that moment when he pressed into her slick entrance and took the invitation she offered, Liam knew that they needed to fall into a delirium together—to fuck and come, to orgasm until life made sense.

He gnashed his molars, and inch by inch, speared her hot tightness. He gripped the back and arm of the couch, perched over her and holding back the thrusts that barked and begged for release.

"Liam—" Her voice caught, rich with bliss, then she left her lips parted.

He drove deeper, flexing between her legs, driving into her sex, until she had his length, and he held still, bracing himself against the delirious pleasure that had him captured.

Her legs snaked up around his thighs, and he withdrew—only enough to make her moan—then gave her his length again. Chelsea purred. Her nails dug into his back as she arched for more.

For one single second, he couldn't move. He couldn't breathe. This was, by far, the deepest, neediest moment of his life. He was sure. Then he pulled back and thrust, again and again.

Her nails bit into his back, and her legs squeezed against his ass. Sweat tickled the nape of his neck, and Liam flew. He fucked. He kissed. He pulled orgasm after moaning, crying, screaming orgasm from her lips until he couldn't take another second of burning lust.

Then he came. The intensity stripped the walls of the world away, leaving him with nothing more than a bucking woman jailed in his arms.

He collapsed. Chelsea was limp. Her pussy muscles clenched and quivered until he could offer nothing but whispered gratitude in her ear.

CHAPTER TWENTY-NINE

SHIVERING, CHELSEA BLINDLY searched for her covers but found nothing but coarse fabric. Half of her body tingled with a chill, but the other half seemed too hot. Her cheek didn't want to move, and she pried an eye open and was surprised by the brightness.

The lights were on. But more importantly, her face was stuck against a man's chest. Her eyes flew open even as the rest of her froze, then the night came crashing back to mind.

She was naked and tangled. Liam lightly snored, his arm and leg hanging off the side of her couch.

Chelsea considered his precarious angle and how sleep had somehow sewed them together, and came up with no solutions on how to get off the couch without him falling—or at the very least, waking.

Oh God. What have we done?

Now wide awake as if she had mainlined a Red Bull, Chelsea assessed her current predicament, having decided there wasn't any way she could escape and hide as though their night had never happened.

She unwound their legs with the attention she might take on dismantling a bomb and propped on her elbow at a snail's speed.

He stirred, not waking, and she took that moment to roll—but failed. *Fudgsicles.*

Liam had flipped his arm across her back and, as if he had absolutely no idea who was naked in his arms, repositioned them so that he was the big spoon and she was the panicking little one.

His snores stopped, but a steady, warm breath tickled the back of her neck, and he squeezed her bare stomach. The distinct, unmistakable thickness of his erection pressed against her backside, and if she ever wanted to live down this day, she had to escape and evade his morning wood while he slept.

His fingers brushed her stomach, making her tingle. Logic wanted her to run away, but apparently her libido thought it was the perfect time to recall their absurd, uncontrolled throes on her couch.

She *had* to move. Chelsea nimbly rolled out of his hold and thudded on the floor.

Cheese and crackers, she hadn't meant to be so loud.

Liam's rhythmic breathing stalled, and even as she lay on the floor, wishing to blend into the carpet, she knew he had awakened.

Chelsea cringed, and she couldn't move, even though the slightest sound of him repositioning on the cushions seemed as loud as a warning alarm.

His sleep-sated chuckle was a preamble to a quick clearing of his throat. "You fall off the couch?"

At least her front was covered, even if that meant her bare backside was front and center between the couch and the coffee table.

"Power's back on," she offered.

He reached over her and pulled the tall glass candle jar to the edge and blew it out.

Oh, this is why people avoid one-night stands and friends with benefits. Right? What does one say to the other? Except they had been deliberate *and* out of control. They hadn't set up hookup rules and didn't have the saving grace of never seeing each other again.

"You know what?"

His rough, quiet voice made her recall the sexy words she'd gone to sleep listening to like a lullaby.

"I'm not sure I want to know," she finally muttered.

He gave a full-out belly laugh. "You've got a really cute ass."

"*What?*"

"That's what I was going to say." He pushed to the far end of the couch and stood. Her clothes dropped over her butt. "I'm going to hit the head."

Okay, I can die now. But not before she dressed then checked on the remaining candles.

The tea lights had burned themselves out, and the remaining decorative candle had burned nearly to the bottom.

After blowing it out, she dressed and had nothing left to do but wait and face this head-on like an adult. Being an adult had sucked a lot lately.

Liam returned, and Chelsea said a quick grateful prayer that he'd pulled on the pants and shirt that she gave him the day before.

The outfit was small, just as he'd pointed out. But she knew just how small now that she'd been up close and personal with his thighs, biceps, and chest.

"We should talk." He sat down and patted the couch, which might forever be known as the scene of the crime.

She joined him and crossed her ankles and arms. "Yeah, we should."

A dark cloud lingered over them. Somehow, that hurt. But then Chelsea remembered their common denominator, the reason they even knew each other, and that hurt even more.

"Last night..." he said but didn't finish.

"Yeah," she offered lamely.

"We messed up, huh?"

Yikes, that hurt. Even though it made sense, to hear him declare their night a mistake hit with the same sting as a slap might. "I don't know what to call it. A doozy."

Liam laughed, but it was nervous, then he rubbed a hand over his face. "Guess it comes down to how much of a doozy."

Confused, she glanced his way.

His eyebrows arched. "We didn't use a condom." Then his forehead pinched. "What did you think we'd messed up?"

Oh, let me make a list. But she stopped short of spouting all her reasons and reassured him. "I get a shot," she explained. "Like a birth control shot. Every few months."

Relief colored his face as though he hadn't inhaled since he'd stopped snoring. "Oh, right." He nodded. "Okay." The nodding continued. "That's great."

If she had to rank their awkwardness, she'd give it an eleven out of ten, and they hadn't even broached the him-and-her talk. *How would that even go?*

Chelsea closed her eyes. Julia died more than a year ago but the guilt was suffocating. Time had passed, but had it been enough? Not that it would ever be long enough to allow them to knock boots.

"So, this guy." Liam pulled the corner of his shirt as if to identify the sweatshirt's owner. "He's not running around, banging everyone or something?"

"What?" She stared blankly—then a blush smacked her. The sex talk. The partner talk. This was a perfectly logical, needed step to take, but she never had one-night stands, and it had taken her far too long to even think about STIs. "I wore the sweats home one day from work when an arrest went bad and the chase took me through a chicken coop."

"A chicken coop?"

"You never know how a day might go. Some days, it's all paperwork, other days..."

"Shit," he offered.

She laughed. "We keep extra sweats in the locker room. Big on me, small on you. And—"

The corner of his eyes crinkled, almost as if he wanted to squint, and Chelsea didn't know how to read that or his silence.

"And..." She pursed her lips. "I haven't had any relationships since my last gyno appointment."

"I'm clean too," he offered.

For a split second, she protectively thought, *He'd better be.* But what did she know of how he'd lived the last year? The idea that he had been with someone hung heavily in her chest.

"I haven't—since..." His jaw tightened as if he'd read Chelsea's mind.

"I'm not sure what to think right now."

"Same."

At least they were on the same honest, confused page.

Liam leaned back and dropped his head against the couch. "Look, a year ago, Julia was my world."

Uncomfortable guilt panged in her. "I know."

He turned to look at her and waited until she looked up at him. He apparently wouldn't let her face away forever. "I haven't noticed anyone since her."

Chelsea's cheeks flamed. "You don't have to say anything else."

"I've always known you were attractive." He ran a hand through his hair. "If someone had asked me about you, I would have said you were hot. But I wasn't attracted to you."

"I get it. I promise." *Please shut your pie hole!* "It's not like I was pining for my best friend's boyfriend."

"I know." He smiled flatly, then after hours seemed to sludge by, he asked, "What now?"

Good question. Though there was only one answer. *Work.* It kept her sane before, it would do the trick now. "We keep an eye on Linda and Frank—if you still want my help."

"Of course I do." He scowled as if she'd lost her mind.

"Okay. Good." She straightened on the couch and wondered what should happen next. *Should I ask him to leave? Offer him a smoothie? Should I go to bed while he takes the couch?* It couldn't have been past five in the morning.

Liam stretched and stood then gave her an innocent peck on her temple. "I'll text you later."

And that was that. The previous night was thoroughly acknowledged, never to be spoken of again. They agreed there'd been an attraction, but there was nothing to it, and they'd confirmed unsaid certainties. Liam would always be considered Julia's boyfriend, and Chelsea would always be the best friend. Truths like that were impossible to change.

CHAPTER THIRTY

THE DAYS LIAM spent keeping an eye on the Nymans eased by. Chance came back to help, assuring Liam that his other commitments were taken care of, and Chelsea went about her work without so much as a passing mention of them in bed—or rather, on the couch. Which was probably best for all when he considered her face when he'd kissed her goodbye. She didn't want to see him. Or maybe she *did.*

Either way, Liam didn't care for how the subject was never to be discussed again.

Maybe he would broach the topic of them later that day. It was the first time he'd be back at her condo, and it would also be the first time they were alone… and sitting where they'd fucked as he never had before…

The DJ on the radio gave another shout to the throwbacks, and Liam's irritation pivoted to aggravation. *How the hell do my favorite bands qualify for old-school shout-outs?* It was as if the DJ who'd dedicated the day to *throwbacks* wanted to remind Liam that time never stopped.

He pinched the bridge of his nose then pulled a U-turn. Chelsea knew he'd be by later, but he wanted to see her now.

"Call Chelsea Kilpatrick," he ordered the Bluetooth.

But she didn't answer, and her voicemail box was filled.

Liam ended the call, still driving her direction. She'd be into the surveillance equipment, and he'd be into… *her.*

"Shit." He blew out his cheeks but still drove toward her condo. As he pulled into her complex, his sour mood lifted enough to wipe away his impatient irritation at nothing that he could pinpoint. Then the corners of his mouth tipped up. *Will a bag of military-grade surveillance equipment feel like Christmas morning to Chelsea too?*

Liam hit the brakes.

"What the…?" Stopped in the middle of the street, he leaned closer to the windshield as if he couldn't see through it. "Hell."

The lights were on in Julia's bedroom windows, illuminated by the darkening fall sky.

Julia had shared a two-bedroom condo with another woman named Maxine. They'd seen each other at the recent remembrance, and he recalled Maxine talking with Linda and Chelsea.

But the last time he'd heard, Linda hadn't moved Julia's things out, and not ready to box Julia's life up, she'd paid rent for the room.

He pulled the Explorer into the closest parking space, threw open the door, and got out. His molars ground together as he slammed the Explorer shut and then raced across the parking lot.

His temples pounded as he ran up the stairs, but Liam held back from tearing off her front door when he heard laughter.

His hostility was rattled, but he threw the door open. Maxine, Linda, and Chelsea jumped. Linda pressed a hand to her chest. Maxine's mouth gaped, and Chelsea nearly threw herself over Linda like Secret Service might protect the President.

When Chelsea saw it was him, she glared.

"You scared the daylights out of us!" Linda cried.

He tried to be grateful that Chelsea had thrown herself in front of Linda to protect her from an unknown assault, but he couldn't see past wondering what they were doing.

"Did you come to help box up?" Maxine asked.

Linda guiltily stammered out an explanation, which he couldn't hear past the noise in his head. *Box up?*

Complete tunnel vision—that was what he had. The contents of Julia's bedroom were stacked in boxes behind the women. He charged by and stopped in the kitchen. A pile of ice was melting in the sink. He pulled open a cabinet door. "It's *empty*."

"Liam," Chelsea called, sounding miles away.

"I'm moving out," Maxine said. "I'm sorry."

He charged out of the kitchen and went to Julia's bedroom. His limbs went cold and the past shattered as he stood at the doorway.

The sheets were stripped off the bed. The mattress and box spring leaned against the wall. Julia's bedroom was neatly dismantled.

"I'm sorry," Linda whispered.

He spun. "Why?"

"I'm moving," Maxine said quietly.

"It had to be done," Linda added.

Over the past year, time sometimes felt slow. Like a day was a decade. Then so much had happened in the past few weeks. He wanted the changes to stop, not caring how bland the world became. "Guess so."

He didn't listen when the three women spoke at the same time and left them to be. Chelsea's voice called for him again, but he didn't stop until he closed the front door of the condo and rushed into the parking lot.

The cold fall air didn't help cool him down. The sky tried to suffocate him with its gloom as he hustled to his Explorer.

"Wait!" Chelsea yelled.

Dammit, he didn't want to talk, but the hurt in her voice resonated.

He shook his head, offering an apology she couldn't hear then closed himself inside his vehicle.

Julia was disappearing. Sometimes he was certain he couldn't remember the exact sound of her voice. Maybe this was punishment for what had happened with Chelsea.

CHAPTER THIRTY-ONE

LIAM ACHED. HE raged. He wanted to fucking cry.

A tornado of confusion and sorrow beat against his chest because he'd enjoyed the night with Chelsea.

Breath racing, he floored the Explorer out of the condo complex. If only he could think—

His cell phone rang. The Bluetooth speakers surrounded him with the repetitive tones, needling his chest. He declined the call without looking to see if it was Chelsea or Linda.

For entirely different reasons, he couldn't speak to either woman.

The phone rang again. He rejected the call, and again the third time.

"God!" He landed a fist on the center console. *Don't they understand?* He had witnessed them tearing apart what had been his life too. It just wasn't anymore…

He deflated. Regret pinched, and his guilt grew. Julia would've expected him to be a pillar of strength. Liam had buried his mother, his teammates, and a friend or two. But he'd never walked in to see their existence being dismantled as he had in Julia's condo.

A lump formed in Liam's throat, and he tried to picture Julia's bedroom. But no matter how hard he tried, he couldn't picture what decorated the furniture or exactly what the bed looked like.

His heart dropped, then the phone rang again. He gave up avoiding the women and pressed the accept button on his steering wheel.

"Finally." Senator Sorenson's brittle coldness poured through his car speakers. "I don't call you for my health."

Can this day get any worse?

"When the phone rings, you answer it," she snapped. "Are we on the same page?"

He didn't have a fight in him, and a headache pounded. "Roger that, ma'am."

The callous senator had been the furthest thing from his mind. If his head didn't ache, he might wonder how she'd crowned herself capable of military orders without a leash, but Liam couldn't muster the desire to give a fuck about her unmitigated power. All he knew was the future didn't look good if he stepped out of line. Sorenson had made that much clear.

"You have one time to answer truthfully."

Man, he didn't want to play games. "What's the question?"

"Have you shared the circumstances of our conversations?"

He cringed and exited the highway. "I have not."

Though have I? Circumstances sounded too vague, like a trap. And why was she asking on his cell phone? Even if her line was secure, his wasn't.

Liam ran through the mental hopscotch and couldn't come up with a reason for her phone call. Sorenson hadn't risen to her high-reaching position with an ignorance of intelligence rules. Even a newbie analyst could point out what she'd done wrong—unless the call was less for him and more to feed their words to someone who might be listening.

Disinformation to Tran Pham, perhaps? Or maybe it served only to ping his location. Liam glanced in his mirrors, monitoring for tail cars. Nothing jumped out as out of place.

"Are you working any other assignments?" she asked.

"No." She'd been clear about that, so perhaps she was testing him. Hell, he didn't know. His level of political and power gamesmanship had always been low. But given his day, he didn't have the patience. "With all due respect, Senator, you wanted me to do nothing, and I'm doing nothing."

Except for Chance, Chelsea, and the surveillance equipment. But other than that... nothing. Chance and Chelsea were smart enough to cover their tracks, and honestly, they didn't have information they shouldn't. So technically, he wasn't doing nothing when his druthers had been to lock the Nymans in a bunker. He was doing as close to nothing as he could, as allowed. Sorenson's plan, which should be called Operation Grin and

Deal, was still intact.

"If that's all..." He flipped on his turn signal.

"Has Mr. Westin contacted you?"

Liam arched an eyebrow. Maybe the senior senator was paranoid. Sorenson and Westin didn't always see eye to eye, but Liam couldn't fathom getting a phone call from that mean-mugging hard-ass. *What would we discuss? The glass room they liked to hold me in? Or maybe how Sorenson's bracelets clink when her aggravation grows?* "No, ma'am."

"If he contacts you, you let me know. Immediately."

"Are we all on the same team?" he asked. "Or not?"

"I won't allow anyone to ruin this operation," she said, ignoring his question. "There's too much on the line."

Yeah, the terrorist that some people didn't believe existed who murdered Julia, might harm the Nymans, and abducted *someone*, though no one would read Liam into that situation. "I get it."

"Our focus is to draw out Pham and *nothing* else."

She was preaching to the choir. "Senator..." Liam gritted his teeth as he pulled into his apartment's parking lot and jerked into a space. "There's no one on earth who wants that fucker as badly as I do."

Sorenson snorted. "It's safer for all if you don't underestimate me."

CHAPTER THIRTY-TWO

CHELSEA INCREASED THE pressure on the gas pedal as she drove to Liam's apartment. She'd tried calling him, but the ring double-beeped, signaling he was on the other line.

"Come on. Answer." But she ended the call when his voicemail picked up.

The first times Liam ignored her phone call, she could understand. No one had meant to blindside him. But he still hadn't answered her calls when she tried again.

Maybe he was on the other line with Linda. Chelsea hadn't said much when she grabbed her purse, only that she'd check on him.

Her phone trilled, and Linda Nyman's name appeared on her Jeep's console display. Chelsea pressed Accept and didn't bother with pleasantries. "Did you talk to him?"

"No. I was hoping you did."

"Nope." She bit her bottom lip.

"He's on the phone with someone," Linda added.

"I know!" *Aren't we both top-notch detectives*? "I'll be there in a bit and will text you after I talk to him."

Linda hummed, and her worry carried through the speakers. "I should've called him again before we started."

They could look back on the day and change things a hundred different times. But hindsight was pointless. "I'll talk to him." She exited the highway. "It'll be fine."

And it would, as soon as she tracked him down. If he wasn't home, she didn't know where to head next. Even if he was home, that was slightly problematic. She had a vague idea of where he lived but couldn't pinpoint his door to save her life.

"Thanks," Linda said before they hung up.

If he hasn't talked to Linda or me, whom did he turn to? An irrational spike of jealousy panged. He could talk to whomever he wanted. But in the pit of her stomach, she wanted to be the person he turned to for comfort.

But he didn't... That said everything—she might even be the reason he hadn't answered her calls. Or, more specifically, because they'd slept together.

Chelsea turned into his apartment complex. Well, she was ninety-nine percent sure it was his, and though she briefly considered using her federal resources to run his name and get an address, she opted out of trolling through government files for personal use.

"Where the corn muffins am I...?" She pinched her lips together as she crept from one parking lot to the next.

A dark Explorer caught her eye. She sped closer and peered at it. It was completely indistinguishable and wasn't parked close to the buildings. Really, it seemed to straddle the line between two of the low-rise, open-hall-style apartment structures.

Every stone entrance and open breezeway was identical. Even the bushes matched one another, mirror images of every building in the complex.

She called his phone again and once again got no answer. "Big surprise."

But she couldn't blame him. After what he'd seen, plus their newfound inexplicable tension, she wasn't sure where his head might be. She didn't even know about hers.

She only knew she had to find him. That, and that her insides hurt because he was hurting. *And* she knew that her arms ached to hold him.

So, actually, she knew a lot.

But she caught herself. "This isn't about you."

Right? Ugh, she didn't know anything other than finding him was important.

All she had to do was let go of her emotions and think. "Where do you live?"

He was likely trained well enough to avoid parking in front of his home. But Liam was also pissed enough to take the first spot he could find.

She visualized him pulling into this parking spot, then she estimated the shortest distance to an apartment breezeway. It was a tough call, but his building had to be the one on the left.

Chelsea parked and stepped out of her Jeep. She headed for a row of mailboxes. They were numbered, not named. "Would've been too easy." At that point, she would knock on every door if she had to.

She analyzed the open-floor setup. Liam wouldn't live in a ground-floor apartment, and with that guess, she skipped up the steps to the second story.

Apartments lined the hall. Twelve units faced each other, then she saw what looked to be another landing and a staircase. Door-to-door, it was. She bypassed the first two on the right. They had cutesy doormats and flowery wreaths, not exactly meeting her mental image of his entryway.

A dog barked from the second door on the left, and she pressed her ear against the first door on the left. A muffled action movie was playing. That was about as good of a guess as she could muster given the circumstances, so she knocked.

The dog next door barked louder, and a woman yelled for the pooch to calm down.

There was no answer on the door she picked. Still, her gut became surer that it was Liam's apartment, and she banged on the door with enough gusto to interrupt whatever blow-stuff-up action flick he had on.

The door *behind* her swung open. An older woman scowled. "What?"

Maybe she'd knocked too loud, but clearly, she wasn't at the woman's door. "Sorry to disturb you."

"Who are you?" The neighbor crossed her arms over the oversized crocheted sweater and drummed her fingers onto its thick knots.

"A friend—"

"What *kind* of friend?"

What kind of friends stopped by? Chelsea's eyebrow arched. "I'm an… old friend."

"If he doesn't want to be bothered, then scram."

Scram. That sounded like something Chelsea might say. "I didn't mean to bother you, but he doesn't have a choice. I'm not leaving."

The neighbor scowled and unfolded her arms, evidently preparing for a hallway battle as she put her hands on her hips with a high-octane glare.

If Liam couldn't hear them, maybe Chelsea had found the wrong door. She wished there were a way to send an SOS text without the obvious last-ditch attempt for him to answer, but she couldn't think of a smooth way to manage it.

"You're just going to stay out here all night, making a racket?" The woman clucked.

"If that's what it takes, I suppose so."

Her nose scrunched. "He's not home."

"He is." She just hoped it was the correct *he*.

She harrumphed. "Maybe not for you."

Chelsea had had enough. She reeled around and banged on the door. "Liam, open up."

A few beats later, footsteps faintly came closer and the door cracked open. Sure as sprinkles were sweet, Liam didn't seem happy to see her.

Too bad. "Hey!" She stepped closer, then whispered, "You should let me in before she calls the cops on me."

Liam glanced over Chelsea's shoulder. "Evening, Mrs. Donovan." Then turned back to her. "What are you doing here?"

Not exactly the response she was hoping for, and the woman behind her made an I-told-you-so noise.

"I tried to send her away," Mrs. Donovan said.

Chelsea grit her teeth.

"It's fine." Liam stepped to the side and offered her safe harbor. "Thanks, Mrs. Donovan."

She didn't bother with a well-mannered smile to the other woman and strode in. His apartment was lit by the television screen and from the doorway of the kitchen. The smell of fresh popcorn hung in the air, and she turned, eyeing the dark leather couch and the coffee table, which held a bowl of popcorn and a bottle of beer.

Water dripped down his cheeks. His wet hair clung to his face as much as the T-shirt stuck to his wet chest. Well, whoops… he hadn't been ignoring her, he'd been showering. She'd read the situation all wrong.

He shut the door behind him, and the yellowish light from the hallway disappeared, leaving him framed by a blank white wall. With the wet, tousled hair, and the clothes clutching his damp muscles, Liam looked like a tall, dark, and… confused superhero.

"You were in the shower?" Chelsea focused on the obvious, because now the idea of chasing him across town seemed foolish.

He half laughed. "Yeah. I was getting out."

She threw her thumb over her shoulder. "I can step out, if you need me to…" *To what? Leave the apartment so he can go back to his bedroom and finish toweling off?* She'd seen him naked, so obviously, standing outside wasn't needed for him to change in another room. *Why do I have to be so awkward?*

"I'm good." He shoved his hands into his pants pockets. "You met the neighborhood welcoming committee."

"Yes." Chelsea grimaced. "She's charming, and by charming, I mean… *intense.*"

"That's putting it nicely." Liam walked to his couch and eased down. His long legs tucked under the coffee table, and he leaned against the back cushion as though getting ready for a double feature.

Gone was the upset man she'd chased across town. Of course he'd be fine. She'd overreacted. He simply needed a breather. Or a phone call… which he didn't answer.

Her stomach tensed. *Am I jealous? Of what?* It didn't make any sense. She'd never been jealous. But at that moment, she didn't know her right from her left. Even though she tried in vain to name her feelings with such basic terms—jealousy, sadness, worry—she couldn't. Everything was so much more complicated, and she didn't know the words to define how she felt.

But as he settled back, pulling a swig of his beer, her disappointment also registered, as did the uncomfortable, selfish realization that she wished she could've been the one he'd called.

"I just wanted to make sure you were okay." She eyed what had clearly been a first-class self-care plan: shower, movie, popcorn, and beer. "But you seem fine." She smiled uncomfortably. "I'll go."

He paused the movie and tilted his head in a way that made her want to curl into his lap.

Hello! Liam wasn't the one who needed comfort. She was!

She was dying for someone to tell her that the day had been rough, but taking apart Julia's bedroom had been needed.

She and Linda had laughed and cried. Similar to the celebration of life, they'd told stories and shared memories.

But now, more than anything, she needed Liam to wrap his arms around her and promise that she was safe from the real world so long as he hid her away.

"Want a beer?" he asked.

She jerked out of her thoughts. Liam had already pushed up. "Yeah—I can get it."

Because standing there, craving safety and warmth that she wasn't sure she was allowed to feel, wasn't what she wanted to do.

His fiery green eyes slid from her eyes to her mouth and lingered.

"Give me a second," she said. "Be right back."

Heading to the kitchen was safer than wondering what that look meant. Was he somersaulting through the same mental gymnastics she was? Or had sleeping together been a primal, basic way to remove her completely from his system?

"You can have whatever you want," he said in a loaded way.

No, she was most certainly not out of his system, and if Liam watched her like that a second longer, she was liable to combust. What was wrong with them? It was as though they couldn't be in the same room together without lighting the air on fire.

Chelsea faltered with a fake smile and beelined for his kitchen. "Go ahead and start the movie again." Maybe that would help alleviate the tension she didn't want to face.

Macho dialogue and revving engines came to life, and she could've said a prayer of thanks that he'd gone back to watching something with cold-packed testosterone.

"I have an important question for you," Liam called.

Oh no. She prepared for the worst. A promise not to eyeball him? A commitment not to chase him home again? "What's that?" She cringed, uncertain of what he'd say and opened his fridge then frowned—condiments, orange juice, and beer. "What do you eat?"

"Food."

She rolled her eyes. This was awful and cliché, in a man-cave way. "You could've fooled me."

He laughed. "There's plenty in the cabinets."

Doubtful, she closed the fridge and snooped. The shelves were packed with high-test bachelor junk. Instead of ramen noodles, she found protein bars and powder, something that looked like high-end jerky, canned meats, and sardines. "Do you have any real food here?"

"Grocery stores are in one of the levels in Dante's hell."

True enough. She went back to the fridge, grabbed a beer, and moseyed back to the couch, taking in the generic nature of his place. Nothing hung on the walls. Nothing showed any personality. "What was your question?"

He moved his legs from the coffee table so she could walk by and smacked the couch cushion next to her. "It's a really important question."

Her nerves came back wearing party hats. She fake-smiled again and sat next to him. "So ask it."

"If you answer wrong, we can't be friends."

A blush heated her cheeks. "Are we friends?"

A second too late, she realized that calling attention to their situation wasn't her best move, and she clung to the beer bottle as if it were a life raft capable of rescuing her from bumbling small talk.

Liam tilted his head and reached for her beer, cracking off the cap. "No idea what you'd call this." He handed her bottle back. "Still. It's an important question."

She wanted to fall over and hide, but she swallowed hard.

His brow furrowed.

Her anxiety was near peak freak out levels. "*What?*"

His eyes narrowed, jaw ticking expectantly. "Is *Die Hard* a Christmas movie?"

What? What! She'd worked herself to a fever pitch over a movie question?

"Well?"

She took a deep breath and smiled, this time not having to fake it. "Is Santa fat and jolly?"

"Good answer." He knocked his beer to hers.

Chelsea felt as if they were in the Twilight Zone. His attention returned to the movie, and she tried to relax, shifting and repositioning until he put his arm behind her and pulled her close. She forgot to breathe.

"Watch the movie, sunshine." He gave her shoulder a squeeze without tearing his gaze from the TV.

She closed her eyes and melted against his chest.

This is us? It was—whatever *this* was. It was him, her, a movie and a beer while cuddling.

He grabbed the bowl of popcorn and settled it between them. It took two on-screen car chases before she relaxed enough to snack with him.

He finished his beer when the movie slowed for dialogue and put the bottle and popcorn bowl on the table. Explosions lit the television screen again and he tucked her back under his arm. Liam pressed his lips to the side of her head. "Thanks for coming over."

Her insides squeezed. "I was worried."

"I was a dick," he muttered.

She leaned into him. "That was a complicated situation to stumble into."

"Tell me about it." He paused the movie. "Everything snowballed."

"Linda said she'd called earlier—"

"She did. I was in a meeting and didn't answer."

Chelsea closed her eyes and listened to the sound of Liam's heartbeat. "Sorry it played out that way."

"I was headed to see you," he said.

She was surprised but let him continue.

"The lights were on in Julia's window." He shook his head as if remembering the moment he'd driven up. "And I couldn't wrap my head around… anything." He let the word hang then added, "I lost my shit."

"I would've, too, probably."

He shrugged.

"Even though we made the best of it," Chelsea said. "My head had been killing me since we started packing." But since Liam had charged into Julia's condo, Chelsea had forgotten about the headache. It thumped back into place once she recalled how the steady thud of pain had been with her all day.

"Maybe you shouldn't drink." Liam pretended to take her beer but chuckled. "There's ibuprofen in the kitchen if you want it."

That wasn't a bad idea. She stood. "Thanks."

He pulled his legs back for her to walk by, and it struck her as funny. She could've walked the two feet around the other side of the coffee table. He didn't have to move. He hadn't had to before. And they were cuddling! All of that should be weird. She tried to read his mind when he grabbed a handful of popcorn but couldn't. "Is this weird?"

He glanced up. "Us?"

"Yes," she said, raising her eyebrows. He knew exactly what she'd meant.

Liam threw the popcorn into his mouth, took his time to chew, then pushed the bowl farther onto the coffee table and stood to face her. Inches separated them. Their closeness *was* weird. But somehow, it was very much *not.* The lack of space was delicious. It made her nipples perk.

When he took a step closer, Chelsea had to angle her chin up to meet his eye.

"Why do you think it feels weird?" he asked.

"Well—" Her mind scattered. Seconds ago, she could've listed the reasons. But now she couldn't articulate a single one.

"Because of earlier at Julia's? Or because we had sex?"

Chelsea blushed. "Both," she answered quietly.

His jaw ticked, and after a contemplative moment, he asked, "Weird's bad?"

"Is it?"

He shook his head. "I don't think so."

Nothing was bad when they were so close.

His body heat quickened her pulse even though they weren't touching. Arousal pooled deep in her core. Touching Liam wasn't required to turn her on. All Chelsea needed was to see the rise and fall of his chest, to recall their time on the couch, how he made her climax over and over, and understand they shouldn't feel guilty.

Whatever *this* was, it was okay.

"All right then," she whispered, unable to remember why she'd stood up.

"Want me to get it?" he asked.

The ibuprofen! "No, I'll get it. Back to your movie."

Her heartbeat slowed as she walked away, and Chelsea checked the kitchen cabinets, deciding he could use a quick lesson in organization.

"Maybe they're in a closet or something?" she asked then went in search of a hallway or linen closet when he muttered maybe.

She found towels, towels, and more towels. Liam seemed to have enough towels to avoid regularly doing laundry. But the search didn't turn up pain relievers.

She turned for the bathroom.

"Hey, Chelsea," Liam called, but the rest was garbled as explosions rang out in the movie.

"What?" She pulled open a drawer but found nothing helpful. Then she pulled open the cabinet mirror door—

Liam came up behind her. "Wait—"

Startled, she jumped and laughed. "You scared me to death!"

The mirror door swung open, and he cursed. In the corner of the top shelf, an open ring box displayed a velvet pillow and a flawless solitaire diamond engagement ring.

CHAPTER THIRTY-THREE

A*N ENGAGEMENT RING.*

Chelsea couldn't breathe—and she shouldn't. She'd slept with her best friend's boyfriend, the same man who'd bought the most perfect diamond for Julia.

Liam leaned against the doorjamb, and he whispered her name so hoarsely that her shock turned into repugnant self-loathing. Her stomach ached, and even as her lungs started to work again, she couldn't face him.

"I'm sorry." He shut the mirror.

Why? Because I saw the ring? She could've guessed that last year, a proposal would've been in their near future. An engagement wouldn't have been a surprise. The only bewildering bombshell was how life twisted, and she had fallen for him.

"Please don't apologize."

They stared at the mirror. The jeweled color in his eyes deepened. She wished that she could read his mind. Chelsea didn't understand their intensity or the way his jaw held tight, almost straining as if he were choking away something more.

She couldn't comprehend how lost and lonely she suddenly felt. The only other time she could remember feeling like this was when Mac had told her what happened. Chelsea's legs wobbled, and her vision blurred, not with tears but with shame.

Nothing could make her true feelings clearer. She had fallen for Liam. No rationale could explain what had happened. She never saw their physical connection coming. And the chemistry, it had scorched her common sense away.

"I have to go." She spun under his arm, unwilling to slow down when he called her.

Liam caught up quickly and clasped her shoulder. She tugged. The hopeless desire to stay and curl into his chest made her want to weep. She didn't know how to fix what didn't feel broken or stop what made her happy.

He blocked her way. His throat bobbed, but nothing came out as he glanced painfully at the bathroom then over her shoulder. "Everything is…"

So different. But neither of them would offer such a pathetic excuse.

"I know." She pinched her lips shut.

"You don't." His expression turned, unreadable and rueful. Liam angled back, not stopping Chelsea as she ran away.

THE DOOR SLAMMED. A hollow echo resounded, and Liam was trapped in his apartment. If the bottoms of his bare feet weren't weighed down by his conflicted remorse, he would chase Chelsea down. But he couldn't.

Losing Julia had crushed his soul. Misery twisted him inside out until he'd gone numb as the months crawled by. He couldn't even look at that ring and had stored it close but in a place that he never used.

It wasn't that he forgot where the ring had been… Except he had. Sometime last year, the pain mutated into a daily bleakness—one that he'd been able to break from with the time spent lately with Chelsea.

He dropped his head back and pictured the anguish on her paling face as she registered the engagement ring. What was wrong with him? She'd run, and he remained like a lead-lined statue.

He pinched the top of his nose then walked toward the bathroom. The mirror forced him to stare at his reflection, and he didn't like the regret and exhaustion facing back.

"She's good for you," he said, then opened the mirror and closed the ring box. Liam shut the door over his sink and turned toward the hall.

The apartment felt sad and empty, with darkness closing in. The farther away Chelsea got, the hollower he became until a simple husk of a man stared at the door she'd fled through.

Liam's phone rang. Hope leaped through him, and suddenly alive, he hustled to take the call. But disappointment grabbed him by the balls when he read Chance's name.

"Yeah?" Liam grumbled.

"*Yeah* to you too." Chance laughed. "Just calling to see if you've had an opportunity to check out the equipment."

Liam's heavy eyelids sank. "More or less, yeah."

"*You're welcome.*"

He squeezed his eyes shut. "Sorry. Thanks."

Chance let his concern show as he waited quietly. But Liam couldn't explain the shithole of confusion he'd dug himself into.

"You good today?" Chance finally asked.

Yes and no, all depending on the time of day. "Fuck if I know."

"I can find someone to cover for me, and we'll go hit the range."

He appreciated the offer to shoot targets but rather stay in. "Nah, I'm okay."

Chance sighed. "I know your hands are tied, but I promise, brother. It'll be okay."

If Chance really had any idea the restraints that Sorenson laid on him, he wouldn't be so sure. Liam rubbed his forehead, still thinking about Chelsea. "Do you ever think life's a test?"

"Not really."

He wasn't so sure. "Like you don't know if you're supposed to pick A over B, because B wasn't an option."

"I don't think it works like that."

"Then what's it like? Because I don't get it."

"What don't you get?"

"She's not coming back." *But who am I thinking about? Julia? Or Chelsea?* Liam walked to a window and flicked apart the blinds. A quick search for her turned up empty.

"What are you talking about?" Chance asked.

Liam pressed the back of his head against the wall as the blinds swayed and clicked against the window. So much time had gone by that Chance didn't realize who Liam might've meant. Restlessness tingled in his shoulders, and he needed to find Chelsea.

"Never mind—but, hey, I've got to go." Liam ended the call without further explanation then called Chelsea.

She didn't answer—*big surprise*—and he rushed out the door.

Mrs. Donovan was sweeping her front mat despite the late hour. She cocked an eyebrow but didn't stop the back-and-forth movement of her broom.

Liam looked down the hall then at the closer set of stairs. "Did you see which way—"

"She used these stairs," Mrs. Donovan shared without slowing the motion of the broom. "I haven't heard any cars race off."

"Thank you." Liam skipped stairs as he ran down the flight and stopped at the edge of the sidewalk. He scanned the dark parking lot. A set of headlights illuminated the back row, and he sprinted that way.

The dull light from a lamp post showed her bowed head resting in her hands.

"Chelsea!"

She jolted at the sound of her name then quickly shoved her Jeep into reverse. Liam thumped his hand on her hood as she inched backward. "Hang on."

But she crept slowly as if she didn't see him or hear the slap on her SUV.

"Hey." He walked to the driver's window and knocked. "We need to talk."

She stopped backing and the glass rolled partially down. "Sure, we should." The fake perkiness in her voice was too much. "But later."

"No—"

The window whirred up.

"Dammit, Chelsea." The window stopped with an inch to spare. Her lips parted, and Liam shoved his fists into his pockets. If he didn't, there was a good chance he'd hold the vehicle still until she spoke to him. "Let's go. We gotta talk."

She slowly shook her head. "I'll text you later."

"Later doesn't work for me."

"Too bad." Chelsea glanced over her shoulder and reversed again.

Liam stayed with her window.

She slammed her brakes. "*What?* Because I'd really like to wallow at home. All right? Is that what you need to hear?"

What the hell do I want to say? He hadn't planned that far out. "I never use that cabinet."

She stared blankly then said, "You don't need to explain."

"That's not..." He ran a hand through his hair. "Not what I need to say."

"Then what?"

"I... don't know."

Seeming exasperated, she exhaled. "It's been a hard day. Just go upstairs, and I'll text you later."

The Jeep inched back, and his irritation multiplied. She couldn't leave! "Dammit, Chelsea. We didn't talk after we fucked."

She slammed the brakes again. Her mouth gaped, but he didn't care. They'd breezed through the no-condom conversation and didn't hit the important stuff. "So we're sure as hell going to talk about this now."

She slapped the Jeep into drive, straightened, then she jumped out as though she might wring his neck. "Are you insane?"

"Yeah, maybe." He stepped into her personal space.

"You can't say that out here!"

"The hell I can't." Now that he had her close, he wasn't sure where to begin. "You know what I'm sick of?"

She glared.

"Do you?" he prompted.

Her furling anger softened, and at least now she didn't look a moment from strangling him. Finally, exhaustion coated her voice. "What?"

"Expectations."

"What does that mean?"

"What I'm supposed to do. You're supposed to think. How we're supposed to act." He paced and shook his head. "Expectations and assumptions. They're all bullshit."

She didn't respond.

He held a breath then tried to find a place to start. "I'm glad you came over tonight."

She fidgeted. "Sure."

He'd needed her—even if he hadn't known at first. "I'm glad you're *still* here."

She shifted against the driver's door as if suddenly needing more space. "But I need to go."

"This you-me thing..." He took a step, erasing their small gap. "It's hard to understand."

"Hard to understand?" Sadness tugged at the corners of her eyes. "I don't even know who I am."

"You're the same person you've always been."

Her hand flew up, and her palm clapped against his cheek with a snap, causing a sharp sting. "I am *not.* Don't you ever say that again."

Liam took the hand that slapped him and ran his thumb across her knuckles.

She balked. "I don't want to talk. Don't you get that?"

Perhaps that was true of the both of them. He didn't want to talk, either. Not really. He wanted everything to simply slip into the easy course he'd always known. "You don't want to talk. I don't want to fight."

"What do you want, Liam?"

To fuck... Everything they needed to know was clear when they stripped away their clothes and didn't hold back.

"I never hoped for this," she whispered.

"You think I don't know that?"

Pain creased her brow. "I would be so happy if she were here. If you two were engaged—" Her voice cracked. "I promise."

"I know."

Everything came back to the bullshit expectations. How they should feel and act. How they could behave or what they couldn't do, where their eyes and hands wandered, how right it felt when they did, and what happened versus what should happen—but who the hell defined *should.*

He'd never been disloyal a day in his life. He'd never cheated and never wanted to. The notion of being with anyone else hadn't occurred to him—until now.

Chelsea waited as if he had to say more. Liam wanted to hash their situation out until it made sense but knew that'd be impossible. He inhaled and held it until his lungs burned, not ready to say he didn't still mourn Julia, or lie about his desire for Chelsea.

"You loved her. I loved her. How can you believe what we've done is okay?" she pressed.

"When we fucked," he said. "Was it just sex?"

Her jaw fell.

"Life is not linear." It was wrecked with ups and down, spins and crashes, but as long as they moved forward, life was as it had to be. Chelsea finding Julia's engagement ring had forced him to think about the future with her, and the irony was not lost. "And I want you to come back inside."

CHAPTER THIRTY-FOUR

LIAM TOOK CHELSEA by the hand, and that was what she needed to leave the side of her Jeep. Not explanations or absolution. Just the simple safety of holding his hand.

She couldn't explain how it became so simple to climb the stairs, but when they came to the landing in front of his door, she was emotionally spent.

The day had been too hard: the bedroom clean-out, the engagement ring, and the confrontation compiling on the heels of their night together.

"It feels like centuries have past." She stepped to the side as he opened the door.

"Since when?" He grazed her arm when she entered.

Chelsea turned toward him and pursed her lips. "I don't know."

He strode closer, and her nerve endings hummed.

"Do you know?" he asked.

"Know what?"

"If it was just sex?" He watched as if he wanted to tear their clothes away.

A zing of electricity raced down her spine. "Does it matter?"

His eyebrows arched. "Yeah. A lot."

Her heart pounded. The hairs at the back of her neck stood. Would it be worse to simply sleep with him? Or to fall for him? Chelsea didn't understand how he didn't feel guilt and spiral with second-guesses.

"Did you need to get laid," he asked. "Or did you need me?"

Him. A thousand times over. She needed him and couldn't escape the riveting pull they shared. "You," she admitted.

He lifted his chin wordlessly, and she didn't know what should happen next. A grand gesture? The ground to open up and swallow her whole?

Instead, he took her hand again and led them to the couch. He plopped down, seemingly unfazed by their conversation, but she couldn't fake his relaxed manner.

The movie was long since over, and the streaming app rotated through suggestions for what he should watch next. Every time the movie suggestion changed on the television, new hues shadowed the boring white walls.

Their legs were close but not like before, and she was too tense to crawl under his arm again.

"I want to show you something," Liam said.

Chelsea choked then laughed. "Haven't I seen enough tonight?"

He chuckled but left the living room. A minute later, he returned with a package.

She scooted to the edge of the cushion as he laid a towel-covered square on the coffee table. Then carefully, as if he were unwrapping the keys to a bygone golden city, he peeled back the fabric cover. Whatever he had hidden, it must be important to him, to keep it under wraps.

Her heart seized. "Liam…"

"I thought you might be looking for this."

She slipped off the couch and kneeled. Her eyes watered. "How… when…"

But it didn't matter. He'd found the draft copy she'd given up on and thrown away after the queso incident. She'd torn out the pages that she didn't think were on par with Julia's work and then destroyed the rest, because even the best part was no good if she couldn't finish the project without her best friend.

Her hands pressed against her chest as if she didn't dare touch the pages that had been patched together and taped.

"This seemed too important to let you shitcan it."

"I don't know what to say."

"That you won't give up," he said.

She wouldn't. The pages blurred, but she didn't want to cry. Instead, she tried to take a quick breath then, with the most delicate touch possible, turned to the first page. *The dedication page.* Heartache sliced as her fingertips drifted over the jagged, repaired rips.

"Dedicated to best friends. *Life is a journey, not a destination.* Ralph Waldo Emerson." He cleared his throat. "You two nailed it."

The tears Chelsea had been holding back slipped free, and she turned the page.

A LETTER FROM THE AUTHORS

She and Julia had written several drafts in which they'd explained how their friendship came years before their books, but the understanding of their friendship had grown with each passing revision. They discussed how real life could seem stranger than fiction, and books were needed to make real life palatable.

Chelsea laughed at a memory. Their first version had read "Real life can seem stranger than fiction, and fiction is needed to make real life palatable." But their editor pointed out that they wrote nonfiction. They'd all had a good laugh.

Their letter from the authors hadn't been finished. After the funeral, Chelsea sat down with a pad of paper and cried as she penned the end of their letter. Liam had taped the crumbled page together.

The end of the letter is signed by the both of us—but we hadn't finished before Julia died.

Yesterday, I buried my best friend. We will never put out another book together. She will never see the end of our hunt for Zee Zee Mars. But none of that matters.

Nothing Julia and I worked on ended the way we expected. That was a hallmark of our beautiful friendship. For every problem, we grew—even if we didn't understand why.

Our first book should've been a standalone title. But Zee Zee Mars remained at large. I couldn't understand how Mars could predict our moves and outwit the Marshals, the FBI, and me, yet a second book was born.

I can't understand Julia's murder. It's given me a fear of the future. But I know I can't hide from each day. There's a "yet..." that will one day come.

So with that belief, I'll share the mantras I now chant: Keep going. Keep growing. Strength will come in ways that are impossible to believe.

Chelsea wiped away the tears. She hadn't read her note since she rushed to put the words on paper. She'd turned it in to her editor, and it wasn't until months later, that she saw it bound in their draft.

Liam put his arm around her shoulder, and she wondered if this was her 'yet' that had been still to come. "Thank you."

He nodded solemnly. Chelsea threw her arms around him. He had no idea the extent to which what he'd done mattered. When she was sure the tears wouldn't come back, she eased away.

"Why did you destroy it?" he asked.

The overwhelming sense of loss had hurt more than she knew how to handle. "Because I couldn't keep going."

She closed the book and vowed to start again where she'd left off. Liam tucked her close on the couch. His strength ensconced her, and even his familiar scent helped to fortify her tumultuous insides. She closed her eyes and hid, protected from the rest of the world when he pulled her close.

"Next time..." His lips pressed to the side of her head. "Just lean on me."

He was strength, in an impossible-to-believe form. Chelsea tilted her chin up. He held her gaze. "Promise?"

Goose bumps raced across her skin. "I promise."

Then he kissed her lips. Sweet and chaste. Chelsea spun as if she'd floated into a kaleidoscope of colors.

Maybe this was what it felt like to fall in love.

CHAPTER THIRTY-FIVE

LIAM TRACED HIS fingers over Chelsea, and they settled into the close embrace on the couch like they had earlier. He turned off the television screen, and they sat in the quiet.

If she'd been surprised that he chased her down, forcing her to admit that arousal wasn't the only reason they'd slept together, she wasn't alone.

The old engagement ring caused him to recognize their truth. Talk about being blindsided. If that hadn't happened, maybe he'd have been content to call their new friendship one of comfort and mind-blowing sex.

"You're staring at me," she pointed out.

He'd spaced and hadn't realized that he was. Liam grinned and focused pointedly on her shoulder then her knee. "What do you want me to look at?"

"I'm serious!" Chelsea elbowed him and gave a quiet, self-conscious giggle. "Don't stare."

He touched her chin, coaxing her to face him again. Only a slip of space remained between their lips. His heart thundered.

She inched away. "You're still staring."

How could he not? "It's fun."

She scoffed and a sexy flush pinked her glowing cheeks. "Be nice."

"Making you laugh *is* nice!" He slid his hand across her thigh. The softness lit him from the inside out. They'd had a heavy night, but now that she melted back into his arms, he needed more of her. "Almost as nice as…"

She sighed. "As what?"

"Making you come."

Chelsea yanked back. "Liam!"

He squeezed the inside of her thigh. "You know I'm right." Then dropped his gaze to her shoulder. "But if you want, I'll stick to staring tonight."

She pushed his chin up, and a dangerous hunger danced in her eyes, threatening to undue his self-control.

"You know what I mean," she said.

"I don't know. Better lay it on me."

Her pink lips pursed then parted. "I…"

"You…" Liam brushed his mouth against her ear and needed to run his tongue from the tips of her breasts to the slit of her pussy. "Have no idea how much I want you."

He couldn't resist the memory of how her fingernails dug into his flesh when she climaxed or the way she bucked on his cock.

Her breathing hitched, and she nuzzled against his neck. "I might."

"Do you know what I want?" he asked.

"Me," she whispered.

"You." He sucked a spot on her neck that made her moan. "Your tits. Your clit. Your eyes locked on mine."

She gripped his shoulders. "Don't tease me."

Liam licked the spot that made her squirm. "Why?"

Her hand slid under his shirt, and the tips of her fingernails lightly scratched down his stomach muscles. Chelsea pressed her forehead to his and held his gaze. "After everything that happened today, I just want to drown in you."

Hell. Her honesty hit him in the chest, raw and real. Not unlike their first time together. That was fueled by lust. Consuming touches and blinding kisses had made them desperate. Nothing but fast and furious, orgasms upon orgasms.

Tonight, he wouldn't tease, but he'd take his time and push her to the brink.

She unfastened her pants—and he caught her hand.

"That doesn't mean you can steal my fun." He lifted her fingers away and loosened her pants.

Chelsea lifted her hips, nipping his lips, urging him on. Liam dipped his hand under her underwear as she squirmed, enjoying her quiet whimper when his fingers teased her wetness.

"Like that," she begged.

He obeyed then circled her clit. Her eyelashes fluttered, and her lips parted.

"Fuck, you're beautiful."

Chelsea's throaty moans grew. Liam eased her pants and underwear lower until they'd been pushed beyond her thighs. Blood rushed to his cock, and he couldn't stay away from the sweetness between her legs. He pulled her pants free. "Lie back."

Chelsea barely moved. He lifted and laid her back on the couch, then lowered himself between her legs.

"Liam," she whispered, thighs clenching his shoulders.

His fingers toyed with her sensitive skin. "Hmm?"

"I—don't know."

Good. Neither did he. Instinct and desire were leading the way. Liam lowered, keeping his eyes locked on hers. Anticipation built then he pressed his lips to her slit.

"Liam," she whispered. Her thighs pinched against his shoulders. "Oh…"

He groaned at the sweet taste of her pussy. The stronger he licked and kissed, the more her hips swayed. His fingers explored, dancing over her clit, rubbing in time with his tongue. She jerked and gasped, and when he wrapped a kiss around her clit, she moaned, promising that her orgasm loomed. "*Liam…*"

Damn, he loved the sound of her crying his name, and he growled his approval.

Her legs quaked. She cried out and came hard against his mouth. Her knees clamped against his head, and she rode the wave of euphoria until her bucking body fell limp.

Everything was right in his world. Liam kissed the inside of her thigh. Her gasping moans dulled to sated murmurs, but Chelsea slid her fingers into his hair and tugged. "Please." Her hoarse voice strained. "I need you inside of me." She pulled him up until his face hovered over hers. "And I need that *now.*"

They fumbled for his pants, and he stripped them away. His erection ached, and Chelsea wrapped her body to his, guiding his cock to the heated slick touch of her entrance. Liam growled, and Chelsea rolled her hips, rubbing the head of his cock against her silky skin. He couldn't wait any longer and thrust into her tightness.

"Yes," she cried. Her muscles clenched then released. "More."

Her arousal coated his shaft, and he fought for control. Liam gritted his teeth, and she moaned. Those sounds stole his control. He flexed again and thrust harder.

"God yes." Her hands bit into his skin, and her hips undulated.

He fucked deeper and deeper, until she took all of him.

Her teeth clamped onto his shoulder. She kissed and cried his name, begging for him to take them higher and harder. Liam rode her sweet body, giving everything she commanded, until his balls tightened and her pussy convulsed.

Chelsea came again and again, then he came, spurting hot semen into her quivering aftershocks.

He collapsed and her thundering spasms milked his dick. Their racing gasps pounded, seesawing as they slowed.

When he could open his eyes, he was positive he'd never witnessed a more powerful, beautiful sight than Chelsea satisfied while he was still buried deep inside her body.

CHAPTER THIRTY-SIX

SOFT MORNING LIGHT urged Chelsea awake in Liam's bed. The night before tumbled back to her mind. Every vivid kiss, each mind-blowing orgasm, and the sweet goodbye kiss he pressed to her forehead before he left for his watch duty at the Nymans'.

She slid her hand over his side of the sheets, wistful that he were still home. She hadn't expected to spend the night in his bed, but they'd somehow found themselves falling asleep for the night without question.

Now, with his comforter tucked under her chin, she needed to do more than register what had happened—*for the second time*. She needed time to contemplate the hidden grace that was buried under the dark cloak of painful change.

Chelsea pulled her hand back and considered rising from the warm cocoon of bedsheets. Sunrise was usually a signal to start her day. But what she had always done didn't match what she wanted to do, and she burrowed into her pillow. The cotton held Liam's clean, masculine scent, and her heart pitter-pattered.

Her decision was made—Chelsea would sleep in. Content in her new-found relaxation, she readjusted and faced the other way. A folded paper with CHELSEA scrawled across the middle waited on the nightstand. Her belly fluttered, and she snatched the note.

Wish I were there when you woke up.

Smitten, she beamed, and clutching the note, she fell back onto the pillow and let herself drift asleep.

A LOW ROAR rumbled. Chelsea shot up. The comforter fell from her naked chest, and she balked at the warm golden sun that poured into Liam's bedroom. *How long have I slept?*

Her gaze dropped to the mostly uncovered man snoring in bed. He was *there*. But her quick burst of excitement dulled. The uneven cadence of his breaths made her worry. It was as if he couldn't relax in his sleep.

Liam snored again then stopped short, and his eyes opened. His sly smile grew, and she'd been busted staring.

Chelsea blushed. "What are you doing here?"

"It's my bedroom," he mumbled then hooked his arm over her side.

She rolled closer. "You know what I mean."

"Chance came back over."

Her brow furrowed. "Why?"

"Why what?" Liam asked.

"He's worked around the clock for the last two days."

"He's not alone. Go back to sleep."

Chelsea inched back. "Who else is working on this? I thought it was only the three of us."

"Now we have Hagan," he said.

"Hagan?"

Liam lifted a shoulder. "Chance's been busting my balls to add a guy he trusts, and now I had reason to be more agreeable to the idea."

"Me?"

He squinted his eyes open. "You."

Her stomach jumped but she still didn't understand the new addition. "*Hagan* just wants to help out on a job we all, basically, don't know anything about?"

"Some things, you don't question."

"Like your buddies pulling extra shifts?" Even good friends didn't offer to pick up unpaid work. She pulled the covers higher and sat up.

"No." He tapped her pillow. "Like the ability to strip naked and dive into bed with you."

"Liam, I'm serious. Why would they do that?"

"Maybe they know I want to be here with you."

She still didn't understand what bound them together, and whether Liam knew or not, he didn't explain.

"Lie down."

The confusion only made her anxious, but she didn't know what there was to protest.

"Chelsea." His fingers stroked her side. "Lie down with me."

Her defenses weren't immune to his sexy, sleep-drenched murmurs, and she had no reason to question Chance and Hagan. But still… "I'll still wonder."

"Wonder later." He squeezed her hip.

A prickling need to press against him clouded her thoughts, and Chelsea relented. "All right. Later."

He tossed his leg over hers and pulled her to his chest, and she was little spoon to his big spoon—little *naked* spoon to his *big naked* spoon.

"Sleep, Sunshine."

"Okay." But she couldn't. Her mind swung from the watch duty to how well their bodies fit together. Spiraling thoughts wound tighter until she focused on the serene quiet and how light bathed the bedroom. "You know why I like the sunrise?"

He snorted quietly. "Because you never went through boot camp?"

She grinned. "No."

"Because you hate sleep?"

"No." Chelsea turned so they were nose to nose. His had a tiny indention and wasn't perfectly straight. She hadn't noticed before, or maybe she'd just not paid attention. But the telltale sign of a once-broken nose reminded her of how much they didn't know about each other.

Though maybe she knew the most important parts. He wasn't a saint but was absolutely a hero. He'd gone through ridiculous steps to ensure Frank and Linda were safe and trusted the people he surrounded himself with, like Chance and Hagan.

"You trust them implicitly?"

He opened his eyes. "The guys?"

She nodded.

"I do Chance, and he does Hagan. So yeah."

That should be enough. Chelsea pressed her lips together.

"And you too." He licked his bottom lip. "I trust you completely."

Her throat tightened. "Likewise."

"Does my trust come as a shock to you?"

Shrugging, she said, "I'm not sure." Chelsea studied the lines on his face. "I was thinking how much I don't know about you."

He laughed. "I still don't know why you like the sunrise."

"Every new morning is a new beginning, and it's impossible not to hope for the best when each day starts fresh."

Liam let out a long sigh. "I'll have to hang on to that." His lips quirked. "What do you want to know about me?"

Where to begin? Chelsea lifted her shoulders again.

"Then go back to sleep." Liam rolled over and pinned her with his naked hips and torso. "Or did you have another idea?"

She didn't know whether it was the sound of his voice or the way his muscular physique held her in place, but Liam cast her worry and wonders away. She heated for his touch, and before a semi-intelligent response passed her lips, he managed to flip her on top of him with deft ease. Chelsea perched, naked and coverless, on his chest. "Liam!"

His gaze smoldered, and his lips curled up into a test-me smile. "You know what I learned about you?"

"What?" She lowered her chest to his and rested her cheek against his shoulder.

He stroked his fingers slowly down her spine then back up and played with her loose hair.

"Tell me," she whispered.

"I thought you were competitive."

Chelsea popped up. "I am."

His hands clasped behind her back, and Liam pulled her close again. "You're ambitious."

"I can be both."

"I guess so, but I see your ambition, and I admire that more."

Her chest squeezed. "Thanks."

"We make a good team because I can anticipate problems, but you plan for the future." He wrapped a lock of her hair around his finger.

"That's not the same thing?" she asked.

"Not really." He let the hair release.

"Did you anticipate this?" Because she had no idea how to map their future.

"No," he said.

"I never planned anything in my personal life," she admitted. Her only focus had been fueled by Zee Zee Mars. Chelsea didn't know how the future would look without a fugitive to dedicate her life to finding. Maybe she figured that one day, everything would slip into place because she'd captured Zee Zee. *Would that change who I am? Would it change how Liam saw me?* Anxiety cooled the hot flash of desire. "Maybe I'm sleepy after all."

He groaned. "I'll have to work on my moves. I didn't think you'd opt for some Zs."

"That's not it!"

"Kidding. Sorta." He winked. "But from here on out, let's keep twenty questions until after we get out of bed."

She held up her hand as though offering God's honest truth. "That *was* an impressive move."

Liam tucked her back to where they first started when he wanted to sleep. "Stick around, Sunshine. I have a couple more that I can share."

CHAPTER THIRTY-SEVEN

THE BELLS THAT hung on the bagel shop's doors jangled, but even if they hadn't announced when Chance walked in, Liam would've known, anyway. Chance had a way about walking into a room full of women that made a hush fall.

Liam tore a chunk off his sliced bagel and dipped it into his peanut butter packet as Chelsea caught sight of his buddy walking in.

"That's him?"

Again, Liam didn't turn to look. "Yup."

"How do you know—"

"Because that book club over there?" He tilted his head back. "Went from a book-talking, boss-busting, homework-bemoaning storm to silent mode."

Her face scrunched, ready to defend the now-quiet group.

"Five bucks says," he continued, "there's a brave one who will try to snap a picture with her phone."

Chelsea slapped her mouth shut.

"You think we don't know?" He winked and tore another piece of bagel and dug it into the peanut butter.

"You can't honestly think that random women take pictures of you guys on the down low."

He laughed. "You should see what happens if there's a dog or kid around."

Chance walked to the counter and placed his order, and Chelsea paused as though imagining the sight then rolled her eyes. "Don't let it go to your head."

He feigned innocence. "Of course not."

"Why don't you use a knife and spread the peanut butter like a normal person?"

"Do you know how cute you are when you don't have a way to win a conversation?" He dunked the bagel in the peanut butter again.

"No one is taking pictures of either of you."

"If you put a book in his hands, he could go viral." Liam popped the smeared bagel piece into his mouth. "I always wonder why they take pictures instead of walking up and saying hey."

"Because as cute as you two might be, it's a gamble if you're worth the trouble."

"Hey, now."

She shook her head. "The book club ladies always know what they're doing."

He arched an eyebrow. "And that is?"

"Staying away from trouble."

He laughed, shaking his head as Chance stepped up to their table.

"Morning." His lazy half grin curled for Chelsea, and he stuck his hand out to introduce himself.

Pleasantries said, Chance turned for his order when it was called.

Chelsea rolled her eyes. "Fine. He'd go viral—with a book, a puppy, or a kid."

Liam chuckled. "At least you agree sneaky pictures exist."

She didn't answer as Chance joined them again with his order and eased into his chair.

They made quick small talk, and Liam wondered if Chelsea would ask Chance what his thoughts were on strangers taking pictures. But the conversation shifted to Chance's watch duty. After a list of possible concerns that weren't problematic, he summarized the update as "Jack shit is happening now, and maybe Hagan will have better luck."

"Nothing happening *is* good luck," Liam pointed out.

Chance shrugged then spread cream cheese across a toasted bagel with a plastic knife.

Chelsea preened, and Liam tore off a larger-than-necessary piece of bagel and rolled it in peanut butter. Her eyebrow lifted, and he tossed the entire messy bite into his mouth.

"Sexy," she muttered.

"That's what I tell him all the time," Chance added, taking a second glance at Chelsea.

Liam balled up his peanut-butter-covered napkin and pegged Chance. "Eyes in your head."

"I wasn't checking her out." Chance tossed his hands up in faux surrender. "Just understanding the dynamic."

They were at work. There was no dynamic. Chelsea straightened and focused on her bagel.

"You two going to set up the new equipment today?" Chance asked.

Liam nodded.

"Want some help?"

He considered how much time Chance's help would save against how much Liam enjoyed time alone with Chelsea.

"Why don't either of you have jobs?" Chelsea asked.

Chance took another bite of bagel then a swig of coffee. "We do."

She scowled. "Why don't you have to *go to them*?"

"Contracting means making your own schedule," he said.

"I thought you were only able to help for a couple days," Chelsea countered.

"At first." Chance left his response at that.

"We're off, and we're on," Liam added, preferring the inquisition to be over. "Contracts change. That's how it goes."

Chance agreed then asked Chelsea, "Are you okay with this?"

"This what? Because I don't know much."

"You have to know something."

Their conversation was making Liam uncomfortable.

"I can help catch Julia's murderer, and two people I love may be in danger. That's all I know."

"Maybe that's for the best," Chance said.

Oh hell. That wasn't the right thing to say to Chelsea.

"*What do you know?*" she asked.

The volume of a muted television that hung in a corner turned up, interrupting the growing tension, and a hush fell over the bagel shop again. Chance, Chelsea, and Liam turned toward the television.

BREAKING NEWS REPORT was emblazoned across the red chyron at the bottom of the screen. A scene of first responders working behind a reporter was playing. Smoke curled from a building behind the woman's dark hair.

"She did it again," Chelsea whispered then pushed out of her chair and asked the woman behind the counter, "Can you turn that up?"

Even as the volume increased, she stepped closer to the TV.

Liam pieced together the report. Zee Zee Mars had struck again, hitting a student center in Kentucky. They showed a picture of Mars and the calling card she'd become known for, a dark calla lily. Chelsea's face reddened. She had her cell phone in hand and was furiously texting.

"What's that all about?" Chance asked.

The incident was tragic, but Chelsea's reaction showed more. It was personal, and she'd been pulled from her work because they'd gone out and gotten drunk together.

Guilt lined his chest. If people died, that might be his fault. Perhaps she could've prevented the bombing. And he'd stopped her while trying to protect his loved ones while other innocents were lost. "She's worked on Zee Zee Mars for years."

"Shit." Chance whistled then looked from the television screen to Chelsea and back. "Squint a little, and it's almost like Chelsea could be Zee Zee Mars, give or take a decade or so."

Liam didn't see a resemblance. "I wonder if they'll need her on the job."

Then they both realized quickly that they were about to be a person down if she had to report into work.

"We can handle it," Liam finally said.

"If we can't, then I know a guy or two that can step in."

Liam rubbed his temples. For a gig that wasn't supposed to exist, keeping an eye on the Nymans was starting to expand more than he was comfortable with. "No more folks."

"My source is solid. They won't ask. Won't tell."

They? "I can't rely on you to provide an endless supply of backup."

Chance let a fist land heavily on the table. "In this case? You do."

Surprised by the truth, Liam agreed. "Appreciate it."

Chelsea returned and folded herself into the chair. She tore a piece off her bagel and jammed it into her cream cheese container. If she didn't look ready to angry-cry or kill, Liam would've called her on the bagel tear-and-dunk.

She swallowed the bagel, and her expression darkened. "I'm *still* benched."

"What?" That couldn't be right. Even if he didn't want to lose her help, it didn't make sense not to call in all hands on deck.

"Something about how Mac has it covered. How I worked it like a lone ranger and now it was my turn to get my head on straight."

"Your head's not on straight?" Chance asked wryly.

She seared him with a laser glare.

"Forget I asked."

Chelsea abruptly pushed out of her chair again and studied the back of the bagel shop then rotated and gave the rest of the shop the same scrutiny.

Chance glanced at Liam, and Liam shrugged. The bombing and her behavior didn't match.

"What's up?"

Her lips flattened, and finally, her search stopped. "I don't know. Nothing I can explain."

That had been their life lately.

"Something's up," Liam pressed.

"Something." She feigned a bullshit smile and sat down again. "Or not."

Both he and Chance hazarded a quick look around, but neither sourced her unease.

Her foot tapped.

The fidgeting unsettled him. "Chelsea?"

"Don't worry about it."

Liam covered her bouncing knee with his hand and stilled it. "What is it?"

"I feel like..." Her lips tightened. "We're being watched."

Was that a possibility? Sorenson? Liam peppered her with casual questions to hone-in on her concern and avoid giving away what he wondered, but she couldn't nail anything other than a vibe.

"Just a strange feeling," she finally said and stopped fidgeting.

Strange feelings were gut punches of instinct. Liam did another once-over as Chelsea gathered the trash from the table. The last time he'd had a bad feeling, all hell broke loose on the Metro. "Guess that means it's time to roll."

CHAPTER THIRTY-EIGHT

THEY LEFT THE bagel shop and planned to meet in the Nymans' neighborhood. Chance drove separately, and Liam stayed in step with Chelsea.

Concern needled him. *What did she sense that I didn't? What did I miss?* Unsettled, he took her hand. Their fingers tangled, but Chelsea eased her hand away then glanced around.

Anxiety spiked. Why didn't he sense a possible threat like she did? "What are you looking for?"

But the nervous glances were different from the bagel shop. Insecurity stiffened her shoulders, and her rigid walked seemed disjointed. "Maybe we shouldn't."

"Shouldn't what?"

"Hold hands," she said under her breath.

Possessiveness made his molars clench, and he stopped abruptly. "I can make you come in a bed but not touch you now? What kind of shit is that?"

Her eyes widened and her cheeks turned red. "I don't know—" She wouldn't meet his glower. "What if someone sees us and wonders—"

"I touched your hand, Chelsea. I didn't label you a harlot."

Her chin snapped up. "Exactly! That's my point."

"What is?"

"Someone could see us."

He threw his arms out. "Anyone can see us. We're not fucking invisible."

Shame and confusion shimmered in her eyes.

Screw those two guilt-baiting feelings. "We talked about this. Us."

She averted her gaze. "I know."

"But...?" He blanked, not understanding the rules or her perception, then decided to lay on the heavy truth. "Want to know something, Chelsea?"

She backed up. "Not sure that I do."

"Oh, you do, babe."

"Don't say anything you'll regret."

Liam could've laughed, but he prowled closer until her back met a brick wall. "I'm crazy about you."

"Does that mean you have to make a scene?"

"Are you listening to anything that I've said?" He bent close as though he might kiss her. "I want your hand in mine as much as I want you naked in my bed."

"I don't think we're supposed to—"

"Supposed to what?"

"Touch," she suggested.

"Sunshine, I have touched you in ways that make my dick jump. I think I can manage holding your hand."

Her eyes widened again. "But is it the right thing to do?"

They'd already hammered this out! Hadn't they? He saw everything clearly. Or, at least, how he felt about her. Why couldn't she hang onto that instead of doubt? Liam towered over her then realized they could talk until they'd both turned blue. She had to see for herself. "If you want to find out, grab hold, and let's figure this shit out."

"Very romantic," she whispered defensively.

His mindset leaned more toward mission objectives than romance. But he wouldn't back from a test. "You want romantic?"

"No," she quickly corrected. "I didn't say that—"

"Didn't you?" He scoped out their surroundings. "I don't do romance, but if that's what you want."

"You don't *do* romance?"

He grinned then broke away. "Excuse me."

No one stood close to them on the sidewalk, but a group of people stepped out of a restaurant across the street. He called to them, "Hey."

A few in the group stopped, uncertain if the crazy asshole intended for them to pay attention.

"This woman…" Liam pointed at Chelsea, who watched, mouth agape. "Is scared—"

"I'm not scared of anything," she hissed. "And this isn't romantic."

"To hold my hand," he continued, now having the full attention of the group. "And I have no idea how to romance the pants off of her—"

Her face now registered a not-so-subtle shade of fuchsia. "My pants have never been more secure around my waist than they are now."

"Is that a challenge?" he asked with a sideways glance.

"Shakespeare," a woman across the street shouted.

Liam turned directly to Chelsea. "Shakespeare, it is."

"You don't know Shakespeare."

"I know that I want you to hold my damn hand."

Chelsea shook her head as if she couldn't believe what he was doing.

Hell, he couldn't either. Especially since he didn't know shit about Shakespeare, other than two punk teenagers killing themselves instead of telling their families to fuck off. There was no need for anyone to be told to screw off, but he could stretch the moral of the story and make a connection to their circumstances.

Liam noticed two women whom he'd spotted at the bagel shop book club, and they were angling to hear Liam's every word. "Got anything to help me out?"

"Kill me now," Chelsea muttered.

He winked at her. "Pretty sure that's not Shakespeare."

"Probably could've been," one book clubber said.

"How about, 'A rose by any other name would smell as sweet,'" the other woman volunteered.

That was the kind of Shakespeare he was talking about. Liam pictured the acting chops he'd seen at his high school's rendition of the play and belted, "A rose by any other name would smell as sweet—"

But that was all he had. Except for that "Romeo, oh, Romeo" line. That didn't seem to fit the moment. He raised an eyebrow, and at least Chelsea laughed.

"Enough! Enough!" She rushed over, failing in spectacular fashion to cover his mouth as he decided the best course of action was to repeat the same line. "Liam!"

"What?" He dropped his chin, still holding himself up with a puffed chest and testing his acting chops. "Not romantic enough?"

Her fists knotted in his shirt, and she tugged. "I'm going to kill you when we don't have witnesses."

"At least I'll die with your hands on me."

"Liam!" She pulled with her body weight, and finally, he bowed to his crowd and backed her up to the brick wall again.

"At least a little romantic?"

"I don't know what to call that." Her long lashes, which curled at the corners of her eyes, fluttered as he caged himself around her.

"Sexy?" he joked.

Her eyes bugged. "What will it take for you to never do that again?"

The list he could come up with given thirty seconds, a pen, and a piece of paper… His nerves skipped, and all his humor was gone. "Do you like how I touch you?"

"Liam—"

"Do you?" He inched his face closer. "Those goose bumps. The way you shiver. Do you like how I make you feel? It's a very basic question."

Chelsea nodded.

"I don't give a fuck who thinks what. Either people accept this—"

"*What is this?*"

"This. Us," he amended as if that clarified things. "Either they accept us, or they mind their business."

She didn't respond.

"You and me? We're not disloyal. We're not done hurting. We're not doing anything except for living. Either friends and family give us the grace to live as something other than a shell of a fucking human being, or they can stick their judgment where the sun doesn't shine."

"I don't want to hurt anyone," she confessed.

"But you will hurt *me*." That was as real as it got.

Her bottom lip trembled.

He dropped his forehead against hers. His forearms still caged her to the brick wall, and he knew that standing on a busy street wasn't the place to ponder how life evolved or question who she was so afraid of disappointing. "I refuse to question why and when we fit. We just do."

"It's just that simple?"

Fuck yes, it was. "It's whatever we make it."

Liam waited a breath of a second, wondering if they were at a fork in their road where their understandings and expectation forged different paths.

"I'm glad I saw you love her," Chelsea said.

His breath hitched. That wasn't at all what he expected her to say if he'd had a hundred lifetimes to guess.

"Because," she continued, "I saw who you were. How you carried her feelings like a responsibility and a privilege."

His throat ached. "Chelsea..."

"You are a good man." She cupped his cheeks. "And I don't want to disrespect others who saw that and loved you because of it."

"Linda and Frank?"

She nodded. "I suppose."

"We'll talk to them."

Chelsea rolled her lips together. "I don't know why that sounds so hard."

"Because you think it changes the past, and it doesn't." He pushed her hair behind her ear. "Make sense?"

Forever seemed to tick by. "Makes sense." Chelsea's fingers found his hand, and she squeezed. "Guess we should catch up with Chance. He probably thinks we got lost."

Liam's chest shook with a quiet rumble.

"What?"

He glanced down, positive she knew what made him chuckle, but her wide eyes waited, her eyebrows arched. She didn't have a clue.

He hummed as they made their way, holding hands, down the block and around the corner to his Explorer, then he opened the back door. "Up and in."

Her confusion hadn't faded in the least. Liam made a note to expand how her thoughts drifted about them in bed—or out of one too. "If we're going to be late, there should be a better reason than Romeo and Juliet."

CHAPTER THIRTY-NINE

LIAM COCKED HIS head, amused at the look Chelsea gave him as she popped into the back seat of his Explorer. Somehow she'd mixed anticipation and a scolding into one smoldering glance, and that did *very* good things to him.

"How old are you?" She pushed across the seat. "Twelve?"

He crawled in behind her and slammed the door shut. "I didn't ask girls to get in my back seat at twelve."

"At *any* age," she cried, pupils dilating. "You're being ridiculous."

"I'm not sure I ever got past second base in the back seat of a car."

She avoided his eye contact. "You're not going to start today."

He couldn't help but imagine what it'd be like if they did.

"Don't look at me like you'll convince me." Though her breathiness and the sexy way she licked her bottom lip said he might have a chance otherwise.

Liam rested his hand on her thigh. "If you don't want to, fine by me."

Chelsea brushed her hair off her shoulder and moved closer. Their legs brushed. His fingers squeezed then inched toward her knee. Outside, the air had been brisk. Now it was still. Charged. Heat pulsed in his blood, and neither made a move to open the door.

He bent his head close enough to kiss her lips. An electricity radiated between them. It tingled on his lips and teased as her hair brushed against his skin.

"Do you want..."

Her eyelashes fluttered.

"...my mouth on yours?"

Chelsea rolled her lips together, and whispered, "That's really an unfair question."

Absolutely, and he didn't care. Liam skimmed his knuckles across her cheek, threading his hand into her hair. He let the silkiness pull through his fingers. "Yes or no, beautiful."

"Of course. I like your mouth on mine."

"Then we can start there." Though he inched away, unable to hide his teasing grin. "Unless you don't want to."

Chelsea placed her hands on his shirt and smoothed up the fabric. Her fingers curled and pulled him back close again. "Have you always been this cocky?"

"Do you always get this feisty?"

Her eyes flared. "Yes."

"Thank God."

Liam groaned as she slid into his lap. He inhaled the fresh citrus perfume that clung to her hair. Their lips met, igniting a firestorm. She slid her tongue into his mouth, breaking away only long enough to admit, "Okay, you convinced me."

He laughed as they kissed. She nibbled his bottom lip, and he couldn't slow his hands. Liam ripped her pants down, baring her below the waist.

She jumped at the chill but intensified their kiss. The backseat didn't offer much room. His legs were too long, and her pants restricted her movements. But the sight of her bare skin went straight to his cock.

Liam cradled her in his arm and pushed his back against the window.

"Touch me," she begged.

He took his time, making sure he held her the way he wanted. She reached for a kiss, but stilled his mouth against hers, slowing their chaotic rush. His fingers feathered across the trim patch of hair, and she shivered.

His tongue slipped along her lips and eased into a slow kiss as he dipped his hand. She mewed as he neared her mound and, when her arousal dampened his fingertips, Chelsea squirmed.

This was what he needed. As much as he had to hold her hand, he had to make her orgasm.

Liam played with her, dancing around her clitoris and spreading her as he explored.

Every touch, every tease, every single fucking time he tried a different pressure and pace, she rewarded him with hungry groans.

Slowly, he tested her entrance with a finger, mesmerized. Chelsea buried her face in his neck, nipping then stilling as he pressed deeper inside.

"More," she whispered, and her legs jerked against the confines of her pants.

Never had he slowed down and watched a woman give herself to pleasure. *To him.*

Chelsea arched. Her muscles clenched and relaxed. Her hips flexed. "This is so very…"

"Good," he answered. It was for both of them. Liam pumped in and out.

Her arousal spread over his knuckles, glistening in the dim back-seat light, and he added another finger, easy and slow, faster and deeper.

Chelsea lifted her hips. Her lips parted, breaths gasping with every tightening, winding thrust. She moaned and writhed, finally gripping his forearm until she rode against his fucking hand as if he were her toy.

Lust had him by the balls. He needed her pussy to quake.

"Please, God," Chelsea cried. "Liam. Please."

His world revolved around hearing his name again. He pumped into her pussy until his forearm flexed with fire and force.

Chelsea gasped and murmured, "Liam," calling it repeatedly until he couldn't hear a word over her moans. She gripped his fingers, and her other hand dug into his chest, choking on his name.

Every time he thought he had a handle on her, she reminded him that he didn't know jack shit about how hard he was falling. Hallelujah for that.

CHAPTER FORTY

EVERY ORGASM LIAM gave her had always been intense, but Chelsea needed more than a climatic rush. She craved the closeness and intimacy that came when they had sex—even if she was in the backseat of his Explorer.

His erection bulged under her bottom, and she shifted to stroke his shaft. Liam's heavy breaths pulled, and his jaw ticked when she gripped his length.

"Unbuckle your pants, handsome." She kicked free of hers.

He made quick work of the clothes and pulled his thickness free, slowly pumping with his fist. "I thought you weren't too sure about my backseat," he teased.

She replaced his hand with hers, caressing his crown with her thumb then mimicked his stroke. "I thought you were smart enough not to ruin a good thing."

"Oh, right." He inhaled sharply, jaw dropping as she increased the pressure. "Consider me smart. Not ruining a damn thing."

Chelsea laughed, and he did too.

"Good. Because I need..." She straddled his lap, trembling as she positioned the head of his erection against her folds.

"To be inside you," he growled.

She eased down, letting his shaft impale her, and nodded, barely able to whisper, "Yes."

His hands gripped her hips, guiding her movement, slickening their connection until she had her arms wrapped around his neck, Liam fully seated inside her.

"Damn, Chelsea," he growled.

She couldn't do much more than nod—until he palmed her backside and lifted her. His muscles rippled as he thrust and ground her down. The sensation overload made her limp and desperate for more. He possessed her, controlled her, owned every flex and thrust, and she could only exist in building pleasure.

Intensity built. She cried and clenched, panting and pushed beyond any brink she'd experienced before. "Oh, God." She clung to him. "Liam, please, God!"

Her orgasm hit like a tidal wave. The blinding pleasure brought pain as she came again and again. Euphoria rolled, and he didn't stop, drawing out a flood of gratification.

Liam's thick arms wrapped tight. He held her, thrusting and grunting until his orgasm came in like a storm. Their spasms made her shiver. Her heart wanted to explode.

She didn't know how long they stayed like that. But it wasn't until a shiver from the temperature, rather than reacting to Liam, did either of them move.

He pressed a sweet kiss to her forehead, then her lips. "This is one hell of a way to start our day."

THE NYMANS' NEIGHBORHOOD was reminiscent of every other block for miles around. Their town was safe and predictable. But the closer they came to Linda and Frank's, the more he found himself watching the bushes and scanning the shadows.

"Are you okay?" Chelsea asked.

He pulled over on the suburban street and shifted into park. "Just wondering what I might miss if I glance the wrong way or focus on something else."

She waited for him to further explain, and when he didn't, she said, "If you're talking about work, you have to realize that you can't see everything." After a beat, she added, "Actually, that just goes for life in general."

True enough. He never saw them happening. Liam gave her hand a squeeze.

Chance appeared, ambling down the sidewalk as though he hadn't been surreptitiously keeping an eye out for them to arrive.

"Time to work." He opened the driver's door as Chelsea stepped out also.

"About time you two showed up." Chance thumped a fist on the Explorer's hood and gave a suspicious glance from Liam to Chelsea and back.

"We're here." Then Liam shot a warning glare.

The nonverbal cue didn't stop Chance from a chuckle. "I was worried I'd have to send out search and rescue."

Chelsea joined them on the sidewalk. Her eyes were crystal clear of the firing arousal Liam had seen less than ten minutes earlier. In a no-nonsense way that defied logic, she said, "We got distracted for a minute."

"I bet," Chance muttered under his breath with a shit-eating grin.

She pressed her lips together, cautioning Chance in a way that had more effect than Liam's. Chance swallowed a laugh, and they waited in silence as Chelsea power-walked down the sidewalk.

"And here I thought you'd carved out some one-on-one time, but maybe not."

Liam jabbed Chance with an elbow.

"Testy." Chance laughed again and muttered something about Chelsea's all-business demeanor.

Liam didn't hang around to hear for certain and rounded to the Explorer's trunk. They had gear to unload.

Chance followed, still amused with himself. "Which is she? All business or—"

"Careful," Liam warned.

"It's like that, huh?"

It was like a million things he didn't know how to explain but could summarize as 'hell yeah, it was like that'. Still, he wasn't in the mood to banter like an old bitty. "That woman could slice and dice your balls off."

"Pfssh. I could take her."

Liam paused with the halfway-open hatchback in hand. He let go and turned to Chance. "You touch her, and I'll be the one who castrates you."

"Easy, man." Chance smirked. "I'm kidding."

No shit, but still, a possessive need nettled Liam, and he wanted to change the subject. "Thanks again for the supplies."

He took the hint. "It was no big deal."

"That's some bullshit." Liam rolled his shoulders. "One day I'll repay the favor."

"You have no idea." Chance shook his head, amused with himself. "Anyway, I can stick around and help set up."

The offer sounded like a great idea for a split second, but Liam wanted more alone time with Chelsea. "We're good."

Chance gave an understanding chin lift. "Did I mention that Hagan hacked the neighbor's lockbox?"

Liam hoisted the duffel bag onto his shoulder and grabbed a box, tilting his head toward the trunk. "What's that mean?"

His buddy shut the hatchback. "For the neighbor's house."

"The one listed for sale?"

Chance nodded. "He changed the showing availability. No drop-bys or scheduled showings until we lift the lock, and we have a connection that can smooth over any problems."

They stepped to the sidewalk, and concern nagged at Liam that their reach was expanding too far. He'd already pushed the line when he asked Chance and Chelsea for help. But then Hagan? And a new connection?

"Are you two coming?" Chelsea called.

He had to trust Chance—and he couldn't help but be grateful they'd now have an undisturbed location to monitor the Nymans. Even if the thought made Liam want to tear off Chelsea's clothes.

"Judging by that look..." Chance slapped Liam on the back. "I'll head out."

They shared an unsaid "thank you" and "no problem," then he hustled to meet his woman, self-imposing a don't-touch-before-the-job-was-done rule.

CHELSEA REACHED FOR the box in Liam's arms and didn't know how to translate the hard set of his jaw or the dark edge in his eyes. They normally shone like deep, rich emeralds. But now, the color eclipsed words. "Is everything all right?"

His curt headshake gave her a sudden silent answer. His look was *desire.* A snap of awareness rolled over her like the first vivid flash of the sun at first light.

"We have to work," he said, reading her mind.

"I know." But she hadn't for a second. Chelsea took a sobering breath, and they crossed the street and walked the remaining half block to the Nymans'. She set the box at their feet as Liam glanced over his shoulder, and Chelsea slipped her house key from her purse. If she'd unlocked that door once, she'd unlocked it a hundred times. The key slid in effortlessly and turned with a soft, sturdy click.

They'd confirmed the Nymans would be at work all day when Liam had called Linda that morning to apologize. As often as Chelsea had used her key to stop by their house over the years, this time made her jittery.

They walked into the living room, ready to install a monitoring system. She took cautious steps that reminded her of the teenage nights when she and Julia would sneak out to sit in the backyard and gossip under the pine trees.

Liam clambered their gear in and set the duffel bag on the couch with a thud.

Chelsea wanted to shush him as though they might get caught then laughed at herself. "Do you think many kids have the kind of relationship Julia did with Linda and Frank?" she asked. "Or even Linda and Frank with Julia's close friends. Like us."

Liam crossed his arms as though he had never realized their lack of blood ties made them different from other families and loved ones. "If they're lucky."

Her heart smiled. The urge to hug him tingled in her chest. "Gosh, you're sweet."

He scowled.

She smiled and shrugged. "Give me my marching orders."

For the next two hours, they worked with nimble fingers and mind-testing patience. They had no room for mistakes. The consequences would be catastrophic.

Finally, she came down the stairs as Liam walked into the living room, balling up plastic wrap from the monitors he'd installed on the perimeter.

"Is that everything?" Chelsea stood on the bottom stair.

Liam shot the ball of plastic wrap into a box on the couch as if it were a basketball. "Think so." He remained planted on the far side of the living room and laid an arm across the top of a high-back chair. "Time to check it all?"

She nodded. "Then a quick recheck."

His lips curled. "Then let's go."

Installing the equipment had been easy. They each had tasks to complete and connect to a main monitoring system. No one could tamper with appliances or the electrical grid in the house without triggering a silent alarm. No one could set foot on the property without their team knowing about it.

Liam led her toward the back of the first floor. Room after room, window after window, they checked their own and each other's work. They inspected and tested the main monitoring system and did the same for the backup. Their dynamic eased into a fluid partnership as soon as they came to the first section to check, and they worked as though they'd been side by side for years.

Well, they had, in an odd way—not on surveillance or on anything that had so much importance, but passing in closely orbiting circles of friends and people they considered family.

Their quiet teamwork meshed well, and Chelsea thought about their work expertise. She didn't know his details but could guess it amounted to blowing things up. Hers was the opposite—hiding in sight, discovering the impossible. Their connection had a yin-yang balance rooted in savagery and sleuthing.

When they finished the final section, covering the Nymans' backyard, she knew their work was solid. They had eyes everywhere.

They finished in the back corner in front of a black wrought-iron bench that had an expansive view of the property. Liam lowered himself onto the bench as a chilly breeze swept up her hair. Chelsea wrapped her chill-bumped arms around herself, rubbing her jacket's sleeves for warmth, and joined him. The cold metal bled through her pants, and she snuggled under his arm.

Liam tossed his arm around her shoulder and rubbed her arm. "Chilly?"

"A little."

But neither made any effort to stand up.

She didn't know where his thoughts were. Despite the brisk fall breeze, the backyard offered calm peacefulness. Never in a million years could Chelsea imagine how they could sit like that in the Nyman's backyard. But never in a million years could she forget how he made her feel.

"Good work," Liam broke the silence.

Their thighs touched, and she tilted her chin to watch his face. "Good company." Then she asked, "Are you okay?"

A small, almost surprised grin formed. "You know what I like most about you?"

"Hm?"

"We can talk about what happened. That we don't have to ignore the past like it's an elephant in the room, and that we can fight about it—"

The hand holding? "I wasn't trying to fight earlier."

He laughed. "I like that it's okay to figure this out."

No matter if the rest of the world would agree, he was right. No one was better suited to find solace and move forward with. "So." She paused. "*Are you* okay?"

"Yeah." He scanned the backyard. "Despite a target on the Nymans and that feeling you had at the bagel shop? I'm okay."

"How about outside of an operational assessment?" She tapped his chest. "In here."

His lips parted, but his gaze averted and held over her shoulder. Chelsea twisted, unsure what to expect.

Liam was trained on a childhood relic that swayed in a pine tree. "What is that?"

She snickered. "That arts-and-crafts beauty?"

"Yeah," he chuckled too. "I always wondered what the hell it was supposed to be. I never asked—" He cut his attention back to her and shrugged. "I never asked…"

Her heart hurt at all the questions he might never have asked. But there was a lesson to be learned in their messy connection. *Don't hold back. Embrace the present.* "It's a wind chime."

"What?" His forehead creased as he took another look. "*Really?*"

"Or maybe a wind-chime-turned-bird-house."

He laughed then squinted. "I can see that—I think."

She tossed her head back and laughed also. "I have no idea why Linda treasures those little projects."

"Because the woman treasures you."

A shallow sigh caught in her throat. Liam's words made her nostalgic for the past and grateful for the Nymans.

"Was it a preschool project or something," he asked.

Chelsea snorted. "We were definitely in our twenties."

"Damn—I mean." He rolled his lips together. "How did… that happen?"

She side-eyed him. "It involved a bottle of wine."

"I can see that."

"We came home one night as a surprise visit from school. Linda and Frank were asleep, but Linda had left out a bag of school supplies."

"And that thing was the result?" he quipped.

She elbowed him. "Linda woke us up the next morning. We'd passed out in a sea of school supplies. Wood glue. Paint. Construction paper. You name it, we'd used it. She didn't have anything she'd needed for the day."

Liam *tsked.*

"But instead of reading us the riot act, she hung it up—" Chelsea couldn't keep from laughing. "And Linda said, 'I've been waiting for you to bring me something home from college to hang up.' She picked it up like it was a Van Gogh but hung it in the tree."

Liam bent down to kiss her. Chelsea froze, so lost in the past that the right now had slipped away.

She didn't pull back, and he hovered, a breath away, while he searched for an answer. She didn't know the question. Every time she thought she did, it changed.

But he didn't push her, not like earlier on the sidewalk with his Romeo act. That was silly, and calling her out had been spot on. This was self-conscious and breathless. She couldn't relax when she forgot about them.

Her heart slammed in her chest, shouting for her to stop thinking and kiss that man. What was wrong with her? They'd talked until they had logical answers. Nothing was wrong with her and Liam! It was Chelsea who couldn't get it together.

She leaned back from his lips. "You know what I like most about you?"

"What?"

Her eyes closed. "The grace you give me." He was a haven each time her tangled emotions had a hang-up. Healing, grieving, and falling in love were not linear. Liam had explained that, now she had to live like she believed him.

A gust of wind rolled, and he brushed her hair back. "That's one hell of a compliment."

"One that you deserve." She gently kissed him and let their lips part and their tongues tangle in that effortless way that made her feel as if they were floating on clouds.

His forehead rolled to hers, their lips hovered close, then Liam stood from the wrought-iron bench and held out his hand.

She believed in them—and Chelsea took his hand. Their fingers locked, and they slowly walked in the direction of her wino-wind chime.

"My family was nothing like theirs," he said.

"Same." Linda ran laps around her actual mother when it came to support and love.

Liam guided her behind the stately pine trees that lined the fence. "My dad should've left my mom."

"Families are hard," she finally said as the silence widened.

The long-sweeping pine branches above and the pine needles on the ground muffled their steps and conversation. She didn't know anything about his family but recalled Linda mentioning how no one blood related had come to Julia's funeral. Her heart ached.

"I became *the man* of the family early on." He scoffed quietly. "What was I? Six? Maybe seven?" They continued to wander, but he didn't elaborate.

"What happened?"

Liam inhaled and let it out slowly. "When…"

She waited for him to find the words. Their walk became a winding trail in and out of the trees at a glacial speed.

"Before my mom died," he said, "adults saddled me with *the man of the family* title when the only concern I should've had was making the first-string peewee team."

The idea of him as a little footballer who'd lost his mom and couldn't escape the pressures of adulthood made her throat tighten. She wrapped her free hand around his arm and held it to her chest. "You don't have to tell me any more."

"My dad was a piece of shit."

"He left you?"

Liam cackled. "I wish."

Chelsea held on to him as if he needed the support, but truthfully, she wasn't sure she could let go until he explained what happened. Even then, she might not be able to let go.

"If you were to look up how my mom died, the record would say she was the victim of random, senseless violence."

She thought that over and asked, "What *should* it say?"

"It'd say—" His voice cracked. "That we weren't supposed to be home."

She wanted him to stop. "You don't have to say anything else."

Pain pinched his features. "I was sick. A cold or a fever—"

Chelsea was terrified to hear more.

"My dad had fallen into a bad spot with some loan sharks." He cleared his throat. "They shot up our house."

Nausea hit her like a tidal wave. Little Liam… "Oh God."

"They were sending him a message." He toed the pine needles until a layer of dark dirt surfaced. "And he heard them, loud and clear. But my mom was collateral damage."

Tears streamed down Chelsea's cheeks. She wrapped her arms around him and prayed to ease his suffering. "I'm so sorry."

He unwound himself, and his pained expression had dulled to emotionless. "Happened a long time ago."

"That doesn't matter."

"True enough," he finally admitted.

His mother and Julia. No wonder he'd embraced their reality quickly. If someone meant something, Liam understood to hold on that second. No one knew how life would change.

He pulled her close and laid his lips on top of her head. It wasn't so much a kiss as him holding her in place.

In the last few weeks, she'd learned more from him than she had anyone—even her partner, Mac—in her life. But it wasn't until then that she realized Liam had taught her the most important of life lessons. Each person was a second away from a different life. Shying away from the seconds was the same as shooting away the future.

Chelsea pushed onto her toes and pressed her lips to his cheek. An urge to share how much he meant was nearly crushing.

His impassive walls faltered. "What was that for?"

"Because I don't know how to pay you back for all that you give to me."

CHAPTER FORTY-ONE

LIAM COULDN'T PLACE his finger on exactly what Chelsea meant by paying him back for all he'd given her, but he had no doubt she'd offered him a compliment that went far beyond polite kudos.

Soft vulnerability had hushed her when she tried to explain the restrained kiss. No matter what her reasoning was, he wanted to keep the tightness in his chest that made his lungs feel as if they might explode.

"Let's get out of here."

"We're done?" She glanced around, nodding to answer her question.

"I can't think of anything we haven't checked and rechecked."

Her hand found his even as she seemed to run through a mental checklist. His shoulders tightened, and he hungered to pull her close, to ward away the harsh memories and the crisp fall air with her naked body wrapped around his.

When she finished her silent review, she said, "You're right."

Liam didn't wait an extra second and hauled her inside to pack up their gear.

He checked his watch when Chelsea zipped the duffel bag. He hadn't explained to her that they had a new vantage point to keep an eye on the Nymans' home for unexpected visitors. "Come on. I want to show you something."

Liam led Chelsea out the front door, waited for her to lock up, and angled her toward the neighbor's house instead of his Explorer.

"What are we doing?" she asked.

Each time they'd been on lookout duty, they'd used their vehicles on the low-traffic road, positioned far enough away that no one would notice a familiar vehicle. The houses had yards large enough to provide a small layer of anonymity, but the setup was far from ideal.

"This way."

Her steps slowed with uncertainty as they cut through the yard, and when they stopped on the neighbor's front porch, her tension was visible.

"Are you a real estate agent and I didn't know it?" she joked with apprehension.

"Not quite." He produced his lockpick kit from the side of the duffel bag and unwrapped the pick and tension wrench from the protective leather hold.

"*Liam*, what are you doing?"

He slid the tools into the lock. "I thought it was evident."

Her phone buzzed, and she yelped as if they had been caught red-handed doing something wrong. She dug into her purse, wincing as the phone rang again.

"Don't freak out."

She snorted. "Why would I when we're breaking and entering? Oh, fudge pops. It's Mac."

Liam stifled an urge to say something smart-ass. It didn't bug him that she had an overbearing partner. The idea of backup always made him more comfortable. But with everything she'd shared, Liam had decided that Mac was a first-class dickwad when he didn't get his way.

"Hey." She turned with the phone pressed to her ear. "Me? Now? Oh, nothing."

The final key tumbler set, and the door unlocked. He swung it wide for her and stepped through to prove the coast was clear.

But she held up her finger, and he understood. She wanted to talk about Zee Zee Mars in private.

Liam let the door shut on its own and turned to drop his stuff.

Wow. The house was staged. The untouched white couches and fragile statues that teetered on top of modern furniture seemed out of place to him. The house had the same layout as the Nymans', though where their house was sincere, inviting, and lived in, the vacant one had been stripped of personality and decorated in an impossible-to-continue style. Houses with so many bedrooms and backyards that called for swing sets shouldn't have white couches and breakable art. They were made for kids to run through and messes to be made. The staging seemed like disappointment ready-to-happen.

The door opened, and Chelsea stepped through, flustered. Her pink cheeks were a different color from the aroused blush he liked. She seemed *pissed.*

"Everything okay?"

Chelsea glowered. "If okay means that there's an incident with a fugitive I've spent years working on, but I am *still* benched, then everything is absolutely okay."

"What's up with that?" Not that he wanted to lose her help, but shit, bring in the experts when they were needed.

Her jaw sawed. "No idea."

"I'd tell Mac to kiss my ass."

"I should, and Calhoun, too," she griped and added, "He's our direct line supervisor."

"Screw 'em all." But his suggestion didn't lighten her mood.

She tossed her phone into her purse. "Why are we in here?"

Liam looked around. "Because it beats sitting in my Explorer all night."

"But *that's* legal."

He had a vision Senator Sorenson cackling if she pressed on the legalities of their work. "We have an exemption."

"I'm serious, Liam."

"So am I."

"We don't have anything that allows us to be in here."

He spread his arms wide. "Yet here we are."

"Don't be a—" She shook her head.

An asshole? A donut hole? But Liam decided not to tease her. "Just trust me."

Her shoulders stiffened. "You ask for a lot."

His eyebrow arched. "Been worth it so far?"

"This is pretty," she said instead of answering then gestured to the living room. "Not very practical, though."

"I thought the same thing. Can you imagine growing up in fear of breaking vases and crap?"

She turned after a quick inspection. "That was how I grew up."

He groaned. "Sorry."

Chelsea shrugged. "It doesn't matter. Anyway. *Why* are we here? This goes way beyond simply keeping an eye on Linda and Frank."

"Think of it like an office."

"Sure. One that could land us in prison."

The comparison got under his skin. "Even if I wanted to explain every detail of this job, I can't."

She rolled her eyes.

"No one will come by while we're here. Okay?"

Her stare hardened. "Even if you could, do you really want to?"

"Tell you?"

"Yes!"

He pinched the bridge of his nose. "Of course. Why can't you trust me on this?"

"I should," she muttered. "I'm already trusting you on everything else."

"What's that supposed to mean?"

"You're treating me like some random chick when I ask for more information. It's not unreasonable that I'd like to know why we're picking locks."

"No, Sunshine. I'm treating you like a partner who I respect *and* a woman I'm terrified to lose."

CHAPTER FORTY-TWO

CHELSEA DIDN'T KNOW how to process Liam's fear of losing her. *Rejoice that I mean that much? Hurt that he's suffered so greatly?*

Liam stayed quiet.

"You're not going to lose me," she whispered. "Not like your mom or Julia."

"I know."

He paced the living room. An internal war was waged as his hulking shoulders bunched and tendons strained.

"What's bothering you? That I'm asking you to share more?"

She received no reply, and he continued his transfixed pace.

"Liam?"

He stopped short. "I don't trust my source."

Her pulse jumped. "Yet we broke into—"

"No, I trust Chance and Hagan. They arranged this. But the source of this entire clusterfuck? I don't know."

Chelsea hated feeling like an outsider. Mac had made her feel that way, and Liam didn't trust her enough with classified intel that Chance and his buddy seemed to have. "Okay."

"Shit," he muttered. "I told you before. It's complicated."

"And classified." Which meant she should understand, but being the last one to know seriously stunk.

He closed their distance. "My source is Samantha Sorenson."

"*Senator* Sorenson?" she asked as though if she whispered too loudly, the power-hungry politician might materialize out of thin air. Chelsea didn't know much about who and what qualified as the topic du jour. She avoided politicians and stuck with central beliefs. When it came time to cast a vote, she wanted to know who checked her personal boxes, not who joined a political party. She didn't listen to talking heads, radio pundits, or people paid to pontificate. But even Chelsea knew that Sorenson thrived in the capital's shark-eat-shark world.

"I don't trust her," he finally said.

"And I don't blame you." She eased against his chest, grateful that he always stepped forward when conversations became hard.

Liam wrapped his arms around her, and they swayed in the stranger's sterile living room as Chelsea tried to make a connection between what they were doing, what happened last year with Julia, and Senator Sorenson. This situation was far beyond one she could dream up. "I'm sorry I pushed you."

"No one else knows about her, and it's best to keep her between us."

"Of course—this is really bad, isn't it?"

"I don't know about bad, but it's complicated." He held her tightly. "We'll get through this, then we can just..."

"Be."

He sighed and gave her another squeeze.

Whenever that day came, when they didn't have to worry about the Nymans' house blowing up, sneaking into empty homes for sale, or even her problems with Mac and Calhoun, she couldn't wait. Chelsea had no doubt that the hiccups they encountered and hills they climbed over would lead to an understanding she couldn't yet comprehend. Now those were some relationship goals.

THE NEXT MORNING arrived far, far too early courtesy of Chelsea's cell phone vibrating until she woke nauseous. Apparently her aversion to phone calls had reached the point that her stomach turned, because waking up early had always been her habit.

The phone stopped vibrating, and the swell of queasiness subsided. Or maybe waking up, locked against Liam, was enough to melt a stressful stomachache away. Either way, she rubbed her eyes and wanted to keep sleeping.

Suddenly, Chelsea panicked and opened her eyes wide. They weren't in her bedroom, and it wasn't his either. Realization dawned. Their night had turned them into real estate squatters.

"I promise." Liam skimmed his palm over her hip and stomach. "No one will bother us. Don't freak out."

Maybe that was easy for him. Who knew the places his career had asked him to bed down. But she didn't sleep in places that she broke into, even if they had the approval of Senator Sorenson.

"Sunshine," he whispered, "I promise."

She clung to his promise. He wouldn't lead her astray.

Then her cell phone buzzed again and her stomach turned. Could it be Mac? Maybe there'd been another situation with Zee Zee? Chelsea's normal rules for ignoring phone calls were put on hold when they came at the break of dawn.

Liam groaned as she made a half-hearted attempt to reach her purse without pulling from his arm. That didn't work—and he wedged his leg between hers. The coarse hairs felt rough against her skin, reviving parts of her that she thought might never feel unsatisfied again.

Last night... The memory of how they made love caused her to shiver.

He kissed the back of her head, and her thoughts of the work she was barred from dwindled away.

Until the phone buzzed again.

"Make it stop." He moved her hair and caressed the back of her neck with a kiss that dared her to do so by answering the call. He nibbled again, and her nipples perked.

"You have to give me a little room to reach my purse."

Liam growled then rolled away. "Someone better have a damn good reason."

A chill slipped across her naked limbs, and she concurred when she found her phone. "It's Mac."

"Fan-fucking-tastic." Liam turned over and buried his face in the pillow as she answered it.

"Hello?"

It took Mac all of two seconds to greet her and demand she come help him at the office.

Of course he needed her help. No one could come close to her Mars expertise. But their previous discussion had been about as good as this one, short-tempered and bossy. Mac ended the call almost as quickly as he made his demand for her to work.

Annoyance tinged with good old-fashioned aggravation. "I have to go in."

"The hell you do." Liam rolled to face her. "You're on leave. *Forced* leave."

She couldn't deny the truth, but she also wanted to get back to work. "Even more of a reason to head in. I can remind Calhoun who is actually the brains behind this investigation." And point out that she wasn't intoxicated. But bringing that up would only cause more frustration.

He scrubbed his hands over his face. "Fine."

"I'm pouting too. Trust me." Leaving Liam naked in a bed was at the bottom of her to-do list.

"I'll drive you." He sat up then raked his gaze across her bare breasts and stomach. "*After* we finish in bed."

That was a compromise she couldn't refuse.

CHAPTER FORTY-THREE

"BYE!" CHELSEA GRABBED the Explorer's door handle to head into the gloomy, raining cold, but Liam pulled her back.

"Not so fast." At the front of the building, in front of God and all to see, he laid a kiss on her so hot the stormy fall day would feel like a summer heat wave.

He ended it with a gentle but seriously sexy nibble of her bottom lip that made her equilibrium seesaw until she saw stars. Then, breathless, limp, and lovestruck, she finally fell away with what had to be a loopy grin.

"Have a good day, Sunshine." He settled back and dangled his wrist over the top of the steering wheel. The stubble shading his cheeks and chin and the dark green in his eyes were the cherries on top of the world's most addictive sundae.

How can he sit there so calm and cool? She needed to uncurl her toes before walking into the building. "You too."

Chelsea floated out of the Explorer, shut the door, and gave a quick wave. He was a miracle worker. Not fifteen seconds before, she'd been lost in a jumble of anxious nerves, prepping what she'd say to Calhoun and how she'd handle Mac. She'd spent half of their drive rehearsing a take-a-stand conversation that could be applied to either man, no matter the topic. Her shoulders had been too tight, and her focus hadn't been on what mattered: Zee Zee Mars.

But now she was positively giddy.

Liam waited until she sashayed up the front stairs of the federal office building, and when she turned to smile and wave, he gave a smolder and salute before he drove away.

There was nothing she couldn't handle today. And maybe that was always the case—or so she hoped—but today she had Liam in her corner to remind her of that truth.

Chelsea entered through the familiar glass door and breezed to the security line. It clipped along until she relinquished her purse and weapon for inspection and said hello to the same guard who'd scanned her badge for years.

"Nice to see you again." He waved her through the Magtron. "Looks like your vacation put a bounce in your step."

She didn't correct him on her forced time off but beamed. That drop-off kiss still radiated in her. "Looks like it did."

He said goodbye with an approving, friendly nod as she collected her belongings. The day wouldn't be so bad. Nothing could turn her smile upside down.

She followed the hallway and waited for the elevator with a woman engrossed in her phone, and two men who worked on the fourth floor.

The elevator opened as a faraway clap of thunder boomed. They murmured small talk that they'd made it inside before a storm crashed.

Just before the elevator doors closed, Mac strode in and glared her way. "Just who I was looking for."

Oh, joy. She might've been saved from one storm but was headed straight toward another one. "Here I am." She angled to face him as he pushed next to her in the small elevator. "In the flesh."

His scowl didn't soften, and Chelsea shifted her purse to the other shoulder.

Still, Mac stared, not side-eyeing her but flat-out facing her direction and glowering.

The elevator crept like it might stop any moment, and she couldn't put up with Mac's attention. "What?"

"You tell me."

Her eyebrow arched. "Tell you *what?*"

"Did you drive in?" he asked.

She squinted, confused, then glanced around at what felt like the slowest elevator on earth. "No. Why?"

"I know."

"Good for you." Her forehead pinched. "What's your problem?"

"Who dropped you off?"

She drew back. "Excuse me?"

"You heard me."

His voice had lowered, but it wasn't as if they had personal space. Everyone could hear everything, maybe even the weird way she was breathing.

"Cool your jets, my friend," Chelsea said.

"I'm your partner, not your friend."

The elevator stopped, and another woman joined them.

"I'll talk to you upstairs." Then Chelsea turned away, though she could feel his gaze boring into the side of her skull. The elevator doors *still* hadn't shut. Chelsea jabbed the door closed button.

Once again, the elevator stopped. This time on the third floor. Both women exited. Mac took the extra room to step into her line of sight.

"*What* is your problem?" she asked again.

The elevator doors inched closed, and Chelsea decided to ignore Mac.

"I know who dropped you off," he shared.

"Good for you." Chelsea clamped her jaw shut.

He crossed his arms as though he'd scored a point in an investigation. The elevator stopped on the fourth floor and emptied. Mac pressed the door closed button.

As soon as they were alone, she snapped. "Stand down, partner."

"As your partner, I need to know what the hell is happening with you."

Coldness chilled her blood. "I could ask the same thing about you."

"Bullshit."

Her throat tightened. This wasn't any of the conversations she had readied to wage. "Stop cursing at me."

But he knew the words didn't matter. She pressed her fingers to her temples. "I haven't even sat down yet, and you're jumping down my throat."

"We have an agreement."

They did, and it revolved around a strict openness in all work and home aspects. Knowing the other's mindset would keep them alive. But it only worked if they both were on board, and Mac definitely wasn't. Chelsea threw her hands out. "You want to throw around our rules? How about you set Calhoun straight about my *drinking problem.*"

"What the hell do I know?"

Furious, Chelsea waved him away. "You know."

"I know you're out cavorting with—"

"*Cavorting?*" She turned, ice shards flowing in her veins. "What kind of accusation is that?"

"A very specific one."

"You have no idea what I'm doing. Back off."

"I know what you should be doing with your best friend's boyfriend. *Nothing.*"

CHAPTER FORTY-FOUR

THE VENOM-SPEWING PARTNER standing in the elevator with Chelsea wasn't the man she knew. Her Mac wasn't hateful. He'd never dip to such lows, and if she hadn't found such confidence with Liam, she might not be able to see the ugly words for what they were. Vicious and self-serving. "What has happened to you?"

He sneered. "Ask yourself that question, would ya, Kilpatrick?"

Bilious stomach pain punched Chelsea with such force that her eyes nearly watered. But he was in the wrong, and she'd die before a single tear could slip free. Mac would never have the satisfaction of making her cry. But—he had a good chance of making her sick.

The elevator doors opened, and Chelsea escaped. She rushed toward the bull pen, only to find know where to sit. She couldn't go to her basement office and still work with Mac, and she didn't know where to head. Agents in the bullpen glanced over, and a wave of nausea ebbed and flowed.

She spun and crashed into Calhoun.

"Kilpatrick," he said as a greeting.

Mac strode up as if he hadn't been a first-class jerk in the elevator. "Ready to get to work?"

"Would you give me a minute?" she snapped.

"I see the congratulations didn't go as expected," Calhoun grumbled.

She reeled back, eyeing both men. "What congratulations?"

Calhoun's eyebrow arched. "Mac's promotion."

What? She thought back to how he hadn't taken up for her against Calhoun, how he hadn't reached out except for after it had been impossible not to when Zee Zee struck again. "You played me for office politics?"

Mac rolled his eyes. "Give me a break."

"You did. Didn't you? You let—"

"It's not like you wanted to move up," he interjected.

"No! I only cared about Zee Zee Mars!"

"Shut it!" Calhoun commanded, and when she and Mac stopped bickering, she realized they had everyone's attention. "Conference room now."

Mac snickered. "I think we both have news to share and celebrate."

Chelsea's jaw fell, and she didn't know what was more shocking—the acerbic sarcasm or how he didn't seem the least bit sad that their partnership was irreparably shattered. The hurt made her physically ill.

Calhoun marched them into the closest conference room. It overlooked the front parking lot, and Chelsea saw Mac's jacket over the back of a chair and his coffee mug on the table. He'd been working in there and saw Liam kiss her goodbye?

It didn't matter. She wasn't hiding—except she felt certain she might be sick. Mac and Calhoun struck up a casual conversation as they took their seats. The banter stopped and their eyes remained on her.

Finally, Calhoun offered "Do you want to take a seat?"

"Thanks," she hoarsely whispered. "But I'm going to run to the ladies' room first."

She prayed that the dizziness would subside, then forced herself down the hall and into the restroom. Chelsea splashed cold water on her face. But that didn't help. Neither did the cold rag she made for the back of her neck.

She gave up and took a deep breath. That didn't help either, and she had nothing left to do but go back to the conference room.

Both men were kicked back in rolling chairs that swiveled and rocked. They stopped mid-sentence when she walked in and stood. Her boss offered her a chair, but she opted for one at the head of the table so that both men would be at her sides.

"Chelsea," Calhoun said, starting uncharacteristically with her first name.

The door cracked, and Dr. Casper walked in. "Good morning."

It was a setup. An ambush. Mac had camouflaged the reason for the meeting so that she would come in.

Dr. Casper shook Calhoun's hand and sat next to Mac, giving the same greeting, as if they were all old friends.

"I thought we shared everything," Chelsea snapped at her partner. "Where's the truth in this?"

All eyes fell on her.

"Chelsea," Calhoun started again, "you remember Dr. Casper?"

"Yes." She pressed her lips together.

"I thought perhaps you would've arranged an appointment with the doctor."

Dr. Casper kept a neutral expression, but nothing was evenhanded when it came to the alliances that had been formed.

"I've been busy," she said.

"I think," Mac interjected, "Chelsea has something else to bring up that's worth discussing."

Mac wouldn't dare bring up Liam. The corners of her eyes pinched, and her molars sawed to their breaking point. "That's between us."

"With your time off, my role has changed. Whether we remain partners or not, I think that it's important for everyone to know—"

"Do *not* finish that thought," Chelsea snapped.

Dr. Casper pulled out a notebook and jotted a note.

For the love of butter cream—notes*?*

"I never took you for one of those guys who'd throw their partner under the bus to rise in the ranks—" Then she felt it necessary to turn to the scribbling doctor. "This is absurd."

Mac cleared his throat. "It's important for us to realize that you're sleeping with Liam Brosnan." He pivoted to Dr. Casper. "Brosnan is her best friend's boyfriend."

"I'm not sure that's warranted," Calhoun muttered, finally sticking up for her.

"Substance abuse and reckless decisions?" Mac replied to their boss but Chelsea could tell his answer was for Dr. Casper's benefit.

She wanted to cry and yell. What was she supposed to say? *Explain that my best friend is dead? That more than a year had passed before she and Liam became romantically involved?* Mac, Calhoun, and Casper didn't need that information.

"Why don't you take a moment to compose yourself," Calhoun suggested.

"I don't need to," she choked.

He shifted in the rolling chair. "You don't look well."

"I've been ambushed, and you think I have a drinking problem!"

"Take it easy," Calhoun demanded.

Chelsea squared her shoulders and tried to settle her emotions. "Fine."

After a minute, Calhoun rubbed his chin and leaned back. "I'd still like you to see Casper."

Unbelievable. She shook her head.

"There's nothing wrong with getting help," Mac offered.

"I don't need help! What the hell is your problem?"

Mac and Calhoun froze as though they couldn't believe she'd cursed, then Calhoun leaned forward. "Maybe this meeting was a bad idea."

Her chin dropped. "Why did you call me in anyway?"

Calhoun cleared his throat. "Mac's going to be overseeing a taskforce that works with several agencies, and he's suggested their first focus be Zee Zee Mars."

He'd thrown her under the bus for clout and seniority, and had to steal her work? She could see how all the pieces fell into place, even if Calhoun or Casper couldn't. Mac knew what he was doing. She smiled weakly. "Congratulations. Even if you didn't earn it."

"Kilpatrick," Calhoun warned.

She stood and didn't care what more Calhoun had to say. "At least I know why I've been accused of a nonexistent drinking problem and the basis for the relationship with my boyfriend has been publicly called into question."

"Boyfriend." Mac snickered.

Calhoun shot Mac a look to stand down, but that didn't change what had happened. She was dangerously close to balling her fists and beating the ever-loving daylights out of her partner. But given the two oh-so-neutral witnesses, she'd probably find herself in lock-up. "I should go."

"I'll give you a buzz if I have any questions about Mars." Mac rocked back. "But I think we have her handled."

That cocky son of a biscuit-eating polar bear. She chewed the inside of her mouth, only when she was certain that speaking wouldn't mean throwing herself across the table to claw his eyes out, Chelsea simply said, "I'm sure."

Mac pursed his lips and glanced at Calhoun.

Calhoun now seemed confused and looked at Dr. Casper, but he was busily scribbling notes.

"I want you to come back when you're ready," Calhoun said.

"Who will make that call?" Her hands clenched again, and her palms would bleed before the *impromptu* meeting ended.

Mac muttered something under his breath, and she did too.

"Enough." Calhoun stood. "You two can't work together, even if you were back on duty today."

"Sir—"

Calhoun waved away her interruption. "Kilpatrick, before you leave, double check with Mac on any missing holes, and then you two, get to different corners."

How could I lose everything I've worked on? Nausea rolled over her again. An unsettling sweat broke out at the back of her neck and between her breasts. Her stomach churned, and she didn't feel as if the room had enough air. She pressed her lips together and tried not to vomit.

"Kilpatrick?" Calhoun's beady eyes narrowed. "Are we going to have another problem?"

Yes... his decisions were making her ill. This absurd situation called for internal affairs to investigate—or something! But a request for an IA investigation could ruin her career, and she tried to see what was important. Catching Zee Zee. That was what Chelsea needed to focus on. She swallowed hard and prayed for team-player strength and the miraculous appearance of a roll of antacids. "Anything to capture Mars."

The corners of Mac's lips turned up slightly. Whatever had happened in Kentucky gave them a break and created a multi-agency taskforce, and she'd never know if Mac didn't share.

"And." Calhoun inhaled and let it out while he made eye contact with the doctor. "Kilpatrick, I think the best way to handle your current situation is to remain as we are. Your benefits will continue while we work this out."

"This is insane," Chelsea protested.

"We've talked enough for today." Calhoun offered a worried look. "*I* want you to come back, but get your life under control first."

CHAPTER FORTY-FIVE

LIAM'S BEDROOM WAS cloaked in darkness. The shadows surprised Chelsea, and she blinked to focus in the dark, fumbling for a lamp. Instead, she knocked something off the nightstand, maybe a metal water bottle. The metallic clang hung in the air like a gong.

The bedroom door cracked open, and the hallway light fell over the bed. "You're awake?"

She winced as the memory of her morning came back. "How long have I been asleep?"

"A while."

She was still wearing her pantsuit but without the jacket, and the last she recalled, the couch had beckoned her to take a self-pitying nap. "When did I come in here?"

"I moved you."

"Ah." She'd called Liam to pick her up earlier than they'd planned and spent the entire ride back to his apartment volleying between righteous fury that made her want to scream and shock over her partner's disloyalty. But now? Even though she'd slept much longer than she planned, she was spent.

"Feeling better?" He picked up the water bottle and offered it to her.

She uncapped the lid and took a long drink then a longer breath. "Yeah. I think so."

He moved to the side of the bed and took the bottle, screwed the lid on, and returned it to the spot she'd knocked it from. "Can I sit?"

"Of course." She scooted from the edge. "I can't believe I slept the day away."

"I can after that kind of shit show."

She quietly snort-laughed.

"What would make it a better day? Chocolate? Booze? Vegging in front of the TV?"

She fell back onto the pillows and barely shook her head. Nothing could make the day any less ugly than it was. Her fingers found his, and he ran his thumb over each one, across her knuckles, then started the design again.

"You," she answered.

"Me what?"

"You'd make my day better."

His hand squeezed hers, and he held her eyes.

"You always do," she whispered.

"I think I can manage to lay down with you." He let her burrow against him then cocooned her in his arms.

Chelsea listened to his heart beat. She skimmed her hand over the soft hair on his forearm and the rigid cords of his muscles. His breathing deepened, and Liam rubbed her back in a hypnotic pattern.

"Thank you," she said.

"For what?"

"Everything and then so much more."

He quietly laughed. "Do you want to get up? Are you hungry?"

"Hmm." Hungry maybe, but more than that, she didn't want to let him go. "In a bit."

"How about I distract you?" Liam unbuttoned the top of her blouse. With every button he undid, he teased and caressed as light as air for only the slightest breeze of a moment before he unfastened another button and then another. "How am I doing?"

She hummed. "I think it's working."

He slid down lower, taking away her pants until nothing but a thin layer of lace and silk covered her breasts and sex. "I think so too."

Then she recalled a low point from the meeting and whispered, "I did something today. I mean, I said something."

His knuckles trailed to her jawbone then her chin. The tips of his fingers ran down her throat to the valley between her breasts. Liam skimmed over her stomach and deftly slid below her lace underwear and curled his fingers against her mound. "What's that?"

She squirmed. "I said you were mine."

"Good. I am." He tore off his shirt and kneeled between her thighs.

"My day's turning around." She unfastened the button and zippers on his pants, and he stripped.

"I'm happy to do my part."

Her sex clenched when he tossed the last of their clothes onto the floor.

Liam's thick erection hung heavily, and she needed him to obliterate the day until there was nothing left to remember except his weight, the sheen of their sweat, and the knowledge that he'd come deep inside her.

His fingers stroked expertly until her eyes slipped shut and his lips met hers. Two thick fingers breached her ready entrance. "All yours." His mouth took hers, harsh and hungry. It mirrored the motion of his hand, spearing her again and again until the intensity became all-consuming.

He sucked her tongue and bit her lip, and she moaned. They were feverish and wild. Her words pleaded and became a tangle of yeses, until she begged him to be inside her. "I need you *now*."

The thick head of his erection nudged, and he speared his tongue into her mouth when he thrust.

She hadn't realized how much she needed his body. He worked his shaft inside her clenching muscles. Inch by inch, he powered between her thighs, and her nails dug into the sinewy muscles in his back. "I need this. *You*."

His eyes shone like he understood, then he slowed until she almost screamed. The intensity was blinding. She gasped and rocked, desperate for the hot flames that were splitting her apart. He thrust again, seated deep, then stilled.

She trembled. "Please."

Then, wild and hot, Liam took her mouth and withdrew his shaft. He drove in again and out, offering hungry, beautiful, painstaking bliss.

Hips writhed against hips. Mouths dueled for kisses and cries. She lost her mind with the rhythmic rapture, teasing and torturing, giving her whirling sensations of complete ecstasy.

Her raspy voice called his name over and over again. A spiral of pleasure drew deeper, and Chelsea bucked, clinging to him for every single maddening, orgasm-swelling stroke.

"Liam!" *God!* Chelsea arched as a volcano of color exploded behind her closed eyes and pleasure as hot as lava ran through her veins.

He didn't slow, driving her higher and higher. Chelsea bit his shoulder, and she came again, cursing and crying.

He wrapped her to his chest, rolling on the bed until he lay on his back, and she draped limply over him. His hands massaged her hips then grabbed her ass as he slowed down, easing in and out with lackadaisical moves as she caught her breath.

The room stopped spinning and her lungs found a normal pattern. She eased up, sitting on his erection, overwhelmed by how his length and thickness filled her. Liam's powerful hands caressed her thighs and slid to her hips as she rocked on him.

His fingers bit into her sides. She wanted nothing more than to hear his pleasure again. She rose and eased down. Violent need clouded her mind.

His hips jerked, and she braced her hands on his shoulders. Liam pounded into her body, and she gasped, losing her breath, her mind, her everything as the wildfire of another orgasm loomed so close.

"Fuck." Liam's rough voice was pinched with brutal need.

That was what she wanted. His orgasm. His cum. She wanted to feel him release inside her.

He thundered into her, wrapping her to his chest and came.

His arms tightened until she almost couldn't breathe, and their bodies spasmed together.

Limp, their breaths seesawed. He stayed inside her. Her hair covered his neck and her face, but they didn't have enough strength between them to move it.

Finally, she slipped her eyes open and pressed a soft kiss to his shoulder. Liam moved from her and rolled them on their sides, spooning around her body.

"Boyfriend," she whispered. "That's what I said."

He kissed the back of her head.

It didn't matter what he would've said or what she had called him. After she tucked into the crook of his arm, using his muscles as a pillow, she let herself drift to sleep again, knowing only one thing with certainty. Liam owned her soul.

CHAPTER FORTY-SIX

CRISP RED LEAVES mixed with yellow and brown ones, and Chelsea drank in the cool morning air. Real fall was upon them, the kind in which Thanksgiving displays popped up before Halloween and frost glazed windshields across the parking lot every morning. The weather was *just* right. She could get away with a pullover but wouldn't mind a jacket.

Truthfully, after a few days of alternating between being in Liam's arms, working on her book project, and monitoring the Nyman residence, Chelsea didn't mind much, even with her semi-lack of employment. She was living her best life. And as a bonus, she was living her best morning, enjoying a fall walk from her condo to the farmer's market.

Chelsea stepped off the footpath across from her condo complex and crossed the street. The shopping center had been transformed into a village of flower tents, fruit and veggie stalls, and rows upon rows of farm-fresh dairy products, baked goods, and heavenly treats. Her stomach growled as she thought of homemade honey buns and iced cinnamon bread. But her first stop was always the same fruit stand run by the same woman, who went by the simplest name—the Apple Lady.

Never in all the years Chelsea had bought her smoothie supplies did she wonder who the Apple Lady was when she left the market—until now. She melted into the crowd and wondered if the kind woman's gentleness was real or simply a role played to sell local fruit, and if her kind eyes and easy smile told of a life that Chelsea was certain smelled like nutmeg and sounded like laughter.

She wondered about everyone else too. *Are there others nearby who lost their best friend? Who are falling for wonderful men?* She couldn't tell simply by looking at the passing faces. Even before she was trained, she had been smart enough to know folks weren't always what they seemed. They were made of sins and scars, love and luck, the darkest darks and the brightest lights. People were decisions, choices, consequences, opportunities, risk, and reward. They were so much more than she could comprehend, and the realization that everyone lived as complex lives as she did made her feel infinitely small and magnificently special.

Sidestepping a gaggle of weekend warriors who were sampling the Apple Lady's apple cider, Chelsea waved hello. "Busy today."

The woman held a large pink apple in one hand and a light-green one in the other. "These two beauties are the reason why."

Chelsea smiled, certain that the Apple Lady's house smelled like brown sugar too. "Why's that?"

"They are everything that fall fruit should be."

That wasn't really an answer, but it somehow fit Chelsea's mood. "I should bring some home. Which one is sweeter?"

She raised the pink apple. "Sweeter and softer. But don't discount this one's tart punch."

Smiling again, Chelsea recalled almost the exact same conversation from the year before and the year before that—though then, Julia had been there too. The cycle of fruit continued. The seasons brought change, and the years offered a repeat of the year before. The more everything changed, the more it stayed the same. "I'll try them both."

The Apple Lady beamed, then other customers at the far end of the fruit stall asked for help with cider. "Keep looking. I'll be back in a few."

Or more than a few. Chelsea regarded the small group, who seemed to have hit the mimosas a little hard that morning. "Take your time."

They shared a knowing laugh, and Chelsea eyed a large bunch of plump grapes and stacks of pears.

"Ohhh." A young girl had her eyes on the same fruits and reached out for them, bumping into Chelsea.

Chelsea grinned and gave the little girl more room as her mother, who had a baby tied to her chest, offered an apology then added, "Look with your eyes. Not your fingers. *Please.*"

It took another *please* before the girl pulled her hands back.

Chelsea tried not to melt from the cuteness as the little girl took her mother's other hand.

It had been just seconds since the mother gave a semi-sweet scolding, and they'd locked hands as if the incident weren't even a faint memory. What a night-and-day difference from how Chelsea had been raised. Just thinking about it made her stiffen.

Not that her mother would've taken her to something as frivolous as a farmer's market, but if she had and Chelsea reached for a grape, the reprimand wouldn't have been cutesy and ended with a handhold.

She watched the little girl chatter about pink apples and go over the moon when her mom produced a bright-yellow one.

Maybe, one day, Chelsea might be that type of heartening mother. Maybe she'd *be* a mom. Her pulse fluttered. *A mom?* She'd never thought about her future like that before, and an unhurried sigh made her feel as squishy as a toasted marshmallow.

And Liam... what kind of father would he be? That marshmallow-y feeling melted into an ooey-gooey delight she'd never experienced.

The girl pulled her mom away. Chelsea's tranquil thoughts drifted as she turned back to the fruit and found a black calla lily.

Ice-cold awareness ripped through her. Chelsea twisted and jumped back, then, far, far too close, Chelsea was face to face with Zee Zee Mars.

Familiarity that she couldn't explain slapped her senseless until Zee Zee's smugness broke their trance. She grabbed a pear with nonchalant coolness that couldn't be faked. Zee Zee tossed the fruit, caught it in her opposite hand, and took a bite. Her pupils dilated, and a hint of a dare turned up the corners of her lips. Never once did she blink. "Chelsea Kilpatrick, in the flesh."

Chelsea's mind raced. She had no backup, not even her purse, as she had a monthly tab with the Apple Lady. She didn't even have so much as a bobby pin to MacGyver into a weapon.

Zee Zee smacked the pear juice from her lips. "I haven't seen you in a while."

"You haven't." She needed to buy time, needed to check her surroundings. "This is unexpected."

"Is it?" Zee Zee studied the pear then held it close to her lips. "You know me better than that—Or maybe you don't know me at all."

Chelsea gaged how quickly she could nab Zee Zee. It wasn't as if she could simply ask her to turn around and put her hands behind her back. *What, then?* Chelsea could ask the Apple Lady for the burlap garland that decorated the fruit stand to secure Zee Zee's wrist.

Zee Zee would run. *Won't she?* "Why are you here?" It made absolutely no sense.

"Those fucking calla lilies," Zee Zee offered instead. "God, I hate those things."

Chelsea did, too, but she wasn't sure that commiserating over flowers would help her understand.

Zee Zee narrowed her eyes. "You do too."

That wasn't a question. Chelsea's skin prickled.

"Did you ever stop to wonder if maybe I've studied you as much as you've studied me?"

"No." Chelsea hoped she was feigning the same level of confidence that Zee Zee seemed to exude. "I assumed your time was spent on more sinister thoughts."

"Sinister?" Zee Zee raised an eyebrow. "It's just a game."

A game. Explosion after explosion over the course of years, and it was just a sick, twisted hobby. "How about we end it now?"

Zee Zee pointed her pear toward their feet. A lone paper bag with its top neatly folded over and stapled rested along a parking space line. "You have two guesses as to what's in there."

Panic bottomed in Chelsea's stomach. Still, she kept her face blank. "Honey buns?"

Zee Zee cocked her head and laughed. "I think we have the same sense of humor too."

"What does that mean?" Chelsea asked.

"For everything you got, for every single opportunity you didn't relish, you would think," Zee Zee snarled, "that you'd have learned something."

Chelsea swallowed over the knot in her throat. Why was the conversation so personal? "What I do know is that you've never targeted a farmer's market, and I don't think you'll start today."

Zee Zee bit into the pear again and chewed slowly. "Actually, that's your choice."

Chelsea skipped the semantics. Everything they knew about Zee Zee seemed to be wrong. "What do you want?"

"You to look in the bag."

"Do I need to?" she asked. "Either it's there, or it's not."

The Apple Lady came over, smiled, then asked Zee Zee, "Can I help you?"

The woman on top of the US Marshal's Most Wanted Fugitive List nailed a fake smile and saccharine sweetness. "The only one who can help me is Chelsea."

"Oh." Confusion crossed the soft lines on her forehead. "Then I'll let you be."

Chelsea wanted to scream, *Run!* The farmer's market needed to be evacuated. "Let everyone leave. Then it's just you and me."

Zee Zee reached into her back pocket then dangled a dead man's switch. "If you make one move to alert anyone..."

The switch hadn't been activated. That was Chelsea's only saving grace.

The little girl from earlier tore by, dragging a large cinnamon broom as her mother trailed behind her, laughing.

Chelsea wanted to weep for them and for everyone nearby. "Just you and me."

Zee Zee lowered her hand but didn't put away the switch. The device was a thumb flick away from detonating the bag at their feet. "Why weren't *you* there?"

Blanking, Chelsea asked, "Where?"

"Kentucky." Zee Zee arched a dark eyebrow as if to question Chelsea's sanity.

"The rest of the world was there." Her best update had come from the news. The FBI, US Marshals, and every ding dang news organization on the planet had descended upon the smoldering bits like fruit flies to a peach.

Zee Zee sawed her teeth. "I don't care about them."

"Me?" She shook her head. "You don't need me to terrorize—"

"*Yes.*" Zee Zee hissed and shook the switch. "I do."

"Careful, please." She held her hands by her side. "Let's go somewhere else."

Zee Zee snorted.

"Come on." Chelsea tilted her head. "We're not on the same page, and I think that's important to you."

"You think!" Zee Zee shouted.

A few people stared. No one knew what she had in her hand. Chelsea wanted to wave them away, but the blast zone would be too large for them to escape.

Their conversation conflicted with everything Chelsea had known for years—the bombings, the motives. *What is the point if not some kind of activism?* Chelsea erased her long-understood beliefs on Zee Zee Mars. "Tell me what I should know."

An agreeable expression softened Zee Zee's face, but she added, "It hurts."

"What does?"

"That all this time, you really didn't know."

Cheese and crackers, know what? "What do I do to make it right?"

"Don't use your education and fancy job to talk down to me," Zee Zee snapped.

Her choices, her opportunities, her education—was this about *her*? "I'm sorry."

Shock brightened in Zee Zee's eyes. "You are?"

Carefully, Chelsea nodded.

"Is everything all right?" the Apple Lady asked at precisely the wrong second.

Zee Zee hardened again—and activated the dead man's switch. "An apology won't make up for it."

"We're fine," Chelsea answered, praying that somehow, the Apple Lady could read between the invisible lines of the two words and clear the farmer's market of people. When that telepathy didn't work and the Apple

Lady walked away, Chelsea tried again. "It's time to leave. You and me. Or let me tell everyone else to go."

"The churches," Zee Zee said. "The law firms."

Chelsea didn't know what to say. Zee Zee wasn't making sense.

"The libraries. The schools."

Zee Zee's pitch had increased, and Chelsea tried to guess how many seconds it would take to transmit the detonation. *Enough that I could save some lives? Should I simply scream, "RUN"?*

"You had all that." Zee Zee dropped her voice low and strained to hold back tears. "You had *her*. And you broke her heart."

"*Who?*" Chelsea sputtered, terrified that she didn't know if shouting or not would save lives. "How?"

Zee Zee's face twisted. "You had everything and threw it away to become a federal agent?"

The words clanged loudly in Chelsea's head. Zee Zee sounded like *her mother.*

Tears streamed down the woman's face. "She should've kept me!"

Chelsea didn't give herself time to process the words. She shot her arm out and clasped Zee Zee's fist in hers. If her hand kept tight, the bomb could not explode.

"Run!" She struggled as Zee Zee fought to release her hand. "Everyone—" A fist snapped against her jaw. "Go!"

To hold a person by just their hand was impossible, but she couldn't let go. Zee Zee screamed. She bit. Hands pulled at Chelsea's back as though she needed to be pulled off Zee Zee.

"Bomb!" Chelsea cried, holding onto Zee Zee's fist for dear life. "Run!"

Zee Zee dug her teeth into Chelsea's shoulder, ripping back and forth like a rabid beast, and beat her head repeatedly.

Bright lights and clouds skewed Chelsea's vision, and she hooked her unbalanced leg behind Zee Zee's knees. They crashed to the asphalt. Zee Zee took the brunt of the fall and gasped as the air was knocked from her lungs.

Their arms were tangled between their stomachs. Chelsea couldn't move her hands to strike, and her grip slipped as they rolled. Their knees jabbed. Zee Zee fisted Chelsea's hair, tearing back as she bit into the soft flesh of her neck.

The brilliant slice of pain paralyzed Chelsea. She was going to die. Zee Zee would rip out her throat and sever her carotid artery, and the bomb would still explode.

Warm wetness slicked over them—her blood—and the same nausea from before roared back. But she couldn't fail. She'd worked too hard to catch Zee Zee. It meant too much to Julia. Living for Liam meant a family one day, and God help her, she wanted to send a message to Mac that he could kiss her sugar plum tail.

Chelsea reared back, tearing free, and head-butted Zee Zee's blood-smeared face. Stars exploded in her eyes, and her stomach turned. All her strength was gone as blackness ebbed. Chelsea blinked hard, ignoring the threatening bile, and pulled the dead man's switch into her hands as Zee Zee fell limp.

CHAPTER FORTY-SEVEN

SIRENS WAILED IN the distance. Chelsea choked and gagged on the metallic taste of her blood and fisted the dead man's switch.

Zee Zee remained unconscious, but there was no telling how long that might last. She could wake up, and if Chelsea had the switch in her hand, she couldn't fight back. But for the moment, she remained still in the middle of a parking space in the eerily silent farmer's market.

Chelsea inched closer and pushed Zee Zee's hair back. The two of them had similarities. The jokes and side comments had always been well-founded. But as she really studied her cheek structure and the point of her chin, her mother's image became clear.

Zee Zee was almost twenty years older than Chelsea. That would mean that when Zee Zee was born, her mother would have been around... *Twelve years old?* If Zee Zee was right, they could be sisters. *What happened to my mother?*

Chelsea never knew her family beyond her mother. She'd never asked. But having a baby when she was still a child—that could explain so much, even how her mother might do anything to make the second chance at a child an unwavering standard of perfection.

The attention and demands had been smothering. But if Zee Zee was a lost daughter looking in, the complete obsession with Chelsea might be enough to drive a person crazy.

Law enforcement appeared, pointing their guns and holding their riot shields and protective barriers up. Now that they were in sight, lightheadedness threatened to pull Chelsea to the dark.

"Federal agent," she identified herself as loudly as she could. "We need a bomb squad."

The next few minutes were an intolerable wait as the officers were pulled back, and she sat alongside the brown bag and the unconscious Zee Zee. Sleep called, and after Chelsea realized she had to slow the flow of her neck wounds, she wilted.

Her lashes fluttered. Her fist cramped, and she wrapped her other hand over it, refusing to cry, and both hands began to ache.

"Chelsea?"

Her chin jutted up. Relief surged through her at the sight of two bomb technicians in thick protective suits coming her way. She might make it out of this… And first things first, she needed to hear Liam's voice.

Then second, Chelsea had to phone her mom for the first time in years. Maybe through the new lens of knowledge. If what Zee Zee had said was true, perhaps she could understand her mother's harshness and drive. Perhaps Chelsea could find a place deep in her soul to offer forgiveness.

The technicians orchestrated a textbook hand-off and departed with the switch and the bag. As soon as they were clear, a flurry of activity appeared at the far lane of the farmer's market. Medics and law enforcement rushed forward.

But not before Chelsea crawled to Zee Zee and ripped the burlap garland off the fruit display. "You are under arrest." She tied the woman's hands behind her back, and a feeling of satisfaction surged. She'd done it. No matter how it happened, she'd wanted to arrest Zee Zee, and now that was done. "You have the right to remain silent…"

Her head bobbed as an officer swooped in to finish what she'd started. EMTs moved into action, and an ambulance pulled forward. But between the chaos of her physical assessment and the officers arranging for Zee Zee's transport, Calhoun stepped forward. He had her complete attention.

"Job well done, Kilpatrick."

Her dry lips parted. "Thank you."

"I owe you an apology."

He owed her more than that, and she tried to organize her thoughts.

Calhoun cleared his throat. "Frankly, I owe you more than that."

He'd read her mind. The medics lifted her onto a stretcher as she tried to understand what she'd just heard. It jostled and shook as it rolled across the asphalt then lurched and clicked into the ambulance. Her boss climbed in also.

Chelsea tried to sit up, but the EMT pushed her down.

Calhoun positioned next to her shoulder. As the driver took off, her head spun, and she closed her eyes.

"I got a lot of things wrong lately." He grumbled. "That shit's not easy for me to say."

Laughter tickled in her, and Chelsea tried to hide her smile.

"Laugh it up," Calhoun said. "I deserve it."

Chelsea sat up and, as politely as she could, waved the medic away, asking for just a moment. "I don't have a drinking—"

He held up his hand and grimaced. "I know. Took me too long to figure out the power play there, and that's on me." His lips flattened. "I hope you'll come back. You won't have to worry about Mac."

The ambulance took a sharp turn that didn't sit well with her and further clouded everything she didn't understand and wasn't privy to about Mac's play for power, but she wanted to come back. Though only *after* she assessed what the future should look like.

★ ★ ★

TICK, TOCK. LIAM'S day crawled by, and he pinched the bridge of his nose wondering how much time he'd wasted. Sorenson had *again* had him hauled into their special meeting place. The location took forever to get to, then the senator made him wait and wait some more. He couldn't even play on his phone to pass the time.

Time didn't seem to be a commodity that Sorenson cared about. She operated in terms of calculated power moves, and even though Liam knew that, he couldn't see what her point was today.

The outer door unlocked and opened, followed by the glass one.

This time Sorenson was joined again by Westin and Black as they entered the glass cube meeting room and took the standard positions, with Sorenson sitting directly across from Liam.

"Good morning," Liam offered.

Curt smiles and nods were the only responses. Something was different about them. The air of disagreement hung heavily, and Liam shifted in the uncomfortable chair. "Or is it good afternoon by now…"

No one smiled, and he made a mental note to keep the passive aggressive jokes to himself.

"How are Frank and Linda?" the senator asked tartly.

"Doing well."

"Anything out of the ordinary?"

Liam played a few ways that question could be taken. After a moment's pause, he decided to take it in a broad, how-are-they-doing way. "Not that I can think of."

She scowled. "That's all you'd like to share?"

Did she want him to explain the surveillance equipment? Too bad. He'd done nothing to tip Pham off, so she could kiss his left nut. "I guess."

"You're keeping tabs on their house," she snipped.

That was less a question and more of an accusation. He offered a closed-mouth smile and didn't say shit.

She glared at Westin then knit her bony fingers together. Her bracelets clinked, and Liam studied their dynamic, unable to read the unsaid conversation.

"We've been over this," Westin said. "Keeping an eye on the house is a smart move."

"And if Pham saw the setup? The equipment?"

"He didn't. Everything installed is military-grade and untraceable. They know what they're doing."

Liam ran his tongue along his teeth. *He* had been under surveillance? And they evaluated his gear? But he kept quiet. If Westin was defending his actions to Sorenson, Liam wouldn't interrupt.

Her thickly mascaraed eyes beaded and lasered his way. "You're working with a team."

Liam shook his head. "A couple friends are helping me keep an eye on the place."

Her bracelets jangled. "That's—"

"That's," Westin interrupted, "not a problem."

"It is if we're ever going to catch Pham," she snapped.

Westin shook his head as if they'd had that argument before.

"Are you two on the same side or not?" Liam stared at the senator. "I'm following your asinine rules. God knows why, when it's *my* life in the crosshairs. A woman *I* loved was murdered. The people *I* care about are the walking targets. I don't see a lot of you invested in Pham, other than the glory from a takedown."

She straightened, gaze widening as if no one had every called her out on her bullshit before. "Watch yourself, Brosnan."

He'd had enough. He wanted to move on with his life, and he'd been able to in every way except one. Sorenson dangled Julia's killer like a juicy slab of meat while promising more harm could come, and Liam couldn't ignore the situation.

"Enough." Westin cracked his knuckles. "The circumstances are farther reaching than you know."

Of course they were. This clusterfuck was nothing but a shadowy cat-and-mouse game. "Which I'm sure no one will share."

Westin frowned, then said, "Since you arrive, we've become aware of a wrinkle in our plan."

Liam angled toward him. "Is it all smoothed out?"

"No." Sorenson steepled her fingers. Her irritating bracelets clinked. "Let's discuss your personal life."

Liam paused, unprepared for the turn in conversation. "What would you like to know?"

"What haven't you shared?"

"All right, cut the shit, Samantha." Westin glared. "Chelsea Kilpatrick?"

His blood went cold. "What about her?"

"We didn't anticipate you might have a new relationship."

Hell, when Sorenson dragged him into their first meeting, he hadn't either. Liam straightened his shoulders. "Don't know how that's possible when you've had eyes on me."

"Not in the way you might realize," Black said.

Liam glanced at him then to Westin. "What's going on?"

Sorenson tapped her fingertips together. "We're playing catch up late in the game—"

"My life is not a game," Liam growled.

"Is it serious?" she asked, then flipped her wrist. "Or are you… blowing off steam?"

His molars sawed. "Yeah. It's serious."

"Shit," Sorenson muttered.

"What does that mean?" Liam jerked from his chair. "Is she in danger?" Of course Chelsea would be in danger. He panicked.

Westin slapped his chest. "Sit."

Liam jerked away.

"*Sit,*" Westin ordered.

Liam planted his fists onto the table. "Is Chelsea in danger—"

An alarm chimed and echoed around as though someone had struck crystal.

Both Westin and Black reacted subtly. Their jaws hardened, and their lips thinned. But it was Sorenson that put fear into Liam's heart.

She cursed then stood and pointed a finger at him. "If we lost Pham because you don't know how to classify your heart from your dick, I will make sure you don't live to see your next birthday."

Chelsea *was* in danger.

The three walked out just as they'd come in, and as many questions as Liam yelled, no answers came his way.

CHAPTER FORTY-EIGHT

AN ANTISEPTIC SMELL coaxed Chelsea awake, but it was a slice of bright light that finally pulled her eyes open. Then pain throbbed.

She fought against the hurt and found her bearings. The light was coming from the space between the hospital curtains.

Chelsea closed her eyes and rolled over. Once her equilibrium settled again, she opened her eyes. The overhead lights were turned off, and the busy sound of a hospital emergency room came into focus, and she touched the thick bandages on her neck. The day came rushing back.

Oh, she ached. Her wound pulsed, and if she turned the wrong way, tape pulled at her skin. *Can't I get a pain killer?*

Then the overwhelming recollection of Zee Zee Mars zapped the last of her strength, churning her stomach. But the threat of another bombing hadn't made her nauseous. Zee Zee believed that they were related.

That they were sisters…

Every bombing had been nothing but a plea for attention from a mother who had given up a child.

How would her mother feel? Chelsea wondered if that was the first time she'd thought of that question. The selfishness made her sick, then an unfamiliar need to speak with her mother made her sit up.

The phone in her emergency room bay wasn't easy to reach, but she grasped it and eased back onto the bed. After a failed attempt to reach an outside line, she connected with the operator and convinced the woman to patch her through to the same phone number Chelsea had had as a child.

After three long rings, her mother answered with prim perfection that had haunted her for decades. "Kilpatrick residence. Hello?"

"Mom?" she croaked through a mixture of emotion and a dry throat.

After a long pause, her mother said, "Chelsea?"

Tears pooled in her eyes and slipped free. Years of resentment and frustration fizzled away with her new understanding, and she didn't know where to start. "I'm so sorry."

"Chelsea?" Worry poured through the phone. "Is that you?"

Her eyes squeezed shut, and she nodded. "I didn't know."

"Know what? Are you okay?" her mother asked, then muttered, "I always knew that job would get you hurt one day."

There was no other way to ask what she needed to know, and she blurted out, "Did you have a baby before me?"

Her mother gasped then scolded her, "Young lady—"

Chelsea sniffled. "I met her today."

The silence on the phone line was a powerful answer, then her mother whispered, "You can't understand. You—" Another painfully long pause. "I couldn't bring a baby into the hell I lived in."

Chelsea didn't know what to say.

"She went to a good place. A good home." The only emotion that Chelsea had ever heard from her mother cracked. "I was—I—"

"You were just a child," Chelsea offered.

"Is she..."

Her mother didn't finish the question, and Chelsea wasn't sure where her thoughts were going. *All right? Alive? A victim? A criminal? Dead?*

Finally, Chelsea promised, "She's going to be all right."

Zee Zee would likely go to prison or maybe a psych facility, but she'd get her mother's attention.

No one could erase the past, but maybe this was the start of a healing process. "Mom?"

After a painfully long wait, her mother whispered, "Yes?"

Chelsea wanted to gather her mom into a hug, even if she couldn't even remember them embracing before. "I want you to know that I—" *Understand? Appreciate? Forgive?* Her heart trembled. "I—"

"I love you, Chelsea. Even if I didn't tell you."

She sobbed, unable to have needed those words any more. "I love you too."

Chelsea wrapped up the phone call with a promise to explain more later. She mustered enough strength to hang up the phone when the curtain pulled back and a woman's concern reached her ears.

"Careful." She extended her hand. "Pleasure to meet you. I'm Dr. Nguyen."

Chelsea scooted back onto her hospital bed, and they shook. "Nice to meet you."

The doctor's pleasant demeanor showed through as she did a quick once over. "I was told you'd spring back up."

Chelsea racked her brain to recall meeting other doctors and nurses earlier, but her memory was hazy. "You weren't here before?"

"No." Dr. Nguyen took a tablet from her white medical coat pocket. "Dr. Due initially assessed you, and Dr. Little from plastic surgery stitched you up. Now you have me."

She raised her eyebrows at her list of doctors. "Oh. Wow."

Dr. Nguyen nodded. "You came in at shift change. Always a bit of a shuffle." She took out her light and had Chelsea follow her finger then ran through a battery of quick tests. "There is a raised concern about infection with human bite marks, but given the day you've had, I'd say that you did well. The news says your quite the hero."

She blushed. "Oh, I, uh…"

"Forget I mentioned it." Dr. Nguyen returned her tablet to her pocket. "Do you have any questions?"

About a thousand, but until that point, none had to do with the pain that dully throbbed in her neck and at the back of her skull. She shifted on the uncomfortable hospital bed. "Are you discharging me?"

"There's no reason to keep you." Dr. Nguyen nodded. "The nurse will come by with your paperwork. How to clean the wound, how often to change the bandage. Other than that, we did a workup, and you are completely healthy. Just make a follow up appointment with your regular doctor immediately. Okay?"

Chelsea could recall learning once how a dog bite was cleaner than a human bite. "I don't need antibiotics?"

"In situations like yours, we prefer to wait out the healing process. If there's a sign of infection, then there are some antibiotics that would be appropriate. But your doctor would know what works best for you."

Who knew neck wounds had their own set of rules?

She also wanted to address her pain. But Chelsea hesitated to ask for pills. Maybe they had read a report from Dr. Casper that said she might have an addiction. Dr. Nguyen might not want to give her a prescription.

Still, the wound was literally a pain in the neck. She pointed at her bandage. "What's the best way to dull this?"

Her doctor smiled. "Great question. You can alternate cold compresses for swelling with a heating pad set to low. The warmth helps improve blood flow."

"That's it?"

"Unless you're fairly high on the pain scale, we don't suggestion pregnant women take pain relievers. But like I said, check in with your regular doctor, and—"

"*What?*"

Dr. Nguyen paused. Her head angled slightly, and she quickly assessed Chelsea's reaction. "You weren't aware that you're pregnant?"

Chelsea grabbed the rails on the side of her bed. "*No.*"

CHAPTER FORTY-NINE

CHELSEA AND DR. Nguyen volleyed questions back and forth until they'd landed on a source of the miscommunication. Her discharging doctor had assumed any are-you-pregnant conversations happened before shift change with the previous doctor.

They had not. At least, not that she could remember.

Then Chelsea assured everyone, even the nurse redrawing her blood and asking her to pee in a cup, that it was impossible she could be pregnant. She had already had a once-in-a-lifetime situation happen earlier that day when she learned of a sister during a bomb scare.

Two absurd circumstances clustered so close together had to be categorically, metaphysically, and statistically impossible.

The nurse bounced in and handed the report to Dr. Nguyen, whom Chelsea hadn't let leave her side, at least for the first test. Apparently, the other took more than two minutes to run.

"You're pregnant." Dr. Nguyen went on to explain hCGs and the process of dating conception, but Chelsea couldn't listen or see straight. "Are you okay?"

Am I okay? Am I *okay?* Forget the bomb scare and the vampire attack—*she was pregnant.*

"Must be," the nurse said. "Look at the smile on her face."

Chelsea touched her cheeks and her lips. That was, indeed, what had to be a painfully huge smile. Aside from the shock and having to tell Liam, she realized that the news made her very, *very* happy. Even if it made no sense.

★ ★ ★

"WOMEN'S CARE FAMILY practice. Can I help you?"

After calling Liam a hundred times in a row, Chelsea could've kissed her ob-gyn's receptionist for answering the phone. "Hi. I need to speak to my doctor. Dr. Doyle, please."

"I can take a message and have—"

"I *need* to speak with Dr. Doyle. It's an emergency." Maybe that was a little dramatic, but given the day she'd had, she was allowed as much theatrics as she wanted. Besides, Chelsea didn't have her cell phone. She could only make phone calls on the hospital line, which meant no return calls. "*Please.*"

"Ma'am, if it's an emergency, you should call 911 and go to the hospital."

"I am *at* the hospital."

"I can put you through to her nurse."

For all the love of cheese doodles. Chelsea took a deep breath. "Sure. Her nurse would be fine."

"Name?"

"Chelsea Kilpatrick—"

"Oh. Okay." The receptionist sounded as though her name came with a warning label. "One moment, please."

The hold music played with tips for women's health—limit caffeine and alcohol.

Take a prenatal vitamin with iron and folic acid. Eat fiber. Avoid foods with high levels of mercury.

Anxiety needled her. A sudden urge to take notes made her twitchy. *How was I supposed to know about mercury if it hadn't been for the hold music? Where's the pregnancy rule book? Could someone give her a Cliff's Notes of dos and don'ts?* Blood loss and human neck bites were sure to be high on the bad list.

What else didn't she know? How do pregnant people act? She couldn't recall spending much time with anyone nurturing another person inside their body. A cold sweat formed at the base of her hairline.

The hold music prattled on. Try whole-wheat toast, dry cereal, or a thin slice of ginger in hot decaf tea to combat morning sickness.

Morning sickness? The times that she thought Mac and Calhoun made her nauseous, she'd had *morning sickness.*

"Chelsea?" A new voice interrupted Chelsea's shock. "You are a hard woman to get ahold of."

"Dr. Doyle?" Chelsea managed. Her thoughts were a roller coaster of how she got pregnant and how to be pregnant. She needed books and blogs. A tutorial. Something.

"Our office has been trying to reach you—"

"I'm pregnant!"

"Chelsea..." There wasn't surprise in the doctor's voice. "You didn't receive our phone calls? The letters?"

Visions of unopened junk mail danced in her head, and if they'd called from a number she didn't know, it hadn't been answered.

"No." She bit her lip. "Maybe. I'm not sure."

Dr. Doyle didn't seem to know what to say. They both knew her shots meant that Chelsea'd had no intention of becoming pregnant. The wait stretched until her doctor repeated, "You're pregnant."

"That's what the tests say—I'm at the hospital."

"Are you okay?"

"It wasn't related. An... accident at work." That was as good of a description as she could come up with on the fly.

"The pharmaceutical company that manufactured your birth control shot issued a recall."

As if the blood and pee tests weren't enough of a confirmation, now she had a reason for how it had happened. "I need an appointment with you."

"Of course," Dr. Doyle said. "We will go through your options—"

"*Options?*" Her thoughts rushed. The hold music tips had been clear. There was no room for error. There were rules. A playbook, perhaps. She was a planner, and planners needed material, task lists, goals—then *options* hit Chelsea like the moment she'd heard *pregnant.*

"I don't need options." Dread interrupted her chaotic tumble of bliss. Would Liam want *options*? The unexpected had taken his girlfriend away, and then more than a year later, the unexpected was about to jerk him to another, different reality.

Until the farmer's market, Chelsea hadn't considered a future outside herself. She closed her eyes and wanted to wish. *But what for? That this hadn't happened?* It had. Chelsea needed to have faith—in herself, in her love for Liam, and in what she hoped for in the future.

Whatever the future had in store, she would survive. That conviction had pulled her through a critical childhood, Julia's death, and it would help her with an unexpected pregnancy.

Her faith didn't beg the future for everything to be okay. It was knowing she'd be okay with what the future gave.

CHAPTER FIFTY

THE HOSPITAL OFFERED Chelsea ill-fitting clothes to wear home. Only then did she realize that her blood-covered clothes were in an evidence bag.

Getting home would be complicated. She had no cell phone to order an Uber, couldn't get a hold of Liam, and wasn't ready to face Linda or Frank.

Chelsea rolled her discharge papers into a tube and wondered if the hospital had a shuttle or could spot her bus change.

"Ma'am?" A man knocked on the other side of her curtain partition as though it were a door.

Everyone else who worked there breezed in and out while announcing themselves, so she guessed he wasn't a hospital employee. "Come in."

The uniformed deputy offered a quick introduction, giving his title formally along with his last name, Odili, and his orders to transport her home when discharged. She knew his type—strict, ordered, and focused—and she could've jumped into his arms and cried.

"Ma'am?" Concern sounded in Odili's voice, but he stood stoic at the sight of her eyes filling with tears. "Are you ready?"

More than she'd ever been.

The drive home was short. Odili offered to walk her in, but she thanked him for the escort, explaining that wasn't necessary.

She floated up the stairs to her condo while reviewing the half-dozen ways she'd thought to explain the baby to Liam.

Chelsea let herself inside her unlocked front door. She'd expected to take less than twenty minutes to run over to the farmer's market for fresh fruit. Several hours later, she had a half-sister, a neck wound, her job back, and a pregnancy. Life moved fast when she was busy making plans.

Her stomach growled, and on the way to the kitchen, she grabbed her waiting cell phone from the counter. A text from Liam waited at the bottom of her notifications from earlier that day.

Unexpected meeting. I never know how long these will last. Call you when I can.

Sweet. But it was the shaky-heart emoji that he signed off with that made *her* heart squeeze.

She reached for a banana and—the hairs at the back of her neck stood on end. She could sense the silent shadow of another person closing in. Without time to drop the banana or the phone, Chelsea jabbed her elbows back and smacked into hard flesh.

A hand wrapped over her nose and mouth. Her angle didn't allow her to kick back for a groin shot. She stomped, hoping for the arches of a foot, but her casual sneakers didn't matter against hard leather boots.

Light-headed, she fought for oxygen. Fighting burned away the last of her breaths, and her lungs felt as if they were on fire.

She stopped thrashing, not to give up—*never* to give up—but to corral the last of her energy.

The hands over her face loosened but didn't let go. Chelsea threw herself back, cracking her skull to his jaw.

His hand dropped. Dizzy, she gulped air and reached onto the counter, searching for a knife, a weapon, anything—her blender.

Chelsea grabbed the handle and twisted, swinging the thick glass carafe with upward momentum and struck the man across his cheek.

He staggered back, hands cupping a bloody nose. Hope exploded, and Chelsea tore out of her kitchen.

An older man blocked the way, pointing an HK 45mm handgun equipped with a silencer.

She jerked back, then her kitchen attacker yanked her arms into his pinching grip.

"Chelsea Kilpatrick?" The older man kept the gun trained on her. His callous tone was unnervingly low-key.

Her training roared to mind. *Be human.* That was the lesson taught above and beyond all else if taken hostage—*do nothing to incite greater animosity, contempt, or aggravation until escape or rescue became a possibility.*

"Yes," she admitted.

Ruthless spite curled on his lips, and he nodded to the man behind her to step away.

"Don't shoot me!" Adrenaline rushed. She couldn't run, couldn't fight. She had nothing—except a hope for compassion. "I'm pregnant."

His eyebrows bit. The finger on the trigger loosened. "Will you have a son or a daughter?"

"I'm not sure yet," she admitted then looked down. Her hands were crossed over her stomach as though she could protect the baby from a bullet.

He lowered his weapon. "When you lose a child, you lose the fear of dying."

Tears slipped free. "Have you lost a child?"

The question seemed to startle him, but only for a second, and he holstered the HK. "Yes."

She trembled. "I'm so sorry."

He moved closer until she could feel his breath on her face. "Do you know why you lose the fear of dying?"

Chelsea pressed her lips together and shook her head. "No."

"Because instead, you fear living the rest of your life, knowing you've outlived your child." He nodded curtly to the other man. "Change of plans. Take her with us."

CHAPTER FIFTY-ONE

THE OUTER AND inner doors opened outside Liam's glass holding cell. He pulled his head off the table and wasn't sure how much time had passed since Sorenson, Westin, and Black walked out. Their expressions were tight and cold, shades far beyond how they left.

Liam's gut tightened. Bad news was coming.

Sorenson made a point of settling herself before she looked Liam's way, and both Westin and Black noticed. Their locked gazes bored into her like missiles on target.

Westin laid a heavy-handed fist on the table, and it was enough that the senator gave Liam her attention.

"Our information was flawed from the start," she said.

"Samantha." Westin worked his jaw from side to side. "So help me God. Tell him everything he needs to know."

The corners of Sorenson's lips tensed.

Liam didn't care about their political battle. "What was the alarm for? Chelsea? Linda and Frank?"

Sorenson faltered, and for that half a heartbeat, Liam needed to scream. Westin lifted his chin at the man across the table.

"Chelsea was abducted," Black said.

Liam's blood went cold. His mind spun. Pham utilized explosions with the rare exception of a shooting and one abduction that no one would speak about. "Pham?"

Westin nodded and cracked his knuckles. "We didn't expect that."

"It's happened before, right? Who?"

"The senator's adult daughter."

Liam's attention swung to Sorenson. She remained unmoved.

Black cleared his throat. "Pham discovered that Sorenson was the reason his negotiations to return his daughter's body failed."

Liam raged. "All of this? This, this… goddamn shit show is your fault?"

Her jaw stiffened, but she remained silent.

Liam's throat ached. "What happened to her?"

"Nothing yet," Sorenson finally said. "Mr. Black believes Pham plans to keep her alive until the last loved one of your team has been killed."

"It's been…" He couldn't wrap his mind around how this had grown.

"Years," Sorenson said. "And I'm ready to bring her home."

"We think there's a chance Pham has dragged the attacks out because he'd found a sense of purpose. Maybe a sick kind of enjoyment," Black explained.

Liam couldn't process the situation. "*Of what?*"

"Stringing Samantha along," Westin said.

"And that's why there was so much time between the attacks? Between Julia and waiting for something to happen to Linda and Frank?"

"Perhaps," Sorenson said. "If Linda and Frank perish, his game is over. My daughter is next. But you gave him another opportunity with Chelsea."

"We didn't expect him to abduct anyone else," Black said. "It doesn't make sense."

"None of this makes sense." Except that he was also to blame for anything that happened to Chelsea. Liam clenched his teeth. "You couldn't come up with a better plan than to bait Pham with civilian lives?"

"Honestly, no," Sorenson offered. "It took us too long to realize what he was doing."

Years… Liam turned to Westin. "What are we going to do?"

"*We* are going to do nothing," Sorenson answered. "This works out best for everyone if we can anticipate Pham's next move. That has to be similar to what happened before."

Before—? With Julia. He might get sick.

"He'll want you there. When he makes his move, we can intercept."

Liam couldn't take her self-serving orders anymore. "No dice. We wait until he takes me to Chelsea."

Sorenson shook her head. “I want him first. *He’s mine.*”

“Go home,” Westin said plainly. “Pham knows how to disappear, and Samantha is correct that the fastest way to locate Pham is to catch him in the act.”

“No—”

“We don’t think he will hurt Chelsea unless you’re there to watch.”

“That’s a huge gamble.” Liam turned to Black. The man had proved himself well versed with numbers and the truth when asked. “You’re certain you know what Pham will do?”

“There’s no such thing as absolute certainty. Quantifying the probability—”

“Is this the best course of action?” Liam asked.

“Listen to the boss man,” Black offered. “That’s what I’d do.”

Again, Liam studied Black then Westin. *Boss man.* “All right then. I’ll follow your orders.”

CHAPTER FIFTY-TWO

THE SHORT DRIVE felt as though it lasted hours. Chelsea had made a last-ditch effort to scream for attention. Maybe someone would call the cops. Maybe Odili hadn't gone far.

But they traveled without incident. The older man had joined her in the back seat, where his muscle man had tied her feet and hands in place. She wished they had locked her in the trunk. At least then, she would have had the chance to kick out the taillights. What she wouldn't give to be pulled over.

When they finally stopped, the back door of the dark SUV opened, and the Muscle Man untied her feet.

"Thanks." Chelsea stepped out of the vehicle and into a large warehouse. The most delicious smell wafted in the air. Her stomach had growled during their journey, and she wasn't sure how she remained upright, given the enormity of the day while taking in next to zero calories.

Muscle Man unfastened her wrists, and not expecting that, Chelsea wanted to make a list of escape possibilities—until the third man appeared and extended her a bag.

"Take it," the older man in charge said. "It's food."

Her mouth watered, and unsure why they would feed her, she carefully took what was offered and peeked inside. The heavenly scent of roasted chicken floated out.

"Thank you," she volunteered then followed the three men and tried to understand their conversation. They led the way across a large warehouse hall, and she couldn't figure out what language they were speaking.

They didn't seem concerned if she heard them or if she followed. They continued without looking back.

Maybe the exits were locked, but more likely they knew she wouldn't run off without eating her meal. They were right. Hunger and strength went hand in hand, and the day had taken everything out of her.

After a few turns, they ambled down an ante-hall and came to a large cage. Her nerves went on high alert.

The walls were constructed with what looked like thick chicken wire, and Muscle Man unlocked a door, directing Chelsea inside.

He was courteous enough, except for the part when he locked her inside the cage. She clung to her bag of food, scared, and turned. That's when she spied the other woman on the far side of the cell.

She sat at a table, surrounded by piles of books and magazines, and she appeared genuinely surprised to have an interruption. The woman didn't acknowledge the men who'd walked by, and their light conversation drifted away as they continued down the hall.

"Hi." The woman stood up, her expression curious.

"Hey." Chelsea didn't know what to make of her. "Are you..." *Another prisoner? A guard?*

"Bored out of my mind," she volunteered. "Soon you will be too."

All-righty. Not what she'd expected to hear. Chelsea made her way to the table.

The woman extended her hand. "I'm Angela."

"Chelsea." Light-headed from hunger, she shook Angela's hand and wondered if starvation and pregnancy could make her hallucinate enough to invent an imaginary friend.

Angela sat and cleared a spot on the table in front of another chair for Chelsea to have her meal.

"I'm not sure what's going on," Chelsea admitted then sat at Angela's urging. She took the food from the bag. "Would you like some?"

"No. I ate earlier tonight."

A well-fed captive?

"But the chicken from that place is amazing," Angela continued.

Really, Chelsea couldn't have been more confused, but she also couldn't contain how hungry she was and dug in.

"Whose kid are you?" Angela asked as Chelsea shoved a mouthful of mashed potatoes and gravy into her mouth.

The full mouth gave her time to think. In the last five minutes, enemies hadn't seemed like enemies, and she didn't know if Angela was trustworthy. "What do you mean?"

Angela shrugged. "I don't know. I'm here because of my mother."

"Who's your mother?"

"Samantha Sorenson."

Chelsea froze. *Senator Sorenson.* Liam's untrustworthy source. It couldn't have been coincidence that Liam had mentioned her and now Chelsea was caged with her daughter. But… Angela flipped through the pages of a magazine as if she wasn't worried.

"How long have you been here?"

"No idea. A few years?"

Chelsea lost her appetite.

But Angela shrugged, then added, "Don't try to count the months, or you'll go batty. Just watch the meals. That's how you know it's day and night."

Chelsea stared blankly.

"You look like you need to eat," Angela prompted.

She did. Even if she'd lost the urge. "Right."

For the next few minutes, Chelsea ate and Angela paged through a magazine. The fog lifted from her mind with every bite, and finally, she asked, "You don't seem… concerned. Or scared."

"I was, but that can only last for so long. Now?" Angela shrugged. "Great food. Good books. I'm not scared. I'm bored."

"They have us for a reason—"

"Of course they do. You can't be *Senator Sorenson's* daughter and make it through life without realizing your mother is ruthless and power-hungry." She leaned over a stack of books and eyed a small container of green goo that had turned Chelsea's stomach. "The creamed spinach is really good."

Chelsea shoved it Angela's way. "They have us here for a reason," she repeated.

"And sometime after the first month or year, I realized that no one was coming to get me. It didn't serve me to be in an anxious fit every day of my life."

"That seems very Zen, considering."

Angela reached into a drawer and withdrew a plastic spork. "Out of my control, and who knows when it's all over." Then she dug into the creamed spinach. "But your arrival is different. Maybe I should be concerned." She stopped mid-mouthful. "Oh, one other thing."

Chelsea arched an eyebrow as she chewed the chicken. "Hm?"

"The old man? I call him Gramps to myself."

She swallowed then asked, "What about him?"

"He likes to come in sometimes and ask questions like I'm his kid." She let the spork hang in her hand. "It'd be creepy if he didn't seem so sad."

CHAPTER FIFTY-THREE

AS WITH EVERY meeting that Liam had with Sorenson at her black site, it ended with DHS agents dropping him off at his Explorer. This time Black did the honors.

He handed over Liam's wallet, keys, and phone. "Good luck, ace. I'm rooting for the both of you."

"Yeah. Thanks." If Liam never had a reason to see any of them again, he'd celebrate.

He jumped into his Explorer and scrolled through the slew of notifications on his cell. The phone calls came from unknown phone numbers, so he was unable to dial back. Instead, he called Chelsea—hoping against hope that everything they'd discussed had been wrong.

His heart ached when her voicemail picked up. The disappointment after that half second of certainty that she would answer sliced him into pieces. Liam called Chance then Hagan. Neither answered. "Fucking hell."

He called Linda.

"Hello?" she answered, and Liam could've jumped for the moon.

"Hey, Linda." He tried to calm his voice. His dry throat and anxiety didn't help. "I'll explain everything later, but please listen to me."

"Oh. Of course." Though hesitation was evident in her words.

"Grab Frank and leave. Don't tell me where. Don't call for reservations. No bags. No Google. Nothing. Just go. Turn your phones off—"

"Liam?"

"Turn your phones off," he repeated. "Leave with only cash, and you have to clean the dollar bills." Frank's career in banking meant he would know what Liam wanted them to do: exchange their currency in cash transactions that couldn't be traced. "Go now."

"Liam," she tried again, more softly. "What's going on? If this is about the other night—"

"You're not safe, and I'm going to kill the motherfucker who took Julia."

That was all the conversation that had to be said. Rattled, Linda hung up quickly after promising to do as he asked.

Why didn't I make them leave before? Why didn't I tell them about the danger? Everything changed when he realized how Sorenson was invested. Liam had fallen for her bullshit song and dance about coaxing out Pham when all he'd had to do was stand in the middle of a parking lot and scream that there was no one left to hurt. *Come and get me.*

And hell, even up to the last moment, he'd thought Westin and Black could be trusted. He didn't know their roles. He had no idea where their loyalties lay. Hell if he didn't trust anyone now. They left him without resources or intelligence. He didn't know where to start.

"Do nothing," Liam muttered and bared his middle fingers against his windshield in case Sorenson was watching him like a hawk. "Not a chance."

Then turned over the engine. *Pham will find me?* Yeah, well, he'd find Pham too.

Even if he didn't know how.

Liam shifted the Explorer into drive and drove toward Chelsea's condo. That was where he would've gone if he hadn't known about the abduction. It seemed like the best place to start.

He floored the vehicle onto the expressway and bobbed through traffic until he hit the left lane, flying. Anger and worry fueled his speed. Liam would get back what was his. Chelsea *and* revenge for Julia. Pham would die. He'd help Sorenson's daughter too.

And as for the senator who chose saving a terrorist before her daughter, she could kiss Liam's ass if she thought it mattered that he handed over Pham alive.

Traffic on the expressway was light. Liam threaded through the lanes and suddenly heard sirens. He checked his rearview mirror and saw flashing lights. "You gotta be kidding me."

Adrenaline surged. *Could I outrun them?* Liam gripped the steering wheel as if he were holding on to the last thread of his sanity. The police sirens pulsed a secondary pull-the-fuck-over warning.

What the hell am I thinking? Liam slapped on his turn signal and jerked onto the shoulder.

The cruiser pulled up close to his rear bumper—too close. It made Liam apprehensive, and despite the dark, he could see that two cops were getting out.

Damn it to hell. He should've pulled over that very first second.

Liam rolled his window down. The officer's dark uniform blended in with the night, but he froze, surprised by who he saw.

Chance leaned in close. "Unlock your doors. Pop the back open." He didn't act as though he'd seen Liam a day before in his life. "And to make this look right, hand over your license and registration."

Liam didn't move. "What are you doing?"

"Do it," Chance said. "Locks and paperwork."

Confused, Liam pressed the hatchback release button and unlocked the doors. The second *officer* moved into Liam's peripheral vision as he turned for his license and registration. When he handed them to Chance, Liam checked his rearview mirror. *Is that… Hagan?*

"Nothing to worry about. Keep lookin' the part." Chance tapped the ID against the side of the door and ambled to the police cruiser.

Liam turned. "Hagan?"

Hagan was *searching* his vehicle and didn't acknowledge that Liam had even spoken until he said, "Eyes up front," then shut the doors and trunk.

Officer Chance returned to the driver-side window and handed over the license, registration, and a ticket.

"What the fuck is going on?" Liam demanded.

Chance gave him that look, the one Liam always saw before shit hit the fan and bullets flew. "Take care of yourself, ace."

The two *cops* ambled back into the night. Seconds later, their cruiser pulled away. He didn't get it. What was he missing? Liam rubbed his temple. Chance's goodbye, on top of this farce, needled under Liam's skin. He unfolded the ticket. The form was blank, but the scrawled message was clear.

We are a go. Check your gear.

Then the thing he couldn't place slammed to mind. *Ace.* Had Chance ever called him that? Never.

His recall hit.

Take care of yourself, ace.
Good luck, ace.
Bravo, ace.

Chance. Black. Westin.

Adrenaline punched in Liam's chest. He slapped on the overhead lights and turned to his back seat. A bug-out bag complete with a Beretta M9 pistol, a Benelli M4 shotgun, and an M4A1 carbine rifle with a night scope had been wedged on the floor. All were the things necessary for a search-and-kill mission.

He raced to check the trunk and found a Kevlar vest, a nylon harness, and small explosive charges for locked-door entries. A pencil-length black box and a note card rested on top. He picked up the blank card and flipped it over.

Sorenson's eyes are only scrambled for five minutes. Dress and drive.

Liam searched the dark sky as highway traffic blasted a swirl of frozen, polluted wind. In the distance, he made out what might've been a drone—or maybe he had lost his mind. He grabbed what he needed, hauled ass for the driver's seat then pulled on the Kevlar and checked the carbine and shotgun for loads in the chambers. He strapped the Beretta pistol to his ankle and secured a knife to his side.

The small box rested in his lap, and he opened it with one hand and glanced down—an ear bud and a comms piece. Liam pulled the equipment free and positioned them but didn't turn it on yet.

Has it been less than five minutes? Fingers crossed. He slammed the gear-shift into drive. His wheels spun gravel, spitting from beneath them, and he merged onto the highway the moment he knew the Explorer could make speed.

Flying, he said a prayer that everything would make sense when he flipped the power on. Then he clicked the tiny switch to turn on his comms.

Dead air clicked over, then he heard the electric buzz of the comm feed in his ear—

"Echo One, this is Zulu Actual," a man interrupted the white noise.

They were the same radio identifiers he'd used while serving in army recon. Liam knew that whoever was on the other end was a friendly.

"Try your mic," the man added.

"Black?" Liam muttered.

"Affirmative, Echo One. This is Zulu Actual. I read you five by five."

Five by five...They heard him loud and clear. Liam swore under his breath. "Who the hell *are* you... *Zulu Actual*?"

"Depends on the day of the week," Black said.

"There's our guy," another man said.

"Chance?"

Chance chuckled. "You looked like you'd seen a ghost."

If Liam understood what was happening, he'd have something to say, but the questions piling upon questions left him stupefied—and hopeful. Suddenly, he dared to wonder if a plan existed, even if he was the last to know. "None of this makes sense."

"I'll tell you what does," another man with a deep voice said. That was the same surly grumble he'd heard in the meetings with Sorenson. That had to be Westin.

"What?" Liam asked.

"There are lines that cannot be crossed. Civilian collateral damage for political gain? Not something we could stand by and watch," Westin said.

"You watched when I dealt with the Nymans," Liam accused.

"You have no idea how much backup you had, brother." Westin grumbled as if offended he'd been questioned. "You duct taped your team together, but we came in with reinforcements."

"And then some," Chance muttered.

"No one could get near the Nymans' house without all hell letting loose," Westin continued. "No matter what Sorenson thought she was doing. That's why we hauled your ass in earlier today."

"You knew Chelsea would be abducted?"

"No but learning about Chelsea changed our play. It would've been fine, but Pham was too close."

"Wherever the hell he's been hiding," Black muttered, frustrated.

Why hadn't Liam mentioned Chelsea before? He was ass over boots in love with the woman, and she didn't even know.

The possibility for regret turned his stomach—but Liam paused. "Hang on." Apprehension stoked his paranoia. "How'd *you* know?"

"You're welcome," Chance answered for Westin and Black.

"What does *that* mean?"

"When it took you two an hour to drive five minutes?" Chance snickered. "I realized Boss Man needed to know about your girl."

The bagel shop? Then Liam paused. *Did Chance just say* Boss Man*?* Liam would pull together the connection between Chance and Westin later, and for the moment, he'd accept what they said because he trusted Chance. "What's the plan?"

He needed to know if they were still following Sorenson's Pham-will-come-to-you strategy. It was ridiculous. *An impossible-to-catch terrorist simply waiting outside Chelsea's condo?* He didn't like those odds.

"Same plan. Pham will come to you," Westin said.

"That's it? That's all you've got?" Liam's grip on the steering wheel tightened.

"Buy us time to juggle Sorenson, and stay live long enough for us to track your location. The rest will be a piece of cake."

CHAPTER FIFTY-FOUR

LIAM EXITED THE highway and drove down the familiar streets toward Chelsea's condo. Maybe he and Westin had extremely different definitions of a cake walk job.

"You'll just have to trust my process," Westin added as though able to read Liam's mind.

He still didn't understand who or what the man was. But Liam trusted Chance, and Chance trusted *Boss Man.*

He grumbled. "Guess I'll trust your process…" *Up to a point.* The closer Liam came to Chelsea's condo, the greater his bloodthirst for Pham raged.

"Keep the end in sight and your focus clear," Westin said. "Pham needs to be taken alive in addition to the rescue."

Liam chewed the inside of his mouth to keep from announcing what he saw clearly. He'd loved and lost. Then he loved again. He'd done so without fault or reservation, without any expectation, because life wasn't linear, and love was never black and white.

He could grieve. He could love. He could rage and want revenge. Liam could do all of those and also kill Tran Pham.

But he didn't know how he was supposed to take Pham alive and rescue two women alone?

Then again, he hadn't been alone this entire time, and tonight, an apparent team stood by, even if only in his ear.

"Do you read me?" Westin requested.

Liam hesitated, uncertain of his backup and not ready to commit to Pham's live capture. But Chelsea and Sorenson's daughter were on the line. He'd figure out how to make everything happen. "Roger that. I have the end in sight."

The entrance to Chelsea's complex loomed. An oncoming SUV cut in front of Liam. He slammed on his brakes. "Shit!"

"Echo One, we're early, but we're a go," Black said.

Liam checked his rearview mirror. Another SUV had boxed him in. A telephone pole and a bike rack blocked the sidewalk on the passenger side, and a third SUV screeched to a stop on the driver's side.

Doors opened, and his enemy appeared. Two, four… Liam counted how many had him surrounded. His adrenaline pumped. Whatever the final count was, it was one against a lot.

Liam reached for the shotgun as a muffled shot fired toward him. The nearest street lamp exploded. Sparks floated, then the dark night became black.

Thump. Thump. His tires exploded under fire. Their air hissed out. *Thump. Thump.* He'd lost his transportation.

"Dammit!" Liam shouted. "A little warning would've been nice, Zulu Actual."

"Even without lights, Sorenson's gonna see this," Black said.

Who cares about Sorenson?

"Do something about it," Westin ordered Black, apparently caring. "Brosnan, you know everything you need. Army recon soldiers are at their best when fighting against an enemy that thinks they have them captured."

He swiveled to check each side. Armed men were closing in on him.

"You know what to do," Westin confirmed. "Now destroy the comms and start this mission, soldier."

Shit. He yanked the mic from his collar and pulled the earpiece. The door of the SUV next to him opened.

Liam readied for his role as a rogue mercenary without any comms or support. He laid the two pieces on the center console and smashed his elbow down.

The other man closed the distance to his door, and Liam swiped the broken pieces aside.

"Here goes nothing." He gripped the carbine and stepped out, meeting the man straight on.

The man from the Metro. Liam knew the hatred in his eyes and could feel the chill of Pham's dead soul. He had a split-second realization that if his life hadn't continued, he'd be a mirror image of the man standing across from him.

The distant *womp, womp* of a low-flying chopper came within earshot. His senses fired. Sorenson knew—and he understood Black's concern. The senator would take Pham before a rescue, and a captured Pham wouldn't give up Chelsea's location to spite them.

They didn't have long. Both men needed to make a move.

"You stole my daughter," Pham accused.

He knew if he gave a single lie, he would never see Chelsea again. "In war."

"Your wars are cowardly."

"In my position, our wars are not mine to judge."

"*Al-jihad fi sabil Allah*—for I strive to walk in the path of God."

"I bet your God hates when you use him as an excuse."

Pham growled. Liam could make out the helicopter drawing near. The interior light of his Explorer flicked on as he heard the sound of his hatch door opening. Dammit, they'd get their hands on his munitions.

One of the men pulled a large case from the trunk and opened it. The other men exchanged rapid-fire shouts. Even Pham let them steal his attention, and Liam turned. A rocket-propelled grenade launcher? What the fuck did he have in there?

The men gestured to the incoming chopper and hastened to put it together.

Liam's stomach dropped. "No!"

Pham and his men jerked their weapons at him. Liam thought about the helicopter and the men and women who would be aboard, carrying out a crazy mission at the behest of a power-hungry politician.

Liam gaged a shootout. They'd kill him if he dove when the launcher fired, but surrounded, they might just kill each other too.

That was the only thing he could do—stand, ready to sacrifice his life for the chopper, ready to pray that a bullet would slice through Tran Pham.

He edged forward. Sweat dampened his chest and back. His mind raced for Chelsea and wept for the chopper.

Foreign words demanded he remain in place. Barrels were pointed at him and jammed in his face. The circle tightened.

One of the men hoisted the RPG to his shoulder. He flipped on the optics and activated the laser targeting. A light glowed green, as though it had a lock on the chopper, but that didn't make sense. Liam racked his mind. He ran every piece of equipment like that he'd ever used. Nothing built like that RPG should've lit as though it were a guided system, ready to control.

The helicopter dove low and close enough that Liam could almost make out a team ready to drop in. He had a split second to decide if Zulu Actual had control over the RPG—and he stood down, believing that Black must.

The RPG fired. The blast shrieked. Its fire burned. The helo pulled upright. If Liam was wrong, escape would be futile.

Impact was imminent. His heart slammed. His pulse screamed.

Then, the red-and-yellow streak jerked. The trajectory arched and angled, and the grenade fired off-target, white hot as it climbed for the heavens.

He hadn't been wrong! Sorenson's chopper aborted their air assault. Pham and his men shouted in disbelief and anger. High above, the grenade blew like a firework in the moonless night sky.

That had to have been Black and Westin. No other possibility existed. They had armed him for every possible situation, controlled everything they could orchestrate, and guided that missile to safety.

The realization was short lived. Pham's men slammed Liam to the ground, disarmed him, then bound his hands and feet. He'd become a captive, and the plan was finally coming into focus.

Pham snapped orders, and men lifted Liam and placed him in the back seat of Pham's vehicle. The three SUVs slowly drove away as if the men hadn't shot up his Explorer and shot off an RPG.

CHAPTER FIFTY-FIVE

PHAM TURNED FROM the casual conversation with his driver to Liam. "You would be happy to know other than the initial interaction, your woman had been treated well."

Liam bit back his reaction. The asshole wanted him to hurt, not Chelsea. "I don't know who you're talking about."

The silence hung in the air until Pham broke it. "Do you know why we meet again?"

Liam's nostrils flared but he kept his rage contained.

"You're responsible for my daughter's death. Quy Long was an innocent casualty to your wars."

"Quy Long wasn't innocent," Liam snapped.

Pham opened his suit jacket, pulled out a thin black container, selected an icepick-like blade, and drove it into Liam's thigh.

He choked as his flesh ripped open, and Pham let the blade remain deep inside his muscle. Blood seeped out. But leaving the knife in place was good, considering. If Pham ripped the blade out, it would do more tissue damage and let him spurt like a geyser, all of which Pham likely knew.

The point was torture and revenge, the same things Liam had come to desire too. Sweat chilled his neck. He tried to control his breaths.

"Do not speak ill of my daughter."

The pain reached a zenith and plateaued. "Maybe you should've considered another line of work for your kid."

Pham snorted. "You continue to surprise me, Captain."

"You haven't seen anything yet." Though Liam didn't have a clue what to do next. The impaled spike wouldn't let him think. Maybe that was

Pham's plan.

They pulled under a bridge, and their SUV skidded to the side. The door flew open. Pham got out, and another man grabbed Liam. With his feet and hands bound, he couldn't do much.

Their SUV spit gravel as its tires spun and tore off. Liam lay on the ground, thigh bleeding, tremendous pain throbbing, while catching his breath.

Two men lifted him. He turned his head, hoping to see the women. But he only saw Pham.

They crossed traffic lanes, and another SUV waited. Pham stepped into the back seat, and Liam was hoisted in alongside. He cursed at the sharp blade then cursed at everyone he could.

A cell phone rang, and the driver answered. Liam couldn't understand the conversation, but it escalated from annoyance to surprise, then the cell phone was handed to Pham.

Liam couldn't understand Pham's conversation either, then Pham cut the discussion off with a cold-hearted "Good. Bring her."

Chelsea? He didn't know how to interpret the only words in English.

The driver eased them from the bridge and merged into traffic. They continued carefully until the vehicle pulled up to a decrepit warehouse, but with the night bathing the building in shadows, details were impossible to make out.

Maybe that was why they hadn't covered his eyes. Or maybe they had no intention of letting him go. Luck hadn't been on his side much that night, but he opted to hope for the first possibility.

Large garage doors opened. Dim light illuminated the cavernous insides, and the SUV drove in and parked.

Is Chelsea here? He couldn't see anything but empty space.

The driver exited and assisted Pham out. Then the man cut Liam's bindings and pulled out the blade.

"Son of a—" He snarled and contained his reaction—or tried to, at least.

With a quick wipe, the man cleaned the slender knife on a dark cloth and returned it to Pham then directed Liam to step out.

There was no telling what awaited. Liam rolled his wrists and moved his feet and regained some circulation as he exited the back seat. He wobbled. Pressure on his wounded leg multiplied, but he choked away the weakness. "Who's joining us?"

No answer.

Chelsea? But asking about her might be the worst thing to do. If Pham wanted to hurt him, then maybe he could convince Pham he couldn't be hurt again.

That might be a stretch. How much did Pham know? Shit, he was too close to the problem, and his personal feelings skewed what should've been tactical ones.

He needed to know more than he currently did. Liam limped closer. "Where are we going?"

"We're going to finish what you started long ago…" Sadistic enjoyment curved across Pham's face. "It's time to watch your loved one die. *Again.*"

CHAPTER FIFTY-SIX

CHELSEA JUMPED FROM her cot when the lock rattled. Angela didn't notice. The even keel of her breathing never changed as she continued to sleep.

The man who'd taken away the chicken-dinner leftovers entered their cage. His demeanor had hardened, and her gut instinct warned her trouble had arrived.

"Angela," Chelsea whispered then nudged her cot. "Wake up."

Angela was slow to rise, but when she did, her eyes widened. Despite how calm and boring she claimed the place to be, a middle-of-the-night visitor visibly alarmed her.

"What's—"

"Put your shoes on," the man ordered.

"Why?" Angela demanded.

He gave the same order again, and his cold demeanor didn't bode well. Chelsea put on her shoes, even as Angela tried to explain that nothing would happen. Nothing *ever* happened.

Sorenson's daughter had become the poster girl for Stockholm Syndrome, and Chelsea explained, "Things never stay the same."

Annoyed, Angela shoved on her shoes. "Can I tell you how thrilled I am to find out my roommate is such a positive presence."

What fluffy cotton-candy cloud did Angela float in on? "I'm not your roommate." Even if Chelsea had somehow managed to excuse the chicken wire, they were locked in a cage, their free will removed. "And this isn't a slumber party."

The man clapped, and Angela jumped. "Jeesh."

After everything Chelsea had survived in the last day, let alone the year and a half, she almost longed for Angela's foolish naivete. But falling into an innocent stupor to hide from reality wouldn't get them out of the warehouse.

They were directed out in a single-file line. Angela trudged and complained, while Chelsea tried to understand what was happening.

The bandage on her neck tugged on her skin with a tacky tightness as she surveyed the barren hall and high rafters. When the man took a phone call, and they paused, she repositioned a layer of tape.

Her neck was warm. The wound ached in a different way than earlier, and she worried it needed to be cleaned. *No*, actually, what she *needed* was to get the double-stacked-pancakes out of that place. Then she could worry about changing the bandages.

By now, Liam knew she was missing, and Chelsea would assume that help was on its way—though that wouldn't keep her for eyeing a possible escape route.

The phone call wrapped up, and they were directed into the open area where she'd first arrived and her hands and feet were untied. Plastic-wrapped pallets lined the walls. The high-reaching stacks created aisles in the cavernous room. A large black SUV was parked in an open space, a few hundred yards away, then another rolled to a stop behind it. Metal clattered, and the garage door slammed shut in the far corner.

Were they going somewhere else?

"This place has never been so busy," Angela said.

Voices echoed and bounced from the other side of the SUVs. Chelsea wasn't sure more people was a good thing.

The driver stepped out the second SUV and opened the back door. He pulled a bound person with a dark hood onto the floor.

"Come," their guard ordered with another clap.

Apprehension flooded her thoughts. The situation was escalating from Angela's long, uneventful stay to new, hood-wearing captives. Chelsea crossed her arms. Her clammy hands tucked into her armpits and her chin trembled as they were ushered closer to the SUVs.

Chelsea couldn't tear her eyes away—and the hood was yanked off the woman on the floor.

"Mom?" Angela stopped abruptly. Her hand clasped Chelsea's arm, and her voice shook. "That's my mother."

That wasn't good, and she hoped Angela was wrong.

Senator Sorenson brushed herself off, seemingly indignant, then turned toward them.

"Oh, God." Angela sprinted toward the senator. "Mom!"

Her sobs rang out when she hugged her mother, and there was no need to convince Angela anymore. This wasn't the slumber party she'd dreamed up after all.

Chelsea kept pace with the man who'd led them there. "The senator. The daughter. The pregnant lady. What on earth do you people want?"

Her escort ignored her question, and they rounded the hood of the SUV and ran into the older man who'd had the HK. He held out his arms as if he were greeting old friends. "The sacrificial lambs."

Chelsea shuddered then caught sight of the other men—"Liam!"

He limped forward, and she bolted toward him. Her guard didn't do a thing to hold her back.

But Liam stopped and froze like he barely knew her.

Stiffly, he offered her an awkward greeting. Concern darkened his eyes. Blood painted his light-colored pants. She didn't care why he didn't react and flung her arms around him.

Liam didn't embrace her in return.

"Liam?"

He pulled back and shifted, then his eyes dropped to her neck. "What'd they do to you?"

Chelsea touched her bandage. "Nothing. I mean—this was from earlier."

He inspected her neck without a word then coldly took another step back.

"What's wrong—"

"If this is who you have..." He tilted his head and cast a side glance her way. "You made a mistake."

Her hands wrapped over lower abdomen. "*What?*"

"I'm not so sure," the older man said.

Liam shrugged, not looking back her way. Unsure what was happening, Chelsea tried to keep a stiff upper lip.

"Believe what you want," Liam said to Pham. "Your intel is wrong." He gestured. "She's not going to bring me to my knees. Try again." Then he turned to her and offered a pacifying half-shrug. "No offense."

Chelsea's eyes darted between the men, and crushing humiliation reddened her cheeks. As her stomach knotted, she tried to make sense of his dismissive nonchalance and came up empty.

Liam would never speak to her like that. He wouldn't do that to *anyone*—but then she fit together pieces that she couldn't see or understand. They'd been called "sacrificial lambs" and the Nymans were in danger because Liam cared about them.

Finally, she understood what he was doing. Little sleep and a bad day were the perfect ingredients for her performance. "You *asshole.*"

She could've sworn Liam's eyebrow twitched when she cursed, and maybe *she* wouldn't, but if the job called for her to shout like a drunken sailor, then Chelsea would trot out whatever it took. Bad words and all.

"I'm the asshole?" He hooked a thumb toward the old man. "I didn't ask him to bring you here. I'm the one with my damn leg sliced open."

Like any woman scorned who'd been abducted to hurt her man, she didn't care. Or so she tried to act. "You think I care he *sliced your leg open*?"

"Enough," the old man called.

Chelsea glared and turned to Liam. "How about you explain '*try again*' like there's someone else?"

"Maybe there is," he said.

"*Enough.*"

She ignored the old man and stomped forward. "Maybe there is?" she mocked like a guest star on a Dr. Phil episode gone bad.

She stopped inches from his face. There, underneath the exhaustion and pain, she could see his emerald-green eyes sparkle for her, *then* she let him have it.

Chelsea screamed and shouted. He yelled and rolled his eyes. Between the faux accusations of clinginess and drunken hookups, they fought as if their lives depended on it. Because they did.

"Enough!" the old man continued to shout. "Enough."

Every eye in the warehouse seemed to burn into them.

Guards pulled them apart. Chelsea kicked and clawed for good measure. Finally, they settled her next to Angela and the senator, who clung together, keeping Liam several feet away.

Chelsea caught her breath as the old man clapped, slowly at first, and then as though he were truly entertained.

Their fight hadn't worked. Her stomach dropped.

The old man motioned for everyone to come close again, and he walked in a tight circle around them, trailed by a bodyguard.

"Closer," he said.

Liam and Chelsea were nudged to the center of the circle, and the old man placed a hand on each of their shoulders.

The bodyguard hovered close, maybe out of habit more than concern.

The old man focused on Chelsea. "I harbor no ill will toward you. It's Captain Brosnan that deserves to suffer."

Did Liam have a grand plan to kick off their escape? She wished he'd kick it off any time now since she hadn't come up with one.

The harsh silence stewed until the old man shook his head—then smiled. "There is one sure way to learn."

Liam's eyes narrowed. "Learn what?"

"What is the truth and what is a lie," he explained.

That didn't make sense—*oh no.* Her stomach dropped again.

"Would you like to tell him, or shall I?" the old man asked.

Chelsea pressed her lips together. Liam would react to news of her pregnancy, and their charade would go up in smoke. Then she would die.

Escape or rescue were their only options. But neither would happen before Liam learned she was pregnant.

Disinterest crossed Liam's expression, and the old man cleared his throat, waiting for an answer.

"Then I will—"

"No." She'd never let Liam find out their news from such an evil man.

Chelsea caught Liam's eye. The rest of the world faded away. He could make her believe it was just them. "I'm pregnant."

CHAPTER FIFTY-SEVEN

PREGNANT. THEIR GAME of wits and deception changed with one word. But Liam's attack plan suddenly became clear. It was as if the world around him paused, and he could map out the steps needed to disarm the room.

Then his mind snapped back, ready to throw a right hook at Pham and immediately disarm his right-hand man—an explosion detonated.

He was blown back. Reverb shook the building. Liam caught himself as another explosion hit.

He and Chelsea had given Zulu Actual time, and now explosions blasted on top of the roof. Smoke and fire rained, and he lunged for Pham. They rolled to the ground. Pham's bodyguard dove onto their pile.

He didn't know whose hands were whose. No one would shoot. Not with Pham in the tussle, and Liam caught the guard with a punch.

The break in the action let Liam pull back just as his peripheral caught the sight of people in tactical gear dropping in on rope lines.

Liam dug his shoulder into Pham, and his guard wrapped a hand around Liam's throat. They fumbled and rolled, then the bodyguard jerked, noticing the fast-moving tactical assault.

Gasping, Liam used the diversion and took the guard's weapon. He jammed the handgun into the soft flesh under Pham's jaw. The bodyguard rolled away, and Liam pulled Pham onto his feet.

"You killed Julia." Liam's blood raced hot. Vengeance tunneled his vision as he remembered the first moment he'd noticed the old man on the Metro.

Eyes bulging, lips snarling, Pham shouted for Liam to pull the trigger. Images of the subway's carpet, soaked with Julia's blood, burned behind

Liam's eyes.

Liam's name reverberated from miles away, but he couldn't break from the need for revenge. He was locked in a trance, tormented by the past and present, by Chelsea's face—her words—their pregnancy.

"Liam." Chelsea grasped his shoulders. "Stop!"

But he couldn't. She was pregnant! He caressed the trigger that would make him safe and sane again.

"Pull the trigger," Pham whispered.

His breath burned, and his teeth clenched. Rage tore him apart—and disgust. Liam shook, throat dry and body sweating. Chelsea was pregnant. *A baby*. Because of that, he couldn't commit murder.

Liam stepped back, his arm dropping down. From far away, he sensed the gun removed from his hands, and he squeezed his eyes shut.

The swish of tactical gear and a gentle touch pulled him back to reality. Chelsea stood in front of him. One hand rested on his cheek, worry coloring her expression.

"It's okay," she said. "Everything is okay."

His hands trembled. Regret and relief battled as he understood what he'd done—*nothing*.

"Liam, look at me."

Wasn't he?

"Liam." Chelsea took his hands in hers. "It's over."

It was. He shook free of vengeful spell that blinded his rational, and he inhaled as though he hadn't taken a breath in hours—then pulled Chelsea to his chest.

She cried in relief and clung like that first night in the bar, when they didn't know the stakes or what was to come.

Liam stroked her hair. "Are you okay?"

She half laughed, half cried. "You're the one with a leg sliced open who dissociated in rage."

"I couldn't kill him."

"You are better than that," she promised. "You did what was right."

Right could mean so many thing, but he knew what it meant for them and would never do anything to jeopardize their future—Chelsea had saved him. Liam dropped his forehead to hers. “I love you.”

Tears streamed down her cheeks. “I know. I love you too.”

Noise and chatter mixed with sirens. New boots rushed in, but nothing would tear him away from her. “You’re pregnant?”

“I didn’t know and—”

“*Sunshine.*” He grinned. “I mean… holy shit. *We’re* going to have a baby.”

She beamed through the tears. “We are.”

EPILOGUE

Seven Months Later

BRIGHTLY COLORED BOXES were stacked to the warehouse-high ceiling. Liam hadn't known big-box stores that catered to baby equipment existed. But there he was, stranded in the middle of a sprawling aisle of strollers.

Picking one didn't have to be so complicated… He drifted farther down the aisle and stopped at another stroller. Truth be told, they all looked the same, but he couldn't tell that to Chelsea or Linda. Especially not after he'd convinced them that he could handle the stroller-choosing task.

Frank had warned Liam that he didn't know what he was getting into, and the man was right. Each stroller had a display and product listing that was not unlike the same lists that he might expect to see if shopping for a new truck.

Rubber-coated wheels for city sidewalks.

Pneumatic wheels for off-roading.

Brakes and shocks.

Cupholders and storage.

Visors, canopies, UV-blockers, rain gear…

He pinched the bridge of his nose. This couldn't be that hard of a decision. Off-roading and cup holders seemed most important.

Then again, he couldn't discount the importance of good brakes. *What have I gotten myself into?* Maybe he should call Frank for backup.

"You don't want that one."

Liam straightened at the familiar voice and pivoted. *Mr. Westin.* "This is unexpected."

The corners of Westin's mouth quirked. "I like to keep folks on their toes."

He eyeballed the stroller aisle. "Never would've guessed you'd be here."

Westin chuckled. "Not my usual."

"Yet you're offering advice." He shoved his hands into his pockets. "You have kids?"

Westin shook his head. "I can't see how that kind of future is in store for me."

Liam shrugged. "You never know. I wouldn't have predicted this a couple years ago."

He laughed. "With my schedule, I would probably have to drop face first into a war zone to find a woman and kid. But crazier things have happened."

An overhead speaker chimed and requested that everyone keep their eye out for an "overly loved pink binkie." Both men shifted awkwardly, and maybe Westin had as much of an understanding of *binkies* as Liam did. His best guess was a blanket shaped like a pinky—but that made no sense. The learning curve on fatherhood would be steep.

Liam tilted his head toward the stroller that first caught his eye. "Why don't I want that one?"

"Because that one over there has more cupholders."

"Good to know." He crossed his arms. "Why are you here?"

"I have a job offer for you, *ace*." Westin cracked a couple knuckles. "With ACES."

Liam snorted. "Yeah, I picked up on that."

Westin smirked. "I was trying it on for size. Asymmetrical Combat Expeditionary Specialists. You report to me. You'll have a home base in Abu Dhabi—"

Liam shook his head. "I have a kid on the way."

"I won't ask you to relocate. Just travel as needed, when you're ready." Westin popped the knuckles on his other hand. "And I pay well."

That sounded like a dream job once upon a time. But now? "Let me think about it and get back to you."

"What's there to think about?"

He chuckled. "I'm going to run decisions that involve pitstops in Abu Dhabi by my wife."

Westin nodded. "I just had lunch with her."

"What?"

"Hell if I was going to offer you a job without getting to know all the players," then translated. "Consider it business research."

He didn't know if Westin was an asshole or smart as hell. Liam also wasn't sure why Chelsea hadn't texted him.

"And she's getting a massage at some fancy-ass place right now. My treat."

His eyebrow arched. "You don't have to do that—"

Westin reached into his pocket then extended a business card in his hand. "You're one lucky SOB with a woman like that."

He already knew that and took the thick cream-colored card. A phone number was center-justified, but the card didn't have any other information. Liam ran his thumb over the raised type then shoved it into his pocket. "You're still working with Chance and Hagan?"

Westin nodded. "And with you, whenever you're ready."

"I didn't say I'd take the job."

"But you will." Then the man whom Mr. Black had called Boss Man strolled down the aisle.

Liam didn't know what his next move should be beyond leaving the store with a stroller. He could only process one monumental decision a day, and todays had been deciding on a name. Catherine *Julia* Brosnan.

He took a deep breath and made another decision. He pulled the order ticket for the stroller with all the cup holders and went to check out. Boss man hadn't led him astray to this point. No reason to second guess him now. ACES it would be.

ABOUT THE AUTHOR

Cristin Harber is a *New York Times* and *USA Today* bestselling romance author. She writes sexy romantic suspense, military romance, new adult, and contemporary romance. Readers voted her onto Amazon's Top Picks for Debut Romance Authors in 2013, and her debut Titan series was both a #1 romantic suspense and #1 military romance bestseller.

Connect with Cristin at www.CristinHarber.com. Join the newsletter! Text TITAN to 66866.

The Titan Series:

Book 1: Winters Heat
Book 1.5: Sweet Girl
Book 2: Garrison's Creed
Book 3: Westin's Chase
Book 4: Gambled and Chased
Book 5: Savage Secrets
Book 6: Hart Attack
Book 7: Sweet One
Book 8: Black Dawn
Book 9: Live Wire
Book 10: Bishop's Queen
Book 12: Locke and Key
Book 12: Jax

The Delta Series:

Book 1: Delta: Retribution
Book 2: Delta: Rescue*
Book 3: Delta: Revenge
Book 4: Delta: Redemption
Book 5: Delta: Ricochet
*The Delta Novella in Liliana Hart's MacKenzie Family Collection

The Only Series:

Book 1: Only for Him

Book 2: Only for Her

Book 3: Only for Us

Book 4: Only Forever

The ACES Series:

The Savior

7 Brides for 7 Soldiers:

Ryder (#1) – Barbara Freethy

Adam (#2) – Roxanne St. Claire

Zane (#3) – Christie Ridgway

Wyatt (#4) – Lynn Raye Harris

Jack (#5) – Julia London

Noah (#6) – Cristin Harber

Ford (#7) – Samantha Chase

Each Titan, Delta, and 7 Brides book can be read as a standalone (except for Sweet Girl), but readers will likely best enjoy the series in order. The Only series must be read in order.

ACKNOWLEDGMENTS

As always, this book would be impossible without the love and support of my family.

Thank you to the wonderful readers who read my books! I will never be able to share how much you mean. I hope you know how thankful I am for you.

Thank you to Marion and Debbie for beta reading and the ladies from Team Titan who were able to read The Savior early. I took everything you said to heart, and I appreciate your help!

This book would not be possible if it weren't for an afternoon with Claudia Connor at a Mexican bar in Denver, Colorado. Inspiration and the God's-honest-truth might be served best with chips, salsa, and margaritas.

A massive shout out to Hot Damn Designs and Kim Killion for the fantastic cover design, Red Adept and Susie for the editing, and Amber Noffke for everything.